LET ME BE YOUR HERO

BOOK FIVE IN THE ASTLEY CHRONICLES

COURTNEY MCCASKILL

HAZEL GROVE BOOKS

THE ASTLEYS OF HARRINGTON HALL

Edward Astley IV, Earl of Cheltenham
Georgiana Astley, Countess of Cheltenham

Edward Astley V, Viscount Fauconbridge, age 27
Harrington Astley, age 26
Anne Cranfield (née Astley), Countess of Morsley, age 24
Caroline Greville (née Astley) Viscountess Thetford, age 20
Lady Lucy Astley, age 19
Lady Isabella Astley, age 19
John Astley, deceased at age 2
Frederick Astley, age 14

First published in 2024 by Hazel Grove Books.

Let Me Be Your Hero Copyright © Courtney McCaskill, 2024.

Excerpt from *Romancing the Rifleman* Copyright © Courtney McCaskill, 2024.

Kindle ISBN: 978-1-63915-037-3

eBook ISBN: 978-1-63915-038-0

Paperback ISBN: 978-1-63915-039-7

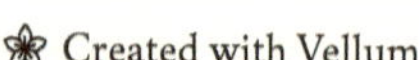 Created with Vellum

CHAPTER 1

London, England
September 1803

It pained Isabella Astley to admit it.

But her mother had been right.

Everyone spoke in hushed whispers about the wickedness that took place in the dark walks of Vauxhall Gardens in a way that made them sound more exciting than dangerous. Illicit rendezvous! Moonlit assignations! A chance to be swept off your feet by a dashing stranger!

What she had found instead was not so much romance as… copulation.

Another feminine moan, this one sounding decidedly feigned, came from the trees on her left. It was accompanied by a rhythmic slapping of skin upon skin and followed by a strangled male cry.

Now, Izzie may have been a virginal young miss. But she was a *curious* virginal young miss who had bribed a housemaid years ago to explain what happened between a man and a woman.

In other words, the source of all that moaning and thumping wasn't exactly a mystery.

She crept along the path, searching for the way out. The dark walks were, for lack of a better term, *dark*, as they were bereft of the famous colorful lamps that illuminated most of the gardens. But she could make her way along the graveled paths well enough by moonlight, at least right now, when the moon was peeking out from behind one of the shifting clouds.

Up ahead, a trio of ladies turned the corner, heading straight for her. Izzie quickly ducked off the path, scurrying behind a tree.

As they strolled past her hiding spot, she saw that they were *ladies* only in the informal sense of the word. Even by moonlight, she could tell that their lips and cheeks were brightly painted and that the one in the middle's hair was an improbable shade of red.

A man—a gentleman, based on the cut of his coat—approached the trio. He took the hand of a woman with curly blonde hair and led her off into the darkness. The cacophony of coupling that ensued was by now familiar. Izzie had seen a half-dozen similar transactions, including two with men she recognized—Lord Ipswitch, whose dissolute reputation was apparently well-deserved, and Andrew Milner, who happened to be one of the Members of Parliament representing her home county of Gloucestershire. Izzie had been surprised to see Mr. Milner there, as he was known for being a high stickler and had won his seat by contrasting his own upright behavior with that of the former incumbent, who was said to consort with the family governess.

The other two women continued along the path. Izzie

was preparing to emerge from behind her tree when a deep voice from the woods behind her made her jump.

"Are they gone?"

"I think so," a man with a Scottish accent answered.

Izzie was debating whether she should stay put or flee when the Englishman said, "So, how soon can you deliver the guns?"

That had her ducking back behind her tree. Guns? What did they mean, guns?

"Look, Cooper," the Scotsman said, "I havnae decided whether I'm going to do this or no."

"Damn it, MacDonald. I promised I would deliver two hundred guns by the first of October."

"Well, that's not my problem, now is it?"

"I'll make it your problem," the first man growled. He paused, clearing his throat, and when he spoke again, it was with a forced joviality. "Come on, now. It's just two hundred guns. The army won't even miss such a trifling amount."

Izzie clung to her tree with white knuckles. So, they were talking about stealing guns from the army. Wasn't that... treason?

"And I'll pay you a pretty penny for your trouble," the first man continued. "You'd be a fool to pass up such easy money."

The Scotsman gave a bleak laugh. "Oh, yes, such an easy decision, it is. Excepting the fact that now I know who those guns are intended for. That's the part I can't stomach."

"You're in too deep," the first man growled, dropping the effort to sound cajoling. "You've already sold me two shipments."

"That was before I knew who you were working for!" the Scotsman protested.

"That's too damned bad. If you don't make this delivery, your superiors are going to receive an anonymous tip about where those weapons you wrote off as *damaged upon receipt* really wound up."

"Don't do this to me," the Scotsman pleaded. "I made a mistake. I don't want to be involved with the—"

"Well, you are involved," the Englishman snapped, cutting the Scotsman off before Izzie could learn the name of his employer. "And you're going to deliver those guns tomorrow, or I'm going to ruin you."

"All right," the Scotsman muttered. "But I don't know that I can come up with the full two hundred by tomorrow."

"How many?"

"I can probably manage fifty."

"Fifty. Good. Same point of delivery as last time."

"All right." The Scotsman's voice was dejected.

"Good. Now, let's get out of here."

Boots crunched against the bed of autumn leaves carpeting the forest floor. Tamping down a squeal, Izzie scurried on tiptoes in a circle around her tree, trying desperately to stay out of sight as they passed.

Just as the first man reached the graveled path, she stepped on a stick, which broke with a sharp snap.

"What was that?" The man who had just emerged from the grove—the Englishman—spun around, facing straight toward her. Izzie had only managed to get halfway behind her tree, but she had no choice but to freeze where she stood. It was dark thanks to the shadows cast by the branches above, but any trace of movement would surely give her away.

The moon was out, but Izzie couldn't make out his face beneath the brim of his hat. He was of average height and slightly bulky with sloping shoulders.

"What was what?" the Scotsman asked, stepping clear of the trees. He removed his hat to wipe his sweaty brow. He was both taller and skinnier than his companion, with light hair and boyish features.

"Thought I heard something." The Englishman was scanning the cluster of trees. Izzie held her breath as he turned toward her hiding place. He did not pause while making his sweep of the trees. That meant he hadn't spotted her.

Didn't it?

"Let's get out of here," the Scotsman muttered. "I've a long night ahead of me to be alone with my guilty conscience."

Grunting, his companion turned and the two of them finally made their way down the path.

Izzie let out a gasping breath. Overhearing men plotting treason was more excitement than she frankly wanted out of her adventure in the dark walks. An adventure she now wanted to come to an end.

Izzie counted to twenty before emerging from behind her tree. Shaking a stray leaf out of her skirts, she hurried toward the front of the gardens. She'd had quite enough adventure for one evening, thank you very—

"Well, well, well," a reedy voice said. "Would you look who it is?"

CHAPTER 2

*I*zzie stiffened, recognizing the voice. She turned, and surely enough, there was Tristan Bassingthwaighte, regarding her from the middle of the path.

Two months ago, Mr. Bassingthwaighte had asked her parents for permission to court her. At first, Izzie had been pleased by the prospect. He had a reputation for being a poet of some talent. She had thought they might pair well together—the poet and the authoress of Gothic novels. Although Mr. Bassingthwaighte was not what you would call plump in the pocket and was likely drawn to her at least in part for her handsome dowry, Izzie hadn't minded. She didn't need palatial surroundings. The most important thing was finding a husband who would support her writing.

Unfortunately, that would not be Mr. Bassingthwaighte. A month into their acquaintance, he had asked to read a chapter of her story. She'd had to copy it out by hand, as she'd been preparing to submit the complete manuscript to The Minerva Press, her dream publisher, which specialized in Gothic novels. She'd passed it to him at a garden party. The next morning, when a footman had announced that Mr.

Bassingthwaighte was there to call upon her, she'd twisted her hands into knots as she glided down the stairs, anxious about his reaction.

At least he had not left her in suspense. "Izzie," he said the second she entered the room, not even bothering to start with a *good morning*, "tell me you have not been wasting your time on this *rubbish*."

They'd fought about it for a good fifteen minutes. Izzie knew her story wasn't rubbish. She'd been writing Gothic novels since she was thirteen and could admit that her early works were best left in the box under her bed where they currently resided.

But she hadn't given up. She had worked hard, and this book was good. She knew it was—an opinion that would be confirmed one week later when The Minerva Press wrote back offering to publish it.

Mr. Bassingthwaighte would hear none of it. Gothic novels were not *serious literature*, a distinction Izzie actually did not mind as writing serious literature had never been her aim. She'd wanted to write something entertaining and enjoyable.

But, according to Mr. Bassingthwaighte, *entertaining* and *enjoyable* were not worthy goals. There was serious literature, and there was rubbish, and Izzie's manuscript fell into the latter category.

Mr. Bassingthwaighte was furious when she asked him to leave and even angrier when she refused to receive him after that. He'd attempted to corner her at a ball—not to apologize, mind you, but to explain again why she was wrong. He'd been so persistent that her brother, Harrington, had eventually noticed and come over to run him off.

That had been two weeks ago. Izzie hadn't spoken to him since.

Nor did she have any desire to renew their acquaintance.

"Mr. Bassingthwaighte," she said coldly. "Do excuse me. I was just leaving."

She turned on her heel and managed to take two steps toward the front of the gardens before she was waylaid by a hand around her upper arm.

"Don't play coy with me," Mr. Bassingthwaighte snarled. "We both know why you're here."

She tried to keep her voice from trembling. "You are mistaken, sir, if you think my reasons for being here have anything to do with you. Now, I will thank you to unhand me."

He only tightened his grip. "You've been leading me on a merry chase these past few weeks, pretending you wanted nothing to do with me."

Izzie tried and failed to yank her arm free. "I *don't* want anything to do with you."

"But tonight," he continued, ignoring her, "when you saw me heading for the dark walks, you decided to follow me."

Izzie gave another futile pull at her arm. "I most certainly did not!"

"Was this your plan from the start? To string me along for a few weeks, then make it up to me tonight? Or were you overcome with jealousy when you saw me slip away, knowing what I would be doing back here and that I would be doing it with a woman other than you?"

"Whoever you met with, she is welcome to you!" she snapped. "I offer her my most profound sympathies. Now, unhand me this instant."

He laughed, but not in a nice way. "That's part of your game, isn't it? You like to act all high and mighty, don't you? To pretend you're too good for the likes of me."

"I am too good for the likes of you! And my reasons for visiting the dark walks have absolutely nothing to do with you."

"Oh, really?" Mr. Bassingthwaighte looked openly skeptical. "There's only one reason people visit these dark walks."

Izzie happened to know that was wrong. To be sure, she had learned tonight that most people visited the dark walks in order to fornicate, for lack of a better term.

But based on what she had overheard, there was a small but persistent minority that came there to discuss acts of treason.

"You wanted an assignation," Mr. Bassingthwaighte continued, leaning in so she could smell the wine on his breath. "That's why you're here."

"Not with *you*," she said without thinking. She quickly realized her error. A planned rendezvous with any man in the dark walks would be enough to ruin her. It would have been better to claim she'd lost her way and hadn't meant to be there at all.

This statement also made Mr. Bassingthwaighte's lips twist cruelly. "So fickle, Lady Isabella? How quickly your affections move from one man to another."

This was patently unfair. She had danced with Mr. Bassingthwaighte a handful of times and had a half-dozen conversations with him. But she had made him no promises, nor had she whispered any words of affection. He had managed to extinguish her budding regard for him when he referred to her book as *rubbish*.

But it did not seem wise to say as much when his hand was gripping her arm in a way that seemed likely to leave a bruise.

"Let me go," she whispered.

He responded by grabbing her other arm and slowly drawing her toward him. "Why should I?"

"My brother will call you out!"

This was normally a potent threat. Harrington was one of the best shots in all of England.

But Mr. Bassingthwaighte just laughed. "No, he won't. What good would it do to shoot me? You would still be ruined. He needs me alive so I can marry you. That will be the only way to quash the rumors."

He continued droning on about how he expected Izzie to be more obedient once she was his wife. Izzie paid him little mind. The future he was describing was not going to happen. She would make sure of it.

He might not be worried about Harrington calling him out. But Harrington was useful in more ways than one and had shown all his sisters precisely where to knee a man for maximum impact.

She marked the moment he became so involved in his speech that his attention started to drift. As he cast a long-suffering gaze toward the trees, she brought her knee up, taking him square in the groin.

Harrington's advice worked better than Izzie could have hoped. Mr. Bassingthwaighte released her at once, clutching his intimate bits with a piteous moan. He crumpled forward, winding up on his knees in the dirt.

Izzie turned and ran, then stopped as she realized she had started in the wrong direction and was heading deeper into the dark walks.

She started to turn but saw that Mr. Bassingthwaighte had struggled to his feet. "You're going to… regret that!" he ground out, staggering toward her.

Oh, dear. He was blocking her best escape route. Now, she had no choice but to flee even deeper into the gardens.

Behind her, she could hear a series of pops as the evening's fireworks display commenced. She came to a crossing and turned left, catching a glimpse of Mr. Bassingthwaighte lurching after her. He was gaining ground in spite of his injury, and she struggled to gather handfuls of her skirts so she could run properly.

He pulled within an arm's length, and she made a quick decision. Without warning, she cut sharply to the left, abandoning the path and taking her chances in the wooded thicket.

It was pitch black in the trees. Izzie couldn't see where she was placing her feet, but she knew she couldn't stop. She stumbled once… twice… but somehow managed to keep her feet. She could hear Mr. Bassingthwaighte crashing through the underbrush behind her, cursing all the while, but she couldn't see well enough to determine how close he might be.

Somehow, she managed not to fall, and after what seemed like an eternity of stumbling blindly through the darkness, she detected the faint red glow of the fireworks display filtering into the woods up ahead.

Surely enough, the path appeared before her. She could have wept with gratitude as moonlight fell upon her face.

And then, after having somehow floundered through the trees in total blackness, *that* was the moment she managed to trip.

What a disaster this night was turning into! She braced herself, expecting to fall face-first in the dirt.

Instead, a pair of strong hands caught her about the waist. Rather than feeling the gritty path against her cheek, she collided with a warm, firm wall covered in soft wool. But no, not a wall.

A man.

Oh, God. It was probably Mr. Bassingthwaighte, and she was out of the frying pan and straight into the fire. Although… Mr. Bassingthwaighte had smelled of cheap wine and sweat. This man smelled clean, like plain white soap and fresh linen that had been dried in the sun.

She tentatively lifted her head and peered at him in the moonlight. "Mr. Nettlethorpe-Ogilvy?"

"Y-yes," answered a familiar, deep voice.

Izzie sagged with relief, clinging to him for purchase. "Oh, thank goodness it's you!"

On one level, almost anybody was better than Tristan Bassingthwaighte. And it was true that she scarcely knew Archibald Nettlethorpe-Ogilvy.

But her entire family held him in high esteem. Her sister, Anne, thought the world of him.

Surely, he would help her.

"Are you all right?" his rich baritone rumbled in her ear.

She answered honestly. "I am, now that you're here."

That must've flummoxed him because he didn't answer. What he did was stand there, steady as an oak, not pawing at her, or dragging her about, but giving her a moment to catch her breath. His hands, warm and gentle, remained at her waist, but strangely, she found their presence reassuring rather than threatening.

She had almost recovered her equilibrium when the sound of someone crashing through the underbrush behind her sent her reeling again. She squealed, glancing over her shoulder, but couldn't tell how close Mr. Bassingthwaighte had drawn in the darkness.

Suddenly, her feet left the ground. Mr. Nettlethorpe-Ogilvy lifted her and turned, reversing their positions so he could shield her with his big body.

Her heart gave a squeeze. After the assortment of vices she had encountered in the dark walks, it was good to remember that there were some decent men left in the world.

Still, if Tristan Bassingthwaighte was going to come crashing out of the underbrush at any second, she needed to take action. She had told him her purpose in visiting the dark walks was to meet another man.

There was another man right here.

"I must ask you for the most terrible favor."

"Anything," he whispered, his breath carrying a hint of cinnamon.

Although… perhaps he was not the right man to ask to help her stage this scene. He was courting Cecilia Chenoweth, after all, and had just taken her off in order to propose marriage when the Duke of Trevissick had arrived at Vauxhall and announced his intention to do the same.

It occurred to her that the fact that he was here in the dark walks, alone, almost certainly meant that Ceci had accepted the duke's proposal, not his.

Still, she found herself asking again, "Are… are you sure?"

"Anything," he said firmly.

The sounds from the underbrush were growing louder. She didn't have time to hem and haw. And, after all, he had said *anything*, not *that depends*, or *what, exactly, did you have in mind?*

Who was she to question him?

So, what she said was, "Oh, thank you!"

And she looped her arms around his neck, rose up on her toes, and kissed him.

So, she does know my name.

That was the last coherent thought to emerge from Archibald's brain before Isabella Astley pressed her lips against his.

He hadn't been sure. When he first made her acquaintance, at the wedding of one of her sisters to Viscount Thetford, he was introduced not to her but to "the twins." Her sister, Lady Lucy, had been the one to say the requisite greetings and carry the conversation while Lady Isabella stared across the room, her lips curved into a bemused half-smile and her thoughts clearly a thousand miles away.

She hadn't been the only one struggling to attend to the conversation. Seeing Isabella Astley for the first time had felt like getting run over by a brace of oxen. She was that beautiful. She had the large, dark blue eyes that were an Astley family trait. But, unlike most of her sisters, her hair was not blonde but a rich, dark brown, which, combined with her pale, creamy skin, made her eyes all the more striking. She was tall for a woman, only an inch shorter than him, and quite slim with only the barest hint of a bosom. She had a delicate quality about her that made him nervous to even bow over her hand out of fear that he might break her with his meaty paw.

All of this combined into an otherworldly quality. He remembered thinking that she did not look human. She looked like the daughter of the fairy king.

Up until that moment, Archibald had spent precisely zero minutes of his life thinking about *the daughter of the fairy king*. His thoughts tended to be consumed with cannons and coal, steam engines and screw-cutting lathes.

Yet, there he was, pining after Isabella Astley like a lovesick schoolboy.

But then, at the wedding breakfast, it got a thousand times worse. Because that was when he finally heard her speak.

She was *so clever*. He had been seated at the next table over, only a few feet away and at such an angle that he could just see her out of the corner of his eye. His assigned dining partner had decided to ignore him in favor of trying to flirt with Lord Graverley across the table. With nothing to distract him and seated in such close proximity, he hadn't been able to help but overhear Isabella Astley's every remark.

She was different from any young lady he had ever encountered. She stated her opinions with an assurance most women twice her age did not possess. She seemed to have little knowledge of the latest gossip. Apparently, she read Gothic novels obsessively and was even trying her own hand at writing them.

When Mrs. Whitcombe informed her that the Gothic novels she loved were "tawdry," Lady Isabella had squealed, pulling a pencil and a little bound notebook from her reticule. "You must have read some very good ones to lead you to such a conclusion. Please, won't you tell me their titles and describe their most tawdry elements?"

Later, Lady Iveson pointedly told her that it wasn't decorous for young ladies to wear bold colors, a thinly veiled criticism of Lady Isabella's red gown.

"Should I meet a decorous young lady," she replied with grave sincerity, "I will be sure to mention it to her."

Then, during the dessert course, Lady Hering complained that the Ancient Egyptian artifacts decorating the bridegroom's family home were "ghastly" and anyone who would choose such a garish theme was "immoral." Lady Isabella replied, "At least my new family-by-marriage's decorations aren't a dead bore, unlike your conversation."

Archibald had to feign a bout of coughing to cover his laughter. She was like a solitary streak of oil paint, vivid and confident, on a sun-faded watercolor. Even though he knew next to nothing about her favorite topics, he could have sat listening to her all day, feeling nothing but delight at the extraordinary sentences that emerged from her rose-pink lips.

She never seemed to notice him over the months and years that followed, not even when he had come to stay as a guest at her family's home. He didn't blame her. How could he expect this ethereal creature to notice the likes of *him*, a glorified blacksmith who spent his days laboring either in his family's iron forge or his own machine shop? It was as ridiculous as expecting Aphrodite to notice Hephaestus.

Well, of course, Aphrodite *had* noticed Hephaestus. Hell, she had even married him.

But everyone knew how *that* had turned out.

So, Archibald had contented himself with admiring Isabella Astley from afar and dreaming about her each night, never expecting her to look at him, much less speak to him.

So tonight, when she threw her arms around his neck and pressed her lips eagerly against his?

His brain ceased functioning, immediately and completely. That was the only explanation for the extreme impropriety of what he did next.

He did not kiss her the way a gentleman should kiss a lady—a restrained, closed-mouth meeting of the lips designed not to unsettle her delicate sensibilities.

Instead, a primitive growl emerged from his throat. *Mine* was the word that echoed through his skull. He proceeded not to kiss her so much as to devour her. She tasted of cherries, sweet and tart and utterly delicious, and he could not get enough of her. She felt so, so perfect in his arms. She was slight compared to his own hulking frame, but it would be a mistake to call her weak, for her kiss crackled with a vivacious energy that left him breathless.

He must have kissed her in thoughtless abandon for some minutes, for when Archibald was next aware of anything, he saw that he had pulled her close, pressing his body against every inch of hers, from throat to thighs. One of his burly arms was wrapped around her waist, and the other snaked across her upper back. His meaty hand was tangled in her hair, depriving her of any chance to escape.

He pulled back, regret and shame flooding him. He was ten times as strong as she, and he had just forced himself on her. "Lady Isabella, I… I'm so sorry."

Her eyelids fluttered open. She was so dazed that she looked almost drunk, but her eyes slowly came into focus.

She stared at him for ten agonizing seconds as he sheepishly disentangled his fingers from her hair.

Just as he was preparing to step back, she said it.

"I'm not."

And then she wrapped her arms around his neck and pulled him back to her.

CHAPTER 4

*W*hy had she never noticed how gorgeous Archibald Nettlethorpe-Ogilvy was?

Perhaps gorgeous was the wrong word. He certainly wasn't pretty, like so many men of the *ton* who flitted about worrying about their meticulously windswept hair or spending a significant proportion of their waking hours trying to transform their cravat into a waterfall.

He was better than *pretty*. He was powerful. Manly.

Virile.

And the way he kissed?

Being a fan of Gothic novels, Izzie knew certain things about kisses. They were supposed to change your life, for one. When you kissed your one true love, you would know it at once.

And a real kiss would make you *feel* things.

Being eager to experience these things for herself, she had specifically sought out opportunities to have one of those magical kisses. She had, in fact, kissed five young men before tonight.

And she had felt things, all right.

Primarily disappointment. But also, upon occasion, boredom, righteous indignation, and the desire to wash her face and hands with lye soap.

But Mr. Nettlethorpe-Ogilvy's kiss was completely different. She loved the way it felt to be cradled against his muscular chest, to have his strong arms surrounding her. Moments ago, she had literally been running for her life, but in his arms, she felt *safe*. He was the sort of man who made you feel absolute confidence in his ability to protect you. And, unlike so many men, he didn't grab and paw at her. Only after she pressed herself against him had he enfolded her in his arms. He took no more than she was willing to give, and there was a reverence in the way he touched her, as if she were a precious treasure. His was a kiss that gave instead of took, that venerated instead of plundered, and it was exactly what she needed after her frightening encounter with Mr. Bassingthwaighte.

And dear lord, the man could kiss! He kissed her as if the explosions going off around them were cannonballs rather than fireworks. As if the world was about to end and kissing her was the last thing he would ever do, and he wanted to make it *count*.

Everyone sneeringly said that he was little more than a *blacksmith*. He was built like a blacksmith, but he reminded Izzie more of a Viking, and she suddenly found herself wishing he would ransack her.

She couldn't seem to stop touching him. God, but his chest was broad, and his shoulders? Magnificent. Every place her hands strayed was so firm, so warm. It made her wish they weren't separated by so many layers of fabric...

Suddenly, he growled, hugging her body against his chest and lifting her off the ground as easily as if she were a rag doll. He carried her to one of the faux Greek ruins along the side of the path. This one looked like a cluster of columns, but, as this was Vauxhall, they were really logs with a little paint slapped on.

One of them had been sawed off at waist level, with a flat, smooth top. As he set her down upon it, it struck Izzie that it looked like an offering table, just the kind of place where the Ancient Greeks might have made a virgin sacrifice. The thought should have terrified her, but suddenly, the notion of sacrificing her virginity to Archibald Nettlethorpe-Ogilvy on a pagan altar in the moonlight did not sound like the absolute worst idea she'd ever had.

Without breaking contact with his lips, she tugged her skirts up so she could get her knees out of the way. He immediately stepped into the cradle of her thighs, and now things were getting *interesting*. Her pulse was flying, and her breath was coming in pants. She made a mewl of protest when he tore his lips from hers, but then he started kissing his way down her neck, which was equally delicious.

She could feel a hard ridge beneath the falls of his trousers. Having snooped through her brother Harrington's room thoroughly enough to find the book of scandalous prints he kept hidden beneath his mattress, she had a fair idea what *that* was, and the notion that Mr. Nettlethorpe-Ogilvy was having those sorts of thoughts while kissing her made her purr with satisfaction.

She scooted even closer to the edge of the column, her curiosity getting the better of her, as usual. He did not retreat but began to circle his hips, grinding his hardness against her softness, and… and… She did not have any words for *that*.

She was gasping for breath as his hand slid up the silk bodice of her dress, his fingertips stroking her nipple through the cloth, and that was when she cried out.

And ruined *everything*.

"Isabella?" a reedy voice called from within the grove of trees behind them. "Isabella, is that you?"

The voice was familiar.

Familiar, and *irritating*.

Surely enough, a few seconds later, Tristan Bassingthwaighte came stumbling out of the woods.

Izzie buried her head in Mr. Nettlethorpe-Ogilvy's neck. It wasn't that she was embarrassed for Mr. Bassingthwaighte to discover them locked in an intimate embrace. She dimly recalled that this had been her original purpose, what felt like a thousand years ago.

But Izzie's nerves were raw, and her emotions were alarmingly close to the surface. She didn't think she could bear to meet anyone's eye at that moment when she was feeling so vulnerable.

Mr. Nettlethorpe-Ogilvy seemed to understand, for he pulled her securely against his chest, cradling her head in one of his marvelously capable hands. She immediately felt comforted.

It appeared that Tristan Bassingthwaighte had not yet spotted them, as they were in the shadow of the archway. "You can stop playing coy, Isabella. You wanted me to chase you, and I did. But now you owe me a favor. And I don't mean just a kiss."

Isabella cringed. That was why she'd been running away, all right.

Beside her, Mr. Nettlethorpe-Ogilvy's brow descended into a ferocious scowl.

"Aha! I recognize those red skirts," Mr. Bassingthwaighte called. "I've found your hiding spot, and now... *Oh.*"

From over Mr. Nettlethorpe-Ogilvy's shoulder, she saw him stop short as he noticed that she was not alone.

The poet scowled. "What are you playing at, Isabella?"

She drew herself up, willing her voice to sound haughty and not terrified. "As I told you earlier, my reasons for visiting the dark walks tonight have nothing to do with *you*. Now, if you will excuse us."

Mr. Bassingthwaighte scowled. "Oh, no. You cannot possibly expect me to believe that you are in any way interested in this crude—"

"He's not crude!" Izzie snapped. "Now, I would appreciate it if you would leave me alone."

"I won't," Mr. Bassingthwaighte said, advancing on her. "Not until I've had my turn."

His *turn*? To think, he had the absolute gall to imagine that he was entitled to a *turn* when she had just told him no!

"She's not a bowl of nuts, and I'm not going to hand her to you when I've had my fill," Archibald snarled. "If she doesn't want your hands on her, then you're not going to put them there. *Full stop.*"

She's not a bowl of nuts. They weren't the words of a poet, such as Mr. Bassingthwaighte.

But Izzie found the sentiment behind them more affecting than the most polished sonnet.

Mr. Bassingthwaighte stopped, his face turning pale in the moonlight. Although he was an inch taller than Mr. Nettlethorpe-Ogilvy, he looked positively scrawny by comparison. He held his hands up, placatingly. "Come, Nettlethorpe-Ogilvy—let's not get all worked up over a bit of muslin."

"A bit of muslin?" Mr. Nettlethorpe-Ogilvy's voice was quiet. Quiet, and *dangerous*. "Did you just refer to Lady Isabella as *a bit of muslin?*"

Izzie sensed that an explosion was about to occur.

Mr. Bassingthwaighte did not seem privy to his impending doom. "You know what I mean."

Archibald snarled. "You will *never* speak about her that way again. In fact"—he glanced down at Izzie—"do you wish to speak to this man again?"

"Never," she confirmed.

He returned his menacing glare to Mr. Bassingthwaighte. "You will never speak *to* her again. If you are standing in a ballroom and she enters, you will fabricate an excuse to leave. You will do everything within your power to make sure that she never has to clap her eyes upon your worthless carcass ever again."

Mr. Bassingthwaighte seemed to have finally comprehended the danger he was in. He was trying to put on a brave front, but his eyes were darting around as if looking for a route of escape. In a nasal voice, he asked, "And if I don't?"

Leaving Izzie sitting on the faux column, Mr. Nettlethorpe-Ogilvy took a slow step toward Mr. Bassingthwaighte, then another.

Izzie could see the whites of Mr. Bassingthwaighte's eyes in the moonlight. He retreated three steps, bumping into one of the columns.

Mr. Nettlethorpe-Ogilvy seized the lapels of his coat in his right hand. Lifting him off the ground with one arm, he slammed him against the faux ruin, holding him in place with his feet dangling off the ground. "If you don't," he said, his voice terrifyingly quiet, "then I will break every bone in your body." His voice crescendoed to a roar as he said, "Which also happens to be what I will do if you breathe a word to *anyone* about her presence here tonight! Have I made myself clear?"

"Yes!" Mr. Bassingthwaighte squeaked.

"Good." Mr. Nettlethorpe-Ogilvy tossed him to the side.

Mr. Bassingthwaighte stumbled but managed to keep his feet. "Lady Isabella, I—"

"Don't talk," Mr. Nettlethorpe-Ogilvy ordered. "Just leave."

Mr. Bassingthwaighte complied, scrambling back into the grove of trees from whence he'd come.

Mr. Nettlethorpe-Ogilvy hurried back to the column where Izzie still sat. An image flashed across her mind of him dressed not in an evening suit but in plate and chainmail.

My knight in shining armor.

"Are you all right?" he asked.

"I am. Thanks to you. He was the one I was running away from when I crashed into you." She swallowed. "He assumed I had come back here looking for him. I panicked and told him I was meeting someone else. So, when I saw you, I… I'm sorry. I probably shouldn't have… you know…"

She trailed off, wondering how he would react. She had admitted that the reason she had kissed him was to stage a scene for Mr. Bassingthwaighte. And it had certainly started off that way.

But by the end… By the end, everything had changed.

Which was exactly what was supposed to happen when you kissed the right man.

Izzie bit her lip, wondering if Mr. Nettlethorpe-Ogilvy really was the right man for her and if she had just given the impression that she hadn't really wanted to kiss him.

He didn't look angry. He nodded sympathetically. "It's all right. He won't bother you again. If he does"—his face turned dark—"just let me know."

Izzie took his hand and pressed it. "I will. Thank you." She wanted him to touch her, wanted him to kiss her again. But it seemed that the usual rules of how a gentleman was supposed to treat a young lady had somehow crept back into place, and she wasn't sure how to overcome them.

The fireworks display had ended, so that you could once again hear the night sounds of the garden.

And other sounds, too. From the front of the gardens, she heard her twin sister's voice. "Izzie?"

A deeper voice. Her brother, Edward. "Izzie, where are you?"

"Isabella Astley, you had better come out of there *right now*, or with God as my witness—"

Izzie bit back a smile. The last one was definitely her mother.

"Come," Mr. Nettlethorpe-Ogilvy said. "You've been missed."

He scooped her off the column as if she were as light as a cushion and gently set her on the ground.

She straightened her skirts. "Do I look all right?"

He tilted his head, looking baffled. "Do you look all right? You always look..." He suddenly turned his head, dropping his voice to a whisper as he added, "... beautiful."

Izzie's heart gave a little squeeze. Maybe he did like her. Maybe she stood a chance.

Maybe she hadn't already ruined everything.

"I meant, are there any obvious signs that we were... you know..."

"*Oh.*" He circled around her, his gaze checking her from head to foot. "Your hair is a little, um..."

She reached up to pat it, and surely enough, her coiffure was listing to the side. "I'll say I snagged it on a tree."

He nodded. "That will serve."

He offered her his arm, and they headed toward the sound of the voices calling out for her. As they neared the front of the gardens, Vauxhall's famous lamps began blinking at them through the trees, making it easier to see.

As they emerged into the crossing of two paths, Isabella saw her mother and sister, Lucy.

Her mother stalked over, steam all but shooting from her ears. "There you are! I told you to stay away from the dark walks!"

"I'm sorry, Mama. I got a bit turned around, and—"

Her mother cast her eyes heavenward. "A bit turned around, my foot. You've been missing for half an hour!"

Izzie was opening her mouth to make some excuse when Archibald laid his hand upon her arm, which was linked with his.

"I came upon Lady Isabella toward the back of the gardens. Her hair was badly snared on a branch." He nodded toward her ruined coiffure. "Even with me there to help, it took some minutes to disentangle her. I am so sorry that you were worried."

Izzie glanced up at him in surprise. He had covered for her. She doubted her mother would have believed the excuse had she uttered it.

But Mr. Nettlethorpe-Ogilvy's reputation was much more upstanding. And everyone was feeling warmly toward him right now for his willingness to offer for Cecilia Chenoweth when her reputation had been in shreds.

Surely enough, her mother's posture eased, and Izzie could almost see the indignation go out of her. She rubbed her brow. "If there is trouble to be found, my Isabella will always manage to find it."

"I'm sorry, Mama. I was actually quite scared when I realized where I was. You cannot imagine my relief when I saw that Mr. Nettlethorpe-Ogilvy was the one who had found me."

She held his eye as she said this, hoping he would see it was the truth.

"Thank you, sir," the countess said. "You have performed yet another great service for us."

The rest of her family had drifted up. Toward the back of the group, she saw the Duke of Trevissick with Cecilia Chenoweth on his arm. They were gazing at each other, lost to the world around them.

Mr. Nettlethorpe-Ogilvy's arm stiffened beneath hers.

She glanced up, and his mournful expression confirmed her suspicions that Ceci had accepted the duke's proposal over his.

He cleared his throat. "Well, then. I'll turn you over to your family."

He started to withdraw his arm, but Izzie instinctively clung to it. She did not like the idea of him being left alone when he was feeling low.

Her mother's expression was arch. "I think it would be better if you walked out with us."

Mr. Nettlethorpe-Ogilvy kept his eyes fixed on the ground. "All right, then. Thank you."

They left the gardens together.

CHAPTER 5

*L*ate the following afternoon, Archibald was working in his machine shop when he received an unexpected caller.

Jimmy, a thirteen-year-old boy who worked as an apprentice metalsmith, was the one to announce him. "Begging your pardon, Mr. Nettlethorpe-Ogilvy, sir. But there's someone here to see you." Jimmy leaned in. "Says he's a duke." He wrinkled his nose, giving the impression that he didn't really believe it.

Archibald grabbed a rag and began wiping his hands. "Thank you, Jimmy."

He might as well talk to whoever this was, duke or otherwise. God knew he wasn't getting a damned thing done today. He usually liked nothing better than finding a few hours to work in his machine shop. Britain had been at war with France for more than a decade, which was excellent for business when you ran an iron works. But it was dull from an engineering perspective. His grandfather had been the one to master the art of boring cannons out of a solid piece of metal, so they were both more accurate and less prone to exploding when in use. Nettlethorpe Iron made the best cannons in the world, and everyone wanted them.

But Archibald had so many ideas. He wanted to build ships out of iron, and bridges out of iron, like the one built at Coalbrookdale the year he was born. But most of all, he wanted to build machines, machines that would build… Well, everything, from screws to locks to steam engines. Machines that would build things *precisely*.

Instead, he built cannons, cannons, and more cannons.

He therefore treasured those scant hours when he could slip away from the forge floor to work on the projects that truly interested him. But today, he wasn't good for much of anything. He could think of nothing but Isabella Astley. He'd almost taken the skin off his thumb with an eighteen-inch file, a tool he normally handled as deftly as an Italian master wielded his brush. Clearly, he needed a break.

He stepped out into the main forge. Surely enough, Marcus Latimer, the Duke of Trevissick, stood waiting for him. He looked entirely out of place with a bejeweled stickpin glinting amongst the folds of his snow-white cravat, standing between a giant pile of coke, a type of coal that burned particularly hot, and a stack of cannons.

"Trevissick," Archibald said, striding up. He started to offer his hand, then paused, noticing how greasy it was. "Maybe we'd better dispense with that."

"That's all right. I was hoping—" The duke jerked to the side as a deafening grind of metal upon metal started up across the forge.

Archibald leaned in and shouted, "They're boring out a cannon. Nothing to worry about." He jerked his head to the side. "Come, we can speak in my office."

He led the way up a flight of stairs and held the door for the duke. His office was a bit more presentable than the forge, but it wasn't what Trevissick was used to. The walls were whitewashed, and there were bare boards on the floor. His desk was nothing fancy, either, not that you could see much of it beneath the papers littered across its surface.

One of the clerks hurried in with a tray bearing a bottle of port and two glasses. He poured the drinks as Archibald gestured for the duke to take a seat. "Thank you, John," he said as the clerk headed for the door.

The duke took a sip, then stared at the glass in surprise. "That's actually quite nice. Is it a Ferreira? The 1798, I believe?"

"I have no idea," Archibald said, stacking papers so they would have someplace to set their glasses. "I told my office manager to get something nice. We have all kinds of people coming through here to place orders."

In this case, *all kinds of people* encompassed literal royalty. When all of Europe was engulfed in war and your factory made the best cannons that money could buy, it was not unusual for princes and kings to come calling.

"Well, it's a good wine." The duke set down his glass. "I'll come straight to the point. I want to apologize for what happened last night."

He didn't have to ask what the duke meant. Archibald had just finished proposing marriage to his friend, Cecilia Chenoweth, whose reputation had been ruined through no fault of her own, when the duke came barreling into the clearing shouting her name, desperate to issue his own proposal, with a flock of curious onlookers trailing behind him.

Thus had several hundred witnesses been present to hear Archibald explain that Cecilia had refused him.

The duke pinched the bridge of his nose. "Such was my desperation to clear up my misunderstanding with Cecilia, I did not consider the possibility that my actions might cause you embarrassment."

Archibald grunted. To be sure, it had been humiliating.

But he was somewhat inured to humiliation. His parents were determined for him to make a society marriage that they hoped would vault the family into the upper echelons of the *ton*.

They did not seem to notice that their son, who felt most comfortable here, at the forge founded by his grandfather, was spectacularly ill-suited for this task. Snide whispers that he was little better than a blacksmith, no matter how substantial the family fortune, followed him every time he walked into a room.

"Thank you for that," Archibald said. "I'm certainly not sorry that she's marrying you. I know you're the one she really wanted, and I want her to be happy."

A wry smirk twisted the duke's lips. "Not *marrying*. We roused the Archbishop of Canterbury from his bed last night. Cecilia is already my duchess."

"Ah." Archibald reached for the decanter and topped off their drinks. "I'll raise a toast to that. To the Duchess of Trevissick."

"To my duchess," the duke agreed, clinking glasses with him. Once he'd taken a sip, he said, "Perhaps now you understand the extent of my regret that I felt compelled to leave my new wife's side in order to apologize."

It was only natural that he would have preferred to spend the day alone with his new wife, engaged in... well. The activities Archibald had *almost* found himself engaged in last night with Isabella Astley.

Suddenly, all he could picture was the way she'd looked in the moonlight. Of course, the only reason she'd been kissing him was so that she could get rid of Tristan Bassingthwaighte. You might say she'd been using him, but Archibald wasn't mad about it. He'd never expected Lady Isabella to so much as look at him. Had there been time for her to tell him the full story, he would have been glad to help her stage her scene. The fact that he'd been permitted to kiss her was an obvious benefit. Even though he knew it had all been for show and had meant nothing to her, he would cherish that memory forever. But just as important, he'd received the opportunity to perform an act of chivalry on her behalf. The notion that she might think well of him, that she might remember him as someone who had helped her in her hour of need, made his heart swell.

The duke was speaking. "If there is anything I can do to make amends, you have but to say the word."

Although... Was it his imagination, or had there been desire clouding her eyes when he pressed her against the archway?

Surely, it was some wistful delusion. Because the notion that *Isabella Astley* would so much as look at *him* was utterly absurd...

"It's a shame you're so bloody rich," the duke continued. "Otherwise, I could at least buy you something."

On the other hand... He could still hear the ferocity in her voice after he'd told her he was sorry for manhandling her, as she replied, *I'm not*. And then she had pulled him back to her. Which, under any other circumstance, he would have interpreted as meaning that she *wanted* to kiss him. Except that couldn't possibly be right...

"Nettlethorpe-Ogilvy!" the duke snapped. "Are you even attending?"

"Sorry." Archibald ran a hand over his face. "You were saying?"

"If there is anything I can do to make up for my poor behavior, you have but to say the word."

Archibald waved this off. "There's not. Or wait—yes. There is something you can do."

The duke leaned forward. "Name it."

"You are very"—he waved a hand, searching for the right word—"influential. Fashionable. Popular."

Trevissick inclined his head regally. "I will not belabor the conversation with false modesty."

"I don't care about all that rot. But my parents do. So, if you could... I don't know... invite them to one of your parties, or speak to them in public, or something like that, I know it would mean a great deal to them."

The duke nodded crisply. "Consider it done." He rose to his feet. "Now, if you will excuse me..."

Archibald waved a hand. "Go on. Get back to your new bride."

After Trevissick left, Archibald sat in his chair, staring at the wall. He wasn't sure it was a good idea for him to go back down to the forge, which was full of hot furnaces, sharp tools, and heavy machinery, in his distracted state.

That evening, he was to attend Lady Waldegrave's ball. Archibald lived in London year-round, as the family business was located just north of town. But for most members of the *ton*, this would be the last hurrah of the Season.

He knew for a fact that the Astleys were planning on leaving town tomorrow to spend the winter at their country estate in Gloucestershire.

This meant two things: one, that he would see Lady Isabella tonight.

And two, that this was the last time he would see her for some months.

He was unsure how he should behave tonight. Were they friends now? Would she expect him to come over and greet her, to ask her for a dance?

That felt a bit presumptuous. She had approached him out of desperation last night. He didn't want to make her feel uncomfortable, or, God forbid, to give the impression that he felt entitled to a repeat performance of their kiss.

He decided he would follow her lead. He certainly wasn't going to cut her. But nor was he going to approach her. If she wished, she could be the one to come up to him. That way, she wouldn't feel cornered.

God. His palms were sweating already, and it was four hours before the party even began. This was a disaster in the making.

CHAPTER 6

"*O*oh—could you pull over up here?" Izzie's twin sister, Lucy, asked the coachman. "I think I see some ducks!"

They were in Hyde Park, taking some autumn air along with their particular friend, Lady Diana Latimer. Their chaperone was Diana's great-aunt Griselda, who was somehow managing to sleep, chin against her chest, while they bumped along in one of the Latimer family's landaus, an open-topped carriage perfect for a leisurely afternoon drive. The three girls took the basket of bread Lucy had brought and headed for the banks of the Serpentine, leaving Lady Griselda napping in the carriage.

It was a lovely afternoon, cool but clear, and Diana had been eager to get out of the house. Her older brother, the Duke of Trevissick, had married Cecilia Chenoweth last night, and although Diana was pleased to have a new sister-in-law, there were some aspects of the match she was not precisely enjoying.

"I had no idea the walls were so thin," she muttered. "I

requested that a bedroom be made up for me in the east wing. That way I might be able to get *some* sleep."

"What sort of sounds are they making?" Lucy asked, her voice full of curiosity.

"All sorts," Diana said. "Groaning. Screaming. Thumping."

"I heard some of that in the dark walks," Izzie said. At Diana and Lucy's startled looks, she added, "It would seem that people go to the dark walks not in search of romance so much as"—she cleared her throat—"a place to fornicate."

Lucy looked horrified. "But you didn't see any of that. Did you, Izzie?"

"No. It was very dark, so I saw nothing of the act itself, thank God. Although…" She lowered her voice to a murmur, even though the two footmen who had accompanied them were hovering at a discreet distance. "You'll never believe who I saw engaging the services of a prostitute. It was Andrew Milner!"

Diana recoiled. "The M.P.?"

Izzie nodded. "The very one."

Diana shook her head, her expression one of disgust. "What a hypocrite. I know some husbands and wives have that kind of arrangement. But Mr. Milner presents himself as a paragon of…"

She trailed off, frowning, raising her hand to shade her eyes as she stared across the expanse of lawn behind them.

"What is it?" Lucy asked.

"Do you see that burgundy carriage? It looks like a hackney—it's scraped up, and you can tell there was once a crest that's been removed from the door."

Izzie squinted across the field. "What about it?"

"I saw it at Hyde Park Corner and again when we went past the parade grounds," Diana said. "I think it's following us."

"Following us?" Lucy asked. "Surely not. What could they want with three girls feeding the ducks?"

"One of those girls happens to be the richest heiress in London," Izzie noted. She was referring to Diana. Over her protests that it would do nothing but attract fortune-hunters, her brother, the duke, had insisted on settling an absurdly large dowry of one hundred thousand pounds upon her. This was in addition to the fortune she would one day inherit from her aunt Griselda, which was probably worth twice that.

Lucy smiled as she tossed bread into the water. "You two have been reading too many Gothic novels. We've a pair of footmen and your aunt Griselda. What could possibly happen?"

"Hmm," Diana said, frowning as the carriage pulled to a halt some fifty yards down the river. Four men piled out.

Diana's shoulders relaxed a trifle when the men started skipping rocks across the water.

Izzie glanced back toward the landau. Lady Griselda was still sleeping soundly.

This was her chance.

She turned to her companions. "I need your advice."

She had already told Lucy in hushed whispers what had transpired last night between her and Mr. Nettlethorpe-Ogilvy. Now, she filled Diana in on what had really occurred in the dark walks.

"He'll be there tonight. At Lady Waldegrave's ball. I would very much like to kiss him again. But I'm not sure how to arrange it."

"He'll ask you to dance," Lucy said.

Izzie rubbed her brow. "I'm not sure that he will. He's never asked me to dance before."

"Of course, he will," Diana said encouragingly. "And then

you can complain of being overheated and ask him to take you for a turn about the balcony."

Izzie wrung her hands. "But what if he doesn't?" It wasn't like her to be such a sheep's heart.

But she found that she cared what Mr. Nettlethorpe-Ogilvy thought of her in a way that she hadn't with any other man.

"Then you'll have to flirt with him," Diana said, taking a handful of bread and scattering it before a pair of passing swans.

She said this as if it were a simple matter, but Izzie found herself at a loss. She was far more accustomed to terrifying men by stating her forthright and often unflattering opinions.

"I haven't much experience with flirting," she admitted. "Before last night, I hadn't found a man I considered to be worthy of flirting with."

"Oh!" Diana looked surprised. "Well, Lucy knows how to do it."

"What? Me?" Lucy jerked her head around, startled. "I haven't the faintest clue."

Diana put her hand upon her hip. "How many proposals have you received this Season?"

Lucy waved this off. "Just six. But that doesn't mean I know how to *flirt*."

"Well, you must be doing something right," Diana argued.

"It's her natural disposition," Izzie said. "Everyone flocks to Lucy."

While Izzie was naturally acerbic, her twin was as sweet as spun sugar. Lucy didn't have to try to flirt because Lucy was naturally interested in people and genuinely thought highly of everyone she met. Men felt flattered when she hung on their every word and peppered them with questions about their interests and accomplishments. Little did they know that Lucy treated the scullery maids the same way. It was just who she was.

Izzie loved her sister more than anything, but she did worry about her. She was far too trusting. The six men who had offered for her had been a mixture of fortune hunters and puffed-up buffoons, and Lucy would have accepted every one of them had Izzie not sat her down and explained precisely why those men were not worthy of her.

"Caro is the one who knows how to flirt," Lucy offered, referring to the second-oldest Astley sister, who was now the Viscountess Thetford.

This was unequivocally true, not that it would help. "But Caro isn't here, and the party is tonight. I need—"

"Where did they go?" Diana asked. Her gaze was fixed upon the hackney carriage parked down the river.

Izzie turned to look. Surely enough, the carriage was still there, but the four men who had been skipping rocks had disappeared.

She felt a cold chill sweep through her. Which was ridiculous, honestly! It was broad daylight, in the middle of Hyde Park.

Yet she could not shake her sense of foreboding.

"They probably just went for a walk," Lucy said. She came over and pressed Diana's hand. "I know you've had to be vigilant for most of your life. But your father is dead now. You can relax."

Diana had grown up with an abusive father who killed her mother by pushing her down a flight of stairs when Diana was two years old. Her older brother, Marcus, had managed to remove Diana from the old duke's grasp by arranging for her to live with her great-aunt Griselda in the far reaches of Yorkshire. But even there, the old duke had proved a danger, once even attempting to kidnap his daughter.

Diana had grown up fencing and shooting under Aunt Griselda's tutelage. The fact that she had been born missing her right hand had not been considered an impediment to her learning to defend herself.

All this meant that Diana was not the relaxing sort.

"I don't like it." Diana stalked over to the landau and shook her great-aunt's arm. "Aunt Griselda. Aunt Griselda, wake up!"

Lady Griselda shouted a few words in her native German before sitting up. "What is it, child?" she asked, her eyes snapping into focus with remarkable speed.

"Do you see that carriage?" Diana asked, pointing. "I think it's been following us. There were four men beside it, skipping rocks. But now they've disappeared."

"Get inside," Lady Griselda said crisply. "We're leaving. Make the horses ready, Charles, and summon the footmen… Wait." She turned her head, her gaze sweeping the riverbank. "Where are the footmen?"

Glancing about, Izzie saw that the footmen had vanished into thin air. Now, her heart was tripping over itself.

Diana was already in the landau. Lucy, at last looking concerned, hurried back from the river.

"Climb up, Lucy," Izzie said, pushing her twin toward the carriage.

Everything happened at once. Four men in dark clothing emerged from behind four trees. One of them rushed up to the horses and grabbed the reins. The other three closed in on Lucy and Izzie, who were not yet in the carriage.

Lucy's foot slipped on the landau's metal step. Izzie caught her, struggling to boost her twin up as Diana grabbed Lucy's hand from above and pulled.

"There she is!" one of the men cried. "Get her!"

Lucy was crying, and everyone was screaming. Just as

Izzie felt someone grab the back of her skirts, a deafening blast from overhead shook the carriage.

The horses reared, squealing in terror. Izzie looked up and saw Lady Griselda standing above her, a smoldering firearm in her hand.

Diana had managed to haul Lucy into the carriage. The man who had grabbed Izzie's skirts fell back, and she managed to get one foot onto the carriage's step.

Lady Griselda grabbed her arm. "Drive!" she shouted to the coachman, not even waiting for Izzie to get all the way into the carriage. Charles urged the horses into a gallop, an order they were all too eager to obey, and Izzie would have gone flying from the landau were it not for Lady Griselda's steely grip on her wrist.

By the time the horses reached the path, Izzie had managed to clamber aboard. Diana reached over and slammed the landau's door shut behind her.

They all turned to look out the back of the carriage. One of the men lay still upon the ground, and the other three were running back toward the hackney.

"Oh, my gracious!" Lucy exclaimed. "Did... did you shoot him?"

Lady Griselda shook her head. "I doubt it. I had to aim high. This is a blunderbuss, a scattershot weapon, you see. I could not shoot them without hitting Lady Isabella."

Lucy was gripping the side of the carriage with white knuckles, but Diana's gaze as she studied their attackers was calm. Assessing. "I'm fairly certain the man who is down is the one who was holding the horses. He probably got kicked when they reared."

They had reached Rotten Row, which was crowded with carriages. Charles had to slow the horses to a trot, but there was no sign of the hackney carriage behind them.

Lucy turned to Diana, her face miserable. "Oh, Diana, I'm

so sorry! I should not have questioned your instincts. I just thought that, with your father dead, surely your troubles had ended."

"Ah," Lady Griselda said, "but they were not after Diana."

"Not after Diana?" Lucy asked. "But they said, *there she is. Get her.* And what could they possibly want with the rest of us?"

Lady Griselda fixed her eyes on Izzie. "That, I do not know. But I do know this—the one they were after is Lady Isabella."

CHAPTER 7

They arrived at Latimer House, the palatial mansion owned by Diana's older brother, just as the duke was disembarking from his own carriage.

He took one look at his sister's pale face and stormed over to the landau. "Diana? What's wrong? What the hell happened?"

They frantically related the story, all four of them talking at once.

No amount of insistence on Lady Griselda's part could shake the duke's conviction that the villains had been after his sister.

"Get Diana inside," he snapped. "I will escort Lady Lucy and Lady Isabella back to Astley House."

Diana rolled her eyes before turning to her friends. "I'll see you tonight at the Waldegrave ball."

"We will not be attending the Waldegrave ball!" her brother snapped. "You will not be setting a foot outside the house until this threat has been eliminated."

"Marcus!" Diana growled. "You are being *entirely* unreasonable. As usual!"

The duke pinched the bridge of his nose. "I am not going to argue with you about this. When it comes to your safety, we will take no chances. Now get inside the house so I can see your friends safely home."

Diana glared mulishly at her brother but allowed the family butler, Ellery, to shepherd her inside.

Once they arrived at Astley House, the duke apologized to Izzie and Lucy's mother. "I am terribly sorry that their proximity to Diana has placed the twins in the crossfire, as it were. Now that my father is dead, I had hoped that the dark cloud that has been hanging over my family would dissipate." He made a bleak sound. "Now I see that is not the case."

"Please," their mother said, "there is no need to apologize. Thank goodness that Lady Griselda is, well, Lady Griselda."

"Thank goodness indeed," the duke said.

"Do you think it was a kidnapping attempt, then?" Lady Cheltenham asked.

"I have very little information at this time. I shall hire a Runner to look into it just as soon as I find out what's become of my footmen. But that seems like the most likely motive, yes."

"We won't keep you," their mother said. "Please give our best wishes to Lady Diana and our thanks to your aunt."

"I will," the duke said.

Their mother called for tea, saying it would be just the thing to restore them to rights. Although the servants were flitting about, packing and making ready for the family to return to their country seat, Harrington Hall, the following morning, the house was quiet by the Astley family's usual standards. Their father had already departed for Gloucestershire that morning. Izzie's eldest brother, Edward, and his wife, Elissa, were out, probably visiting some museum or library, as there was nothing the pair of classicists liked better than crumbling bits of parchment more than a thousand years old.

Her second-oldest brother, Harrington, had recently purchased a lieutenant's commission in the 95th Rifles and would remain with his regiment rather than journey home with the family. Izzie was going to miss him terribly. She and Harrington were the black sheep of the family; now, she supposed she would become the sole target for her father's improving lectures.

Izzie and Lucy also had two older sisters, Anne and Caro, but they were both married and had households of their own, and neither happened to be visiting this afternoon. And, of course, her youngest brother, Freddie, was away at Eton.

So, it was just Lucy, Izzie, and Lady Cheltenham who settled around the tea table. "Gracious, girls," their mother said as Lucy poured them each a cup, "this was an eventful afternoon even by Izzie's standards."

Izzie found herself feeling uncommonly taciturn and took her time chewing a lemon biscuit.

Lucy finally said, "You know, Mama, Lady Griselda was convinced that it wasn't Diana those men were after. She said they were after Izzie."

Her mother froze, her cup halfway to her mouth. It took a moment for her to regain her composure. "And what do you girls think?"

Izzie's tongue felt thick in her mouth. She *wanted* Lady Griselda to be wrong. Not that she wanted Diana to be those men's true target.

But she found herself clinging to the hope that it had been a random act of street crime, a group of cutpurses who had noticed their fancy carriage and assumed they would have something worth stealing. That she had not been a *target* in the literal sense.

That it was unlikely to happen again.

"It's difficult to say," Lucy said in answer to their mother's question. "Everything happened so fast."

Her mother's eyes were sympathetic. "Izzie, there's no reason these men would have for attacking you. Is there, darling?"

Izzie choked on her biscuit. Suddenly, the words she had overheard in the dark walks echoed through her head.

How soon can you deliver the guns?

The army won't even miss such a trifling amount.

I know who those guns are intended for.

You're in too deep.

If those men had spotted her, there was a very good reason someone might now want to kill her.

But if she were to tell her mother that, she would have to tell her the truth. That she hadn't lost her way last night. That she hadn't been delayed due to her hair being snarled in a tree.

That, like Pandora, she had been unable to tamp down her curiosity, and now she desperately wished she could force those secrets she had never wanted to hear back inside the box.

And after all, Lucy had a point. Everything had happened very quickly.

Maybe it really had been a gang of cutpurses.

"Nothing comes to mind," she lied, setting her cup down upon its saucer. "I am feeling shaken, though. If it's all right, I'd like to lie down."

"Of course, darling," her mother said.

Izzie went upstairs. Her maid helped her loosen her gown, and she lay down on the bed.

But sleep did not come.

CHAPTER 8

$\mathcal{A}$ few blocks to the north, Archibald arrived at his family's townhouse, a hulking Gothic monstrosity designed to look like a haunted castle, complete with bars over the windows, crenelated walls, and turrets on each corner. It was his mother's notion of fashionable architecture, and it was apropos in that it blended in with the sedate Georgian townhouses that surrounded it about as well as Archibald himself blended in at a ball.

He handed his coat and hat to the butler, Giddings. "How is he?"

Giddings understood precisely to whom he referred. "He's been resting for most of the afternoon. Shall I send up some tea?"

Archibald flexed his hands, sore from working all day at the forge. "Please. In case he wakes up."

Giddings bowed. "At once, sir."

Archibald made his way up two flights of stairs to a room in one of the circular corner towers. He rapped lightly on the door. There was no answer, but he pushed it open, anyway.

Inside he found his grandfather, John Nettlethorpe, lying

on the bed. The doctors had found a tumor in his chest two months ago. They had cut it out, but the surgery had not slowed his grandfather's decline.

Today, like most days these past two weeks, his grandfather's eyes were closed. On days when he was awake, he would ask Archibald how things were at Nettlethorpe Iron, the business he had founded some fifty years ago. His grandfather gave him better advice than anyone. Archibald understood everything about running Nettlethorpe Iron from an engineering perspective. But he was still getting used to the business side of things, which his grandfather had always overseen, and which was just as complex as any high-pressure steam engine. They would talk for a half-hour or so until his grandfather grew tired.

He placed his hand upon his grandfather's forehead, gently, so as not to wake him. He wasn't feverish. He seemed to be resting peacefully.

Archibald pulled a shield-backed chair beside the bed, intending to stay a while in case his grandfather awakened. He glanced around the room that would be his grandfather's final home. It was grand but spartan, with curved stone walls, a high ceiling, and brilliant stained-glass windows. His grandfather had requested this room over one of the bedrooms, all of which had been overenthusiastically decorated by his parents in the Gothic style, because he was a simple man, and the sparseness of the plain stone walls suited him. But Archibald insisted on moving a particular pendulum clock into the room, positioning it facing the foot of the bed where his grandfather might see it.

It happened to be *the* clock, the one that had started it all. Even as a five-year-old, Archibald had liked to know how things worked. That was how it came to pass that one spring morning, his parents had walked into the front parlor and discovered their son sitting in the middle of the Axminster carpet with a screwdriver in his hand and the pieces of their brand-new clock scattered around him.

His nursemaid was promptly dismissed for failing to mind him sufficiently. His mother was fluttering about the room in despair when John Nettlethorpe appeared in the doorway, just in time to hear his grandson protest, "But, Mama, I can put it back together!"

"Put it back together!" his mother cried, wringing her hands.

"Archie, my boy," his father said, "do you have any idea how much that clock cost?"

"I *can* rebuild it," five-year-old Archibald insisted. "I've done it three times already."

His grandfather chose this moment to stride into the room. "Let's see ye do it, then."

That hadn't stopped his parents' fretting. But, with John Nettlethorpe watching in silence, young Archibald had, indeed, reassembled the clock.

"Oh, thank *goodness!*" his mother cried when the clock was once again ticking away.

"You must promise me you'll never take the clock apart again, Archie," his father said.

"But Papa!" To be sure, he had some nice toys in his nursery. But nothing nearly so interesting as the clock. "I've showed you I can put it back together."

"Promise yer father," his grandfather said firmly.

Archibald winced. He had hoped Grandfather would take his side. Grandfather was the only one who didn't seem to disapprove of his curious nature. "I—I promise," he whispered.

His mother was back to wringing her hands. "We'll find a new nurserymaid by tomorrow. But who will watch you today?"

Archibald remembered perking up, wondering if this meant he might get to spend the day with his mother.

"I'll get one of the kitchen maids to do it, I suppose," she said, and Archibald's heart sank.

"Don't bother," John Nettlethorpe said, going down on one knee so he and Archibald were at eye level. He fixed his grandson with his blue-grey gaze. "You, my boy, are coming with me."

"With *you*?" his mother cried in the same breath that his father said, "Out of the question!"

At the time, Archibald hadn't understood why they were so upset. He hadn't understood that his grandfather was the worst thing you could possibly be, according to his parents, anyway: a working man. He hadn't understood that John Nettlethorpe represented everything they were trying to leave behind.

But John Nettlethorpe's money also paid for their lavish lifestyle, so when he calmly threatened to cut them off, the argument ended in an instant.

In short order, Archibald found himself climbing into the plain brown carriage his grandfather used to get around town.

"Where are we going?" he asked breathlessly.

His grandfather's eyes twinkled. "To the best place in all of London. Nettlethorpe Iron. And don't you worry, Archibald." He leaned forward, holding his grandson's gaze. "I have *much* more interesting machines to show ye than that clock…"

Archibald blinked back into focus. He must have nodded off. The shadows had grown longer in the room. Someone had brought in a pot of tea, but it had gone cold.

His grandfather was still asleep. He straightened the blankets, then slipped from the room.

He was heading to his bedroom to dress for the Waldegrave ball when his mother emerged from the portrait gallery.

"Archie!" his mother called. "Oh, Archie, come and see!"

Although he was careful to keep his face neutral, the name *Archie* grated against his ears, as it always did.

It wasn't that there was anything wrong with the name Archie. But "Archie" sounded like a young man with a mop of blond curls and soft white hands. "Archie" enjoyed racing his highflyer at reckless speeds and was known for the elegant flourish with which he opened his snuffbox.

Meanwhile, Archibald had to use lye soap to get the grease out of his knuckles at the end of each day. He was burly, swarthy, *and* hairy and had not only calluses but burn scars on both of his hands. The closest thing he had to an elegant hobby was boxing, but he hadn't learned to box at Gentleman Jackson's, as one did. Oh, no, growing up, he had learned to box by sparring with the boys his age who were apprenticed at his grandfather's forge.

Sparring against actual ironworkers had prepared him a little too well, and when, at his parents' urging, he finally did show his face at Gentleman Jackson's, he'd managed to make the wrong impression by knocking his sparring partner unconscious within the first ten seconds of their bout.

He hadn't meant to. He hadn't even hit him that hard. Did the man not know how to move his feet? But nobody had wanted to partner with him after that, and so, his days at Gentleman Jackson's had been put on hiatus for a few years until Michael Cranfield, the Earl of Morsley, whom Archibald knew from serving on the board of the Ladies' Society for the Relief of the Destitute, had invited him to go a few rounds.

Morsley was six and a half feet tall and had spent the past few years living on the frontier in Upper Canada. He was as strong as an ox and had a similar problem in that no one wanted to spar with him, either. And so, they began boxing together a few times a week. They were a well-matched pair. Morsley had the reach advantage, but Archibald was faster, and, most importantly, neither of them were going to fly into hysterics if the other one landed a blow.

Depending on the time of day, they usually went for a coffee or stopped in a chophouse for lunch afterward. Morsley was by far the most down-to-earth peer Archibald had met, and they had a similar disinterest in the pointless extravagance of the *ton*.

They had become friends, and, as far as Archibald's parents were concerned, befriending an earl, even a slightly odd one who preferred a log cabin in the Canadian wilderness to a glittering palace, was the best thing Archibald had ever done.

Archibald obediently followed his mother into the gallery. He found his father already inside, grinning broadly as he stood next to a life-sized statue of white marble.

"There you are, Archie, my boy!" his father exclaimed. "Look what arrived today!"

The statue showed a man in Roman-style armor with breastplate, sandals, and a plumed helmet. He was posed as if standing upon a mountaintop, front knee bent, sword at his side as he heroically surveyed his demesne.

"It's Alexander the Great," his father explained.

Ah, Alexander the Great. He could see that. But there was something off about the statue. Greek or Roman statues were usually old and weathered. This one was a pristine white and looked brand new.

That was when Archibald noticed that "Alexander's" facial features were a perfect copy of his father's.

"You—you've commissioned a statue of yourself as Alexander the Great?" he sputtered.

"Yes!" his father exclaimed. "Isn't it marvelous?"

Marvelous was not the word Archibald would have chosen. His parents longed to be welcomed into the upper echelons of high society. Archibald received the occasional invitation because he was both obscenely wealthy and unmarried. He had the potential to be useful in the form of bringing an influx of capital into some debt-ridden family's coffers.

But high society had quickly decided that it had no use for his parents. Meanwhile, they seemed to believe that the key to their entrée into the *ton* was to demonstrate how rich they were through extravagant spending.

Archibald did not pretend to be any great expert on how to impress members of the upper echelons.

But he was fairly certain that commissioning a statue of yourself as Alexander the Great was not it.

His parents were beaming at him, eagerly awaiting his reaction. "It's, um." He cleared his throat. "It's really something."

"Isn't it?" his father exclaimed. "My only regret is that I didn't think to request a pose on horseback."

"Oh, my sweet," his mother cried, "would but you had thought of that!"

"I know, it's a shame, isn't it?" His father shook his head. "I'll just have to commission another one."

Archibald rubbed his brow. *Dear God.* He hadn't thought anything could be worse than the time his parents had paid more than a thousand pounds for an Ancient Egyptian statue of the jackal god Anubis. It didn't sound so bad until you saw that it was in a state of ruination such that the only part remaining was the arse.

That one was on display in the foyer, so that a statue of a

man's arse was the first thing you saw when you came into the house. Which made it awkward to host visitors, to say the least.

But even the Arse of Anubis was easier to explain away than *this*.

"I'm pleased that you're happy," Archibald said. That, at least, was true.

His parents might be the most gauche people in the British Isles. But they did love him, in a fumbling sort of way. And he wanted them to be happy.

"I've managed to secure an invitation to the Waldegrave ball," Archibald announced. "I'd best go and change."

His father laughed. "I'll say. You can hardly walk into a ballroom looking like *that*."

Archibald bit back a sigh. If he was being honest, the comment rankled. Of course, his parents, whose dearest wish was to be accepted in lofty circles, despaired of the sight of him in all his dirt.

But at the same time, they wanted to live lavishly, and the thing that supported their ostentatious lifestyle was, ironically, the thing they hated the most—his work at Nettlethorpe Iron. Pleasing his parents was literally impossible. They didn't *want* him to be in trade, yet they *needed* him to be in trade. And it was crushing, sometimes, the knowledge that no matter what he did, it would never be enough, that they would never be truly proud to have him as their son.

He was stuck between two worlds, fitting in nowhere.

"Say, Archie," his mother said, breaking his reverie. "Have you set your eye on any young ladies? Since things with Miss Chenoweth didn't work out?"

His parents had been thrilled by the news that Cecilia Chenoweth had refused him. They would much prefer that he marry someone with the word *Lady* in front of her name and had despaired at the news that he intended to propose to a mere vicar's daughter.

Isabella Astley's face flashed across his mind, the way she'd looked last night, eyes hazy with... pleasure? Confusion? Distress?

Hell, he didn't know. But he wasn't about to mention her to his parents. They would fly into a frenzy at the thought of him marrying the likes of Isabella Astley.

But that was never going to happen.

"Not yet," he lied. "It will probably have to wait for next year. This is the last event of the Season, so most of the *ton* will be heading to their country homes soon."

"Oh." His mother did not bother to conceal her disappointment.

"Well, aim a little higher next time, son," his father said with an exaggerated wink.

Archibald thought Cecilia Chenoweth was a fine lady, an opinion that would seem to have been borne out by the fact that she was now a duchess. But he gave a slight bow. "I'll try, Father."

He went to his room, a huge space that had been decorated by his mother in the Gothic style. In Archibald's opinion, it looked like the lair of the villain in some medieval melodrama. Its vaulted ceiling was supported by elaborately carved columns made of stone. Red velvet curtains framed tall, arched windows. The room was dominated by the bed, which was raised upon a dais. As if there was any danger of missing it—it was black and hulking, with a canopy carved into pointed arches and spires on each corner. It weighed close to a ton and even had a scarlet silk counterpane.

His valet, Jack, was brushing a coat of black superfine. Jack used to be employed by Nettlethorpe Iron, but he had injured his shoulder lifting a cannon. It never healed well enough for him to return to the heavy work required at the forge. But Archibald had happened to be in need of a valet, so he had offered the job to Jack so he wouldn't find himself out on the street.

After all, how hard could being a valet possibly be?

Archibald cast a dubious look at the set of clothes Jack had laid out. He preferred to dress quite plainly. The coat was dark, but the trousers were cream, and the waistcoat was garnet silk brocaded with gold thread.

"Couldn't I wear this waistcoat?" he asked, pulling one in grey tweed from his wardrobe.

"Don't go touching nothing 'til you've washed up!" Jack snarled, snatching the grey waistcoat from his grasp.

Archibald sighed, but headed for the bathing tub, which was laid out before the fire. He had constructed it himself, and unlike the tiny hipbaths most members of even the upper classes made do with, Archibald fit inside this one with ease.

When you did the sort of work Archibald performed, it became imperative to have proper facilities for washing up. He knew hauling cans of hot water up the stairs for his daily bath was a lot of work for the servants. He had an idea to install a tank of water on the roof with a set of pipes that would enable him to fill the tub himself. He could even add a gas heater to warm the water. The design wouldn't be all that complex; it was just a matter of finding the time to build anything other than cannons.

Once he had undressed and stepped in, he took up a bar of plain white soap and a scrub brush and went to work. As he lathered up his chest, he eyed the waistcoat askance. "Don't you think that one's a bit garish?"

Jack crossed his arms. His expression was mulish. "Bastian says you have to wear this one and all this other shit to go with it."

Bastian was the Duke of Trevissick's valet. One week ago,

he had arrived uninvited and swept through Archibald's closet like a tornado, upending everything and even forcing him to submit to a haircut.

It was probably a good thing. Isabella's older sister, Caroline, was one of the *ton's* leading tastemakers, and she had assured him that both the haircut and Bastian's wardrobe choices were *de rigueur*. She would certainly know better than he would. But Bastian had apparently come to coach Jack on the art of being a valet every day since, and now everything was *Bastian says this* and *Bastian says that*.

Archibald couldn't help but note that Bastian's tastes ran toward clothing that was extremely... fitted. He'd always preferred something a bit looser, to draw emphasis away from his brawny frame. A gentleman was supposed to be athletic, to be sure, but athletic in the *right* way. It was one thing to have strong legs from days spent in the saddle, like Lord Thetford, or the subtle musculature the Duke of Trevissick had developed through hours of practice at fencing.

But Archibald's body was all wrong. His muscles were huge and bulky from lifting cannons. They served as a constant reminder to everyone who looked at him that, for all his wealth, he spent his days performing heavy manual labor. For all of Bastian's assurances that his new style was the height of fashion, Archibald could not help but feel self-conscious wearing such tight-fitting clothes.

Groaning, he sank beneath the water to dampen his hair. Once he was satisfied that he no longer smelled like he'd been working in a forge all day, he toweled off and padded over to the mirror so Jack could help him dress.

When it came time to do his cravat, Jack yanked his collar points all the way up to his ears. "Do you have to pull those up so high?" Archibald grumbled, twisting his neck in an effort to force them back down.

Jack glowered at him, jerking them even higher. "I do. Bastian says—"

"Bastian says, right, right. I hope I don't have to suddenly turn my head. You've put so much starch in these things, I'm liable to stab myself in the eye."

Jack gave one final yank on his cravat, then stepped back, giving a grunt of approval. "Well, if that's the thing that kills you, at least you'll look good at your funeral."

"That will be a great comfort to my mother," Archibald grumbled as he strode out the door.

CHAPTER 9

*I*zzie spotted Mr. Nettlethorpe-Ogilvy as soon as she arrived at Lady Waldegrave's house.

He looked *magnificent* in a black coat, cream breeches, and a garnet-red waistcoat. The clothes were similar to what every other gentleman in attendance had on. But *lud*—she had never seen a man who could fill out a coat like *that*!

Standing with her mother and sister, she fanned herself patiently, waiting for the chance to catch his eye and send him a smile. But he didn't look her way, not even once.

The supper dance that marked the midpoint of the ball came and went. Izzie danced twice more, still paying more attention to the man standing alone in the corner than to her actual partner.

The ball was almost over, and he hadn't so much as looked at her.

It was time to take matters into her own hands.

As a country dance ended, she saw him slip from the room, heading down a deserted hallway.

"Oh, dear!" she cried to her partner. "My, um… sister! She needs me."

Lord Cuthbert, who was heir to the Marquess of Lindisfarne and whose shoulders compared very poorly indeed with those of Mr. Nettlethorpe-Ogilvy, glanced around. "Do you mean Lady Lucy? I don't see her anywhere."

Izzie pressed a hand to her heart. "I don't have to see my sister to know when she is in"—she paused, staring into the distance, as if communing with some mystical power—"not distress, precisely, but... We're twins, you see. Do excuse me!"

She left Lord Cuthbert looking extremely confused in the middle of the ballroom and threaded her way through the crowd.

The corridor Mr. Nettlethorpe-Ogilvy had entered wasn't dark, but it was sparsely lit, suggesting that this was not the main area intended for guests. Izzie checked a few doors along the way but found the rooms deserted.

Finally, just as she was reaching the end of the hallway, a door clicked open, and her quarry stepped into the shadowy corridor.

"Mr. Nettlethorpe-Ogilvy!" she exclaimed, rushing over. "I've been looking for you all night."

"M-me?" he asked, pointing to his chest, then looking around as if there could possibly be someone else with the last name of *Nettlethorpe-Ogilvy* in the deserted hallway.

"Of course," she said, giving him her most brilliant smile.

They lapsed into silence. This flirting business was more difficult than it looked. Izzie cast about for a topic. "What brought you down this way?" she finally asked.

His ears turned as red as his waistcoat. "Oh, um. I was just visiting the, um... You know."

Suddenly, Izzie's face felt warm as well. *Perfect.* She had cornered him while he'd been using the necessary.

Very romantic, Isabella!

Oh, well. Sometimes you had to make a silk purse out of a sow's ear, so she smiled at him again.

He cleared his throat. "What, um… What are you doing down this way?"

She decided that fortune favored the bold. "Waiting for you to ask me to dance."

"*Oh!*" His whole body jerked, as if something had crept up behind him and bitten him on the leg. "I… I… Would you grant me the pleasure of a dance, Lady Isabella?"

He was so masculine, unquestionably a man, not a boy. But he really did look adorable with that befuddled expression.

Isabella smiled. "No."

He looked not annoyed so much as perplexed. "No? But you just said—"

She seized both of his hands in hers, smiling coquettishly as she walked backward, pulling him along after her. "Now that I think on it, I find that I would much prefer a turn about the gardens."

He tripped over his own foot. "A turn about the—" He stared at their joined hands, his expression one of complete and utter confusion. "Are… Are you *flirting* with me?"

She gave a bleak laugh as she turned to face forward, looping her arm through his. "Not very effectively if you have to ask that question."

"I didn't mean to suggest it was ineffective so much as incomprehensible," he muttered.

They entered the ballroom. *Incomprehensible.* How she hoped that didn't mean that he thought her a little fool who wasted her time writing silly Gothic novels, and the notion that an important man like him would ever be interested in the likes of *her* was patently absurd.

Steeling herself, she asked, "Incomprehensible in what way?"

"Just look at you," he said, sounding shocked that she had

asked. "You're the most beautiful woman ever to live. And I'm…"

He trailed off, his ears reddening again. Izzie felt a pleasant thrum in the center of her chest. *The most beautiful woman ever to live*—was that truly how he saw her? What a marvelous development!

She was so glad she had summoned the courage to corner him outside the gentlemen's retiring room.

Archibald tried not to trip over his own feet—*again*—and embarrass himself as Lady Isabella steered him straight across the ballroom and out the French doors that led to the balcony.

She didn't stop there but made for the stone steps that led down into the gardens. "I am embarrassed to say that I don't know much about you, Mr. Nettlethorpe-Ogilvy. I have heard that you are a blacksmith. Is that correct?"

It was rare for someone to say that to his face. He glanced at her, expecting the worst, but her expression was all sincerity. She looked… genuinely curious. And she had not imbued the word with the usual note of derision. She said it as if being a blacksmith was no better or worse than being a duke, an earl, or a naval captain.

"I do some smithing, yes," he said cautiously. "It is often necessary to create the things I want to build. But I primarily consider myself to be an engineer."

She chuckled. "I fear I don't know much about what that entails, either. What kind of engineering do you do?"

She was leading him deep into the garden as if this were completely ordinary and not something that could very easily lead to her ruination. "I build machines."

"That sounds fascinating. What kind of machines?" she asked, tugging him through a stone arch.

The machine he was most proud of was his screw-cutting lathe. He'd been working on it for the past three years, and now had it to the point that it was ready to replicate. Once he had a dozen of them, he planned to open a factory dedicated to manufacturing machine-cut screws.

The machine represented his greatest goal as an engineer: to introduce true precision into manufacturing. His screw-cutting lathes could make precisely the same size of screws every single time, and they could do it at a volume impossible for a single craftsman working by hand to dream of.

Some people would say they were just screws. And they were, but this was merely the first step. The breakthrough was that they were built with precision. And the possibilities...

The possibilities if he could build things with precision were *endless*.

But however excited Archibald was about the progress he had made, he had learned the hard way that no young lady, much less the likes of Isabella Astley, who had the quickest wit of anyone he knew, would be impressed to learn that his life's work involved making *screws*.

"I wouldn't want to bore you," he muttered. "But what about you? I understand that you write Gothic novels?"

They had come to a little stone bench. The rose bushes had been pruned back in anticipation of the coming winter weather, but it was still lovely.

Lovely... and secluded.

"That's correct," she said, taking a seat on the bench and pulling him down next to her.

"Won't you tell me about them?" he asked.

She peered at him uncertainly. "Are you truly interested?"

Did she really have to ask? He could sit and listen to this woman read whatever the most boring book in the world might be... *Debrett's Peerage*, most probably... for hours. The chance to hear her talk about the thing that excited her most in the world?

Priceless.

"I am."

"Well," she said hesitantly, "I recently finished a story about a poor young priest who takes up residence in a crumbling Welsh castle..."

It was Archibald's dream come true. Isabella Astley was talking to *him*. She started out hesitatingly, eyeing him as if she were nervous about his reaction. Needless to say, he hung on her every word. As she saw that he was genuinely interested, her manner slowly became more open, like a flower unfurling its petals to the sun.

Her book sounded like a madcap romp, full of the vivacious energy he associated with her.

"And then," she said, leaning forward, "the Marquis de Valeur discovers that his father, the Duke de Meritè, was not killed in the Terror after all, and is, in fact, the ghost living at the bottom of the well!"

"What?" Archibald said, laughing. "How did he manage to go so long without being discovered?"

Her eyes were solemn, but the corner of her mouth twitched. "There's a guard bear."

"A guard bear?" He threw back his head and laughed. "That's marvelous! How did you think that up?"

He noticed her shiver, so he started peeling off his coat.

"I don't know, I— Oh, thank you!" she said, sounding surprised but also delighted as he draped it about her shoulders.

He found he liked the sight of Isabella Astley wrapping herself snugly in his coat, a soft smile upon her rose-pink lips, but her expression suddenly turned solemn. "You don't think it's too ridiculous?"

"Of course, it's ridiculous but delightfully so. That's the point." He paused as it occurred to him that he might have misunderstood. God, he hoped he hadn't just offended her. "Isn't it?" he asked hesitantly.

"Precisely!" she exclaimed, leaning forward and squeezing his forearm with both hands. "The plot is admittedly outrageous—"

"Which is what makes it so entertaining," he finished.

"I'm so pleased you think so." She squeezed her eyes shut. "This is such a relief!"

He tilted his head. "A relief? Why?"

She waved this off. "It's just... Most people tell me that Gothic novels are a waste of time. That I should devote myself to *serious* literature, instead of writing this"—she suddenly looked down—"this *rubbish*."

Archibald wanted to ask who these people were, where they lived, and what time they would be home so he could go to their house and punch them in the face. "Well, they're wrong. To be sure, there's a time and place for serious literature. But it's books like yours that lift people's spirits, that let them forget their troubles for a time. That is not to be discounted."

She smiled at him, and his heart tripped. "That's one of the nicest things anyone has ever said to me."

He rubbed the back of his head, feeling as bashful as a schoolboy. "I'd quite like to read it." It occurred to him in a flash that she probably only had one copy. "If it's not too much trouble," he added hastily.

She bit her lip. "Can you keep a secret?"

Could he keep a secret? He would fight a horde of angry Vikings for this woman. "I can."

She dropped her voice to a hushed whisper, even though

they were alone. "It's being published by the Minerva Press."

"Izzie!" he exclaimed. "That's wonderful! I mean…" It occurred to him in a flash that he shouldn't have called her by her first name. "I'm sorry. *Lady Isabella—*"

"No, you can call me Izzie. In fact"—she glanced up at him, her eyes suddenly shy—"I would like it if you did."

He couldn't believe this was happening. This was the best night of his life. "And you must call me Archibald."

She nodded. "Very well. Archibald."

God, but he liked the sound of his name on her lips. He cleared his throat. "What is the title?"

"*The Castle of Brynberian.* I had to publish it anonymously, as writing Gothic romances is not a remotely appropriate undertaking for the daughter of an earl. It's coming out next week."

"I will be the first in line to get a copy," he promised. "And you must sign it for me."

"I will. Except…" Her face fell. "Except it will have to wait until next Season as I'm returning to Gloucestershire tomorrow."

"*Oh.*" He had known that, of course. He had even been thinking about how much he would miss her.

But suddenly, her leaving felt like a full-blown tragedy.

"Could I write to you?" he asked. It occurred to him immediately that the answer was probably no. "Or would that be considered improper?"

"It would be completely improper. But that has never stopped me before." She tapped her lip, lost in thought, then perked up. "Address your letters to my sister-in-law, Elissa. She and Edward will be staying at the Dower House down the lane. She'll pass them to me. I know she will."

"Perfect. That's what I'll do."

They lapsed into silence. After a moment, Izzie chuckled.

"Look at us. I didn't drag you out here so we could sit here, feeling morose."

His heartbeat ratcheted up a notch. "Why did you drag me out here, then?"

She looked up at him, her eyes both eager and shy. "I dragged you out here hoping you would kiss me aga—"

His lips were on hers before she could even finish the sentence.

CHAPTER 10

The first time Archibald had kissed her, it had been so good that Izzie wondered if she'd dreamed the whole thing up.

She hadn't. This time was just as good. Although it was… different.

It took her a moment to pinpoint what it was. His lips were still hot and greedy against hers, making her head swirl.

But he wasn't touching her anywhere else.

She peeked down and saw that he was gripping the sides of the stone bench with white knuckles.

"Touch me," she whispered, stroking her fingertips across his jaw, which felt smooth but was already showing a touch of shadow.

He was breathing hard. "I can't."

She trailed kisses up his jawline toward his ear. "You can. I want you to."

He gasped. "I can't. I want you"—he moaned as she nipped his earlobe—"too much. I'm afraid I'll forget myself again, the way I did last night."

She smiled against his cheek. "I liked it when you forgot yourself."

"It wasn't… wasn't proper."

She pulled back enough to give him a wry look. "Do I strike you as *proper*?"

He didn't seem to have an answer for that, which was just as well because she was already kissing him again. But this time, she had a new purpose.

She was going to make him break.

"You don't mind," she said between kisses, "if I touch you, do you?"

"No," he gasped. "No, that's fin—"

He moaned instead of finishing his sentence because that was the moment she slid into his lap, pressing her body against his.

He wasn't wearing a coat, as he'd given it to her, which meant that his perfectly sculpted torso was separated from her eager fingers by only the thin linen of his shirt.

"Izzie," he gasped as she explored absolutely every inch of his magnificent chest and arms. When she reached his forearms, she found them hard as iron as he clung to the bench for dear life. Smiling into his neck, she tickled the inside of his wrist, and he let go for a fraction of a second. But he managed to wrap his fingers around the edge of the bench again.

She was already moving on, sweeping her hands over his bulging biceps to the breadth of his shoulders. *God*, she wanted to see what he looked like without a shirt on. Just the thought had her squirming in his lap.

His waistcoat was in her way, so she unbuttoned it, leaving it to sag open. She trailed her fingers across the broad planes of his chest and down to his stomach, which was as hard as the stone bench and covered with fascinating ridges. By now, he was gritting his teeth and moaning as if he were in agony. And perhaps he was, but she hoped it was agony of the very best kind.

She tugged the hem of his shirt free from his breeches and slipped her hand beneath the linen. She could feel a trail of hair running down the center of his stomach, but otherwise his skin was warm and as smooth as satin. Fascinated, she shifted her leg so she was straddling him, all the better to explore this brave new world with both hands.

His eyes were squeezed shut as she slid her hands higher and higher, and his body had gone as hard as sculpted marble. When she found his nipples beneath his shirt and traced them with curious fingers, he made a sound that was more animal than human. She stayed there a moment, torturing him, then continued to sweep her fingers over his magnificent shoulders.

She stroked back downward, fascinated by the bulges that covered his stomach. Although... those weren't the only bulges that interested her. From her vantage point in his lap, she could feel a certain part of him straining toward her beneath the falls of his trousers.

They say that curiosity killed the cat, and it would certainly be the ruin of Isabella Astley. Unable to resist, she inched her hands lower... and lower... and lower, until she was stroking his shape through the wool of his breeches.

Dear God, how thick is he? was the last coherent thought she had before Archibald seized her wrists in an iron grip. The next thing she knew, she was flat on her back on the stone bench, her arms pinned over her head by one of his hands. He held her in place with his hips and hovered above her, his eyes wild.

Oh, she liked this! She liked this a little bit *too* much, the notion of this powerful man wanting her to desperation.

She let her legs fall open and rolled her hips against the same bulge she'd been exploring with her fingers just moments earlier. "I can't decide whether I want you to let me go or not," she panted. "Part of me wants to keep touching you. But part of me likes this *so much*…"

"God, Izzie," he said, his voice shaking with a potent mix of desperation, desire, and despair. "You're going to be the death of me."

"Yes, but will you die a happy man?" she asked, giving a little moan as she found a particularly good angle at which to rub herself against him.

He gave a bleak sort of laugh. "The happiest man on the face of this earth, if we see this through to its natural conclusion. But I can't take your *maidenhead* on a *stone bench*."

"I know," she sighed. "But part of me really, *really* wishes that you could and that you would hold my wrists while you do it, just. Like. *This*."

He made a strangled sound, and his lips found hers, and even better, his free hand landed, firm and hot, on the side of her waist. Inch by agonizing inch, he slid it up, slowly, much too slowly, until his meaty palm covered her breast.

He released her wrists then, but she didn't even mind because the reason was so he could draw her bodice down, exposing her straining nipple to the cool night air.

Without giving her time to catch her breath, he put his lips over it, and *oh*! The *sensations* Archibald was evoking in her! She threaded her fingers through his hair, nails scouring his scalp as she desperately tried to hold him in place. There was no need. He wasn't going anywhere. He worshipped her with kisses and nips and long pulls that had her writhing on the bench, and it was a good thing his strong, capable hands were at her ribcage, holding her in place, or else she would have tumbled to the ground.

"So good," she gasped. "So good! Archibald…"

With a growl, he came up and seized her lips, and she squirmed beneath him on the bench as he kissed her ferociously and touched every inch of her torso with his strong, warm hands. She was lost to everything but him. The only thing she could feel was his touch. The only thing she could hear was his guttural breathing…

Wait… A hazy thought formed in the far reaches of her brain. Shouldn't…

Shouldn't she also be able to hear the orchestra?

He seemed to realize it in the same instant, because he stopped kissing her, pressed his forehead against the cold stone bench, and muttered a curse.

He immediately cringed. "I'm sorry. I shouldn't have said that."

"That's all right," Izzie gasped. "My brother says that word all the time. I mean my brother Harrington. Not Edward, obviously."

His expression was pained as he pushed himself up. "Obviously." Taking her hands in his, he helped her sit up, too. "It sounds like the party has ended. You've got to get back inside before you're missed."

Sighing, she tugged her bodice back into place. "I suppose I should."

He squeezed his eyes shut. "I don't suppose there are any circumstances in which your parents could be persuaded to let me marry you tomorrow instead of taking you back to Gloucestershire?"

Her heart skipped a beat. It was a little bit frightening how quickly she was falling for this man, although really, who could blame her? It wasn't merely that he was the finest physical specimen in all of London. He seemed genuinely interested in her book, and he kissed her like he would die if he couldn't possess her. It was a heady combination.

And she knew herself well enough to know that she had a tendency to rush into things, and that this tendency occasionally led to disaster. And she was well aware that she scarcely knew this man. And yet…

Archibald didn't feel wrong. He felt…

Perfect. Perfect for *her*.

"Probably not," she said in answer to his question. "In fact, my father departed for Cheltenham this morning, so he isn't even available to ask."

She sighed. It was most likely for the best that the end of the Season was about to push them apart, at least for a few months. It would prevent her from doing something rash, would force her to slow down enough to see if this glittering, gossamer-thin thread that had sprung up, tentatively binding her heart to his, would prove strong enough to hold.

He nodded, staring at the ground, then stood. "I am going to write to you. I'm going to write to you every day. And when we see each other again—"

"Yes," she said. "However you were going to finish that sentence, the answer is yes."

He framed her face with those hands that were so strong, yet so gentle, and brought his lips to hers. He touched her the way an archaeologist would touch a two-thousand-year-old Greek vase, as if she were rare and precious.

She even felt his fingers tremble. How was it possible that *she* could make this hulking man tremble?

Suddenly, he stepped back. "Go on. I'll wait out here a while. No one will know we were together."

"All right." Suddenly her vision was blurry. She didn't want to, but she knew she had to go. "Thank you."

She handed him his coat. Before she could change her mind, she spun on her heel and started toward the house, forcing herself not to look back.

CHAPTER 11

*I*zzie was in a state of distraction as she made her way through the gardens. It felt like a tragedy of the first order that she would be parted from Archibald for months on end when she had just found him.

Her thoughts were awhirl and her eyes were blurred with tears, which explained why the attackers were able to sneak up on her so easily.

A hand emerged from the shadows, grabbing her dress where the neckline met the cap sleeve and jerking her around so quickly that she stumbled. She barely had time to scream before a second man seized her from behind, clamping his filthy, foul-smelling hand over her mouth. He trapped both of her arms in his other hand, twisting them behind her back.

She peered at the first man, the one still grasping a handful of her blue silk gown. She realized with a start that he was one of the four men who had attacked her in the park that afternoon.

"Lady Isabella," he sneered in an East London accent. "At last. You're a lot of trouble for a slip of a girl. Or, I should say, your friends are." He leaned in close so she could smell the foulness of his breath upon her face. "But you're all alone now, aren't you?"

It happened that she wasn't entirely alone. Archibald was in the walled rose garden just behind them. Had he heard her scream? It had been more of a squeak, to be honest. That was as much sound as she'd been able to make before the man had clamped his hand over her mouth, but perhaps he had heard it.

More men emerged from the darkness, a half-dozen or more. Even if Archibald had heard her scream, he could hardly be expected to fight them all. But maybe he could run and fetch the… the brute squad. Did London have a brute squad? She wasn't sure, but there must be *someone* he could fetch, and—

The sound of a meaty hand slapping around the wrist of the man who held her dress answered her question about whether Archibald had heard her scream.

He had heard, all right.

And his eyes were *murderous*.

Audible beneath his snarl was the sound of bone snapping, crisp in the silent garden, as Archibald wrenched the miscreant's offending hand from her person. It was accompanied by the sound of her dress rending, followed closely by a high-pitched scream as her would-be kidnapper stumbled back, his hand flopping unnaturally atop his broken wrist.

The man who'd been holding Izzie from behind let her go, but he wasn't fast enough. Archibald's fist connected with his temple with a hollow *thump*, and he crumpled to the ground.

More men advanced on them from the darkness. Archibald stepped in front of her without the slightest hesitation. One man leaped at him, a knife raised over his head. Archibald caught him with two hands to his chest and hurled him head-first into the garden's stone wall, which he slid down before settling in a heap on the ground.

Two men charged him at once. He grabbed them, one in each hand, and smashed their heads together. They collapsed insensible on the grass.

The final two attackers froze, then turned in unison and sprinted off into the darkness, followed by the man with the broken wrist.

It would appear that she had been mistaken. Archibald didn't need the brute squad.

Archibald *was* the brute squad.

As soon as he had satisfied himself that they were gone, he wheeled around to face her. Gone was the vicious expression he had worn mere seconds before. His eyes held nothing but consternation.

"Izzie!" he cried, framing her face. "Are you all right?"

Before she could answer, a rustling sound emerged from the ground at their feet; one of the attackers was stirring. An annoyed scowl crossed Archibald's face. Glancing down, he delivered a single sharp kick. There was the thump of his boot, then the more muffled sound of a body collapsing on the grass.

Archibald returned his gaze to hers, his eyes once again anguished. "Did they hurt you anywhere, anywhere at all?"

She meant to answer him, really, she did. But the words that emerged unbidden from her lips were, "That was *wildly* attractive."

He blinked at her, confused, then shook his head as if to clear it. "Izzie, darling, are you injured?"

Before she could answer, half of the party came streaming around the corner of the hedgerow, no doubt drawn by the percussive cacophony of Archibald's fists.

Izzie performed a quick survey of what they would see.

At least Archibald had managed to restore his clothing to rights after her departure. But the bodice of her dress had torn when Archibald ripped the attacker's hand from her person and was now gaping open—not that you could really see anything, as she wore a petticoat, corset, and chemise beneath it.

But still, it was bad. It was very bad. Just the fact that she had been caught alone in the garden with Archibald was enough to ruin her.

Well. Unless one considered the insensible bodies of her four assailants to be suitable chaperones.

She spied her mother in the throng. Clearing her throat, she said, "Suffice to say, Mama, Lady Griselda was right about those men who attacked us today in the park. It would appear that I am the one they are after."

CHAPTER 12

$\mathcal{A}$rchibald called at Astley House the following day at the extremely unfashionable hour of eight in the morning. He'd been unable to sleep the previous night, but that didn't matter. The important thing was to find out if Izzie was safe.

Last night, his heart had all but fallen out of his chest when she revealed that she'd been attacked in the park that afternoon. He'd tried to ask her what, exactly, she meant. But, of course, her mother was frantic, demanding to know what had just happened, and while Izzie was busy explaining how she was set upon in the garden, someone had shown up with the local constable. He'd had to explain to the constable why he had beaten four men badly enough to knock them insensible—and deliver the unwelcome news that there was another criminal at large whose wrist had been snapped like a twig, accompanied by two friends who had escaped scot-free. Then a Bow Street Runner had shown up, so he'd been obliged to repeat the whole story over again, and by the time he'd finished speaking to the authorities, Izzie's family had taken her home, and he didn't know what the hell was going on or if she was all right.

The first thing he noticed as he stepped out of his carriage was the crunch of broken glass beneath his boots. He looked up and saw that one of the ground-floor windows was boarded up. His stomach sank as he jogged up the front steps. Something was definitely not right here.

The door was opened not by Yarwood, the Astley family's butler, but by his friend and boxing partner, Morsley, who appeared to be standing guard, along with a half dozen footmen wearing four different sets of livery. "You're here. Good," Morsley said in a clipped voice. "Izzie's been asking for you."

"What the hell is going on? It looks like someone tried to break in." He froze as Morsley's words sank in. "Izzie's been asking for me?"

"Someone did try to break in," Morsley confirmed. "Around five o'clock. That's when she said, 'I wish Archibald was here.'"

"Then why the hell didn't you send for me?" Archibald snapped.

Morsley looked taken aback. "As I said, it was at five o'clock in the—"

"I would've come. Where is she?"

Morsley was giving him a speaking look but let the matter drop as he led the way up the stairs to a parlor on the first floor. "We've managed to assemble about two dozen footmen, between my house, Thetford's, the Duke of Trevissick's, and Peter Ferguson's. I'm watching the front door, Trevissick is pacing the eastern front with his sword, and Lady Griselda is patrolling the back side of the house with a blunderbuss and a pack of dogs. But it's all but impossible to guard a house like this," he said, gesturing to one of the tall windows that lined each and every room on the ground floor.

Morsley showed him which parlor the family was gathered in, then jogged down the stairs to resume his post. Archibald found the entire extended Astley family and a smattering of their closest friends assembled, looking drawn and uncharacteristically silent. His eyes scanned the room until he spotted Izzie, seated next to her twin, who was quietly crying, on a yellow-striped sofa.

Izzie sat up. "Archibald! You—you came."

"Of course, I came," he said, hurrying to her side. He paused as there was nowhere to sit.

"Come here, Luce," Harrington Astley called from a chaise-longue in the corner. "You can cry on me."

Lucy gave him a watery smile as she stood. Archibald nodded his thanks to Harrington and took the seat next to Izzie. "Tell me what's happened," he said in a quiet voice.

She did, from her near miss in the park yesterday, the one she'd been hoping against hope was a coincidence, to everything that had transpired since they parted last night.

"Mama said the best course was to get out right away," Izzie explained. "We didn't even bother to pack. She, Lucy, and I just got in the carriage at four in the morning, the idea being that we would be halfway home before they even realized we'd left."

"What happened?" Archibald asked, knowing the answer couldn't be anything good.

"We didn't even make it out of Mayfair. Armed riders descended on the carriage. The outriders managed to fight them off, but we were lucky no one was hurt. As it was, we barely made it back to the house. And then, an hour later, someone tried to force their way in."

"I saw the window," he confirmed.

She rubbed her brow. She looked exhausted and terrified,

two things he never wanted to see on Isabella Astley's face. "We don't know what to do."

"Do you have any idea who might be behind this?" he asked quietly.

"I've a fair idea. The trouble started while I was at Vauxhall the other night. I overheard some things in the dark walks, you see…"

She told him about the frightening encounter she'd had in the dark walks before he arrived, and everything she could recall about the two men whispering about stealing guns from the army.

"I've wracked my brain trying to remember their names," Izzie said. "The first one, the one who wanted the guns, was named Cooper. I'm almost certain of it. And the man who had access to the guns was a Scotsman—Mac something or the other. McDaniel, maybe? Or McDonald, or McDougal?" Her shoulders slumped. "I wish I could be sure."

"It sounds like he works for the Office of Ordnance." Archibald's mind was flying. He had contacts at the Office of Ordnance. They were Nettlethorpe Iron's biggest customer. His contacts specialized in cannons, of course, not the small firearms it sounded like this Cooper fellow wanted. But that was probably for the best. It certainly increased the odds that the people he knew wouldn't be involved in this scheme…

"Anne has all kinds of contacts through her charity work," Izzie explained. She was referring to Morsley's wife, the founder of the Ladies' Society for the Relief of the Destitute, who did indeed work in some very rough neighborhoods and who kept a number of potential informants on her payroll. "They haven't found any leads yet. I know they're asking around, but it feels like we're grasping at straws."

"I know some people at the Office of Ordnance I can ask," Archibald said.

Izzie looked up, startled. "You… you do?"

"I do. Nettlethorpe Iron sells them quite a lot of cannons."

From across the room, Edward Astley groaned. "Of course you do. Why didn't we think of that?"

"To be fair," Harrington noted, "we've been extremely busy flying into a panic."

Izzie gazed at him with wide eyes. "You make cannons?" she whispered.

"Hmm? Oh, yes. It's been most of our business these past few years, what with the war."

Archibald was trying to decide whom he was going to approach. Smalley, he decided. Robert Smalley seemed as upright as the day was long. Of course, one could never be sure.

But if it came down to it, if Smalley was on the take, no one could top the price Archibald would be willing to pay to secure Izzie's safety...

"You've given me hope," Izzie said. "At least we have a lead. It's terrifying that I have to hole up here like a sitting duck, but I'd much rather do it for days than weeks." She gave a great sniff. "And I've put my entire family in danger. That's the worst part."

He wanted to take her in his arms and comfort her, but he could hardly do so with everyone looking on.

One thing was clear—Izzie wasn't safe here, not even for a matter of days. It was hard enough to guard a house with this many windows during the day. Once darkness fell, it would be ten times worse.

What they needed was a fortress.

Archibald froze. A fortress... like the one in which he happened to live...

"There is a solution," he said slowly. He rose from the sofa and began to pace the room.

The more he thought about it, the more pieces fell into

place. It was *perfect*. If he could convince them, then Izzie would be safe. That was the most important thing.

And he? He would achieve his fondest wish, his most impossible dream.

"The problem is twofold," he announced. "Of primary concern, naturally, is the threat to Lady Isabella's life. It is imperative that we find a way to protect her."

He reached the mantelpiece and turned back the other way. "But do not forget that Lady Isabella has also been ruined by last night's events. She was discovered by several dozen onlookers, alone in the garden with a man—me—with her dress torn. If she does not marry, her reputation will be in tatters, and Lady Lucy will find herself suffering the consequences as well."

Having reached the center of the room, he turned to face the assembled Astleys, who were regarding him with surprise. "What Lady Isabella needs is not just anyone who can protect her. She needs a *husband* who can protect her."

He turned to face Izzie, looking her square in the eye. "And that husband is me."

It seemed that everyone in the room was too shocked to speak. Archibald continued, "I believe last night I demonstrated some facility for dealing with these cretins. I hope I have shown my willingness to do whatever it takes to keep Lady Isabella safe." He kept his eyes locked on hers. "Because I will."

Lady Cheltenham seemed to have recovered from her shock. "And we appreciate everything you did for Izzie last night."

Murmurs of agreement filled the room. Once they died down, Archibald continued, "But it is not merely my brute strength that makes me uniquely suited to this role. Excepting the Tower of London, my house is the closest thing you will find to a fortress for fifty miles. The windows are small, and there are bars on them. Unpickable locks on every door that I designed myself and built by hand. Thick stone walls. Towers on every corner. My house can be defended, and not only that, I have the men to defend it."

He turned to Lady Cheltenham. "My forge employs five hundred ironworkers. The most hardened criminals in Newgate Prison are not a tenth as hard as my men. I treat them well, and I pay them some of the best wages in London. For every opening we have, we receive a hundred applicants. These men are loyal to *me*. And I can afford to pay however many of them are needed to guard my house around the clock, both inside and out."

"As for the rest of it, it is no secret that I have been looking to marry." He returned his gaze to Izzie, who looked very small, and very alone, on the yellow-striped sofa. He tried to convey everything he felt for her with his eyes. "And I would be very happy, indeed, to find myself married to Lady Isabella."

Silence fell over the room. It was finally broken by Lady Cheltenham. "I must admit, it is a far better solution than anything we've come up with." There were a few reluctant murmurs of agreement. Once they died down, Lady Cheltenham continued, "But what do you think about all of this, Izzie?"

Archibald studied her, trying to read her face. He would describe her expression as thoughtful but also hesitant.

After an interminable duration that was probably no more than ten seconds, Isabella said, "Might I have a few minutes to speak to Mr. Nettlethorpe-Ogilvy in private?"

CHAPTER 13

*I*zzie nodded and smiled and did her best impersonation of an obedient daughter as her mother firmly informed her that she would be returning to the room in fifteen minutes. Then, everyone filed out of the yellow parlor, leaving her alone with Archibald.

As soon as the door closed, Izzie scurried across the room and turned the key in the lock.

Archibald stared at her with wide eyes. "I know your mother agreed to let us have fifteen minutes. But I don't think she would approve of us locking the door."

It was all Izzie could do to tamp down a crazed laugh. Leaving the door unlocked was well and good for a standard sort of proposal.

But the concern she was about to express to Archibald required... exceptional measures.

"Well, it's a good thing I'm already ruined, then," she said crisply.

She began pacing the room, wondering where to begin. What she was about to confess would be a difficult admission, to say the least.

After her second circuit of the room, Archibald cleared his throat. "If you are desirous of reassurances of affection on my part—"

"It's not that," she said crisply, then regretted interrupting him when he stopped short. Even though that wasn't the issue at hand, it would have been nice to hear.

"Perhaps you are wondering how I intend to treat my future wife?"

She waved this off. "It's not that, either."

She needed to come to the point, no matter how much embarrassment she felt. They had few enough minutes as it was. Steeling herself, Izzie stopped in the middle of the room, squeezed her eyes shut, and curled her hands into fists. "There is a *particular* concern I have that I would prefer to have addressed before I agree to marry any man."

"Of course." He crossed the room in three strides, coming to stand in front of her. "You have but to name it."

"Last night," she began haltingly, "physical relations between us seemed… promising."

His voice dropped half an octave. "A fair sight more than promising, I would say."

She could see her reflection in the mirror hanging beside the fireplace. Her cheeks were scarlet. "This is the area I wish to discuss."

He waited for her to elaborate. When she did not, he asked, "Are you worried that I might engage in physical relations outside of our marriage? Allow me to assure you that I will not."

"No, it's not that."

He tilted his head. "Are you trying to tell me that you have engaged in, er, *relations*, prior to marriage?"

She blew out a frustrated breath. "It's not that, either."

He was studying her more closely than was comfortable. He took a step closer, and his voice was gentle as he said,

"It wouldn't put me off, Izzie. I would still want to marry you."

"I appreciate that. But my maidenhead is intact." She swallowed, wishing he wasn't standing so close because this was going to be humiliating enough as it was. But at this point, she was wasting time, a commodity of which they had too little to begin with.

She'd best just come out and say it. She stared at the wall behind him. "My concern is this. I am afraid"—she squeezed her eyes shut—"that I am frigid."

~

Archibald couldn't help it.

He laughed.

When Izzie opened her eyes, they were full of poison.

"I'm sorry," he said swiftly. "But... Really, Izzie. You are quite possibly the least frigid person I have ever met."

"I wish I could share in your confidence!" she snapped. "But I... I..." She looked away, rubbing her elbow awkwardly.

He seized her hand and led her over to the sofa. Once they were settled, he said, "Tell me the reason for your concerns."

Her face was a portrait of mortification. "I told you. I'm *frigid.*"

He studied her profile. If she hadn't been with another man, that seemed to leave only one option. "Are you saying that you tried touching yourself?"

Her cheeks were scarlet. "*Yes.*"

He squeezed her hand. "It's nothing to be embarrassed about. It's normal to be curious. I take it you did not find your satisfaction?"

"*No.*"

She still wouldn't look at him, but at least they were

getting somewhere. "All right. What all did you attempt to do?"

Panic filled her eyes. "I… I…" She swallowed. *You know.*

"No, I don't."

She squeezed her eyes shut. "The point is, it didn't work. *At all.*"

"All right. But, as you noted, things between us seemed promising. *Very* promising," he added.

She looked at him then, but her expression remained one of consternation. "But what if it turns out that we're wrong? Marriage is for life, and I feel uncomfortable tying myself permanently to a man if we might not be, er…"

"Physically compatible?" Archibald supplied.

"Yes," Izzie muttered, looking away.

It was difficult for Archibald to imagine being more compatible with someone than he had been with Izzie last night. He could certainly speak for himself, and given the way Izzie had cried out when he kissed her breasts, and began instinctively grinding her core against him, it certainly seemed like she had felt something similar.

But right now, she was in distress.

"I have to be sure," she said.

It seemed that nothing he could say would reassure her. He was going to have to show her how good they could be together.

"Let me make sure I understand," he said slowly. "If I can bring you to climax, right here, right now, you'll agree to marry me?"

Izzie peered up at him, cringing. "It would make me feel considerably better about the prospect, yes."

Archibald glanced at the clock.

Eleven minutes.

That was how long he would have.

CHAPTER 14

*A*rchibald considered the task at hand.

He had only eleven minutes to bring an innocent to climax. An innocent who had tried and failed to find pleasure on her own.

But he did have some advantages on his side.

One—Archibald liked to know how things worked. He'd had two previous lovers—experienced widows with whom he'd entered into a temporary financial arrangement—and he had asked both of them questions.

Lots of questions.

He therefore had several ideas where he could start when it came to Izzie.

Two—she was naturally attracted to him. He knew she was.

And three—Archibald was a craftsman.

Which meant he was *very good* with his hands.

Without warning, he pulled Izzie onto his lap.

Normally, he would have started with a little more finesse. But he only had eleven minutes, damn it, so finesse would just have to wait.

He kissed her fiercely, the way he thought she liked, and allowed his hands to rove over all the delicate places to which he had denied himself access last night.

He could feel her stomach trembling with nervous energy, like a bumblebee's wings. As he stroked his way up her delicate torso, she shivered. And when his calloused thumb found a nipple, already peaked, through the silk of her gown, Izzie moaned into his mouth.

Recalling what she had said last night about loving the feeling of him holding her down, he pressed her back against the cushions of the sofa, pinning her in place with his hips. He caught both of her wrists in one hand and brought them up over her head, restraining her.

Rather than trying to be gentle, he let go. He kissed her like he wanted to devour her, which he did. He let his free hand rove over her body, the way he'd been dreaming of doing for years. With a snarl, he yanked the front of her bodice down, exposing the delicate curves of her breasts to his hungry gaze.

He worried he was being too rough, but as he kissed his way across her collarbone, her chest rose and fell in rapid pants. Her cheeks were flushed, but not, he thought, with embarrassment. No, the dazed look in her eyes bespoke arousal.

Encouraged, he bent down and sucked a perfect, dusky rose nipple into his mouth. She gave a soft cry, her hips bucking against him.

All signs seemed extremely promising. How he would've liked to linger on her breasts, to tease her until she was out of her mind with pleasure and crying out for what came next. But, seeing as time was of the essence, he went ahead and started drawing up her skirts. He had to release her wrists in order to kneel on the floor between her legs.

Izzie sat halfway up. "Archibald?" she asked, suddenly

looking nervous again. "Won't I bleed if you take my—my maidenhead?"

He'd reached the skin on her thighs, which was the color of cream and as soft as satin. "You would. But I'm not going to take your maidenhead."

She frowned but didn't offer any resistance as he pressed her thighs open. God, she was gorgeous here, too, flushed and pink and already slick for him. She even smelled like heaven.

He started kissing his way up the inside of her thighs.

"But if you're not going to take my maidenhead, how are you going to—oh. Oh. *Oh!*"

His tongue found the little bud at the juncture of her thighs, and Izzie didn't ask any more questions for some time.

Izzie didn't see how Archibald was going to bring her pleasure without taking her maidenhead. The maid she had paid a shilling to answer her questions when she was fourteen had told her she would find her enjoyment from a man's cock, sliding in and out of her passage.

But as soon as Archibald started flicking his tongue over that *amazing* spot, Izzie realized that there were quite a few things the maid had failed to mention.

It felt *beautiful*, it felt *beyond* beautiful, and she understood in an instant that this was it, the thing the poets sang about, the reason people did foolish things in pursuit of this pleasure, even when it brought them to ruin.

Everything seemed to crescendo. Helpless sounds of bliss emerged from her lips, and the panicked thought that her *mother* was probably listening at the door flitted across her dazed mind. But she couldn't seem to stop making them, any more than she could stop the trembling of her thighs.

Suddenly, Archibald's hand appeared next to her mouth but not to clamp down over her lips. She realized with a start that he was offering her the heel of his hand to bite down on. She availed herself of his offer, wrapping her lips over her teeth so she wouldn't hurt him… although, who knew if she even could have, given the thick callouses covering his palm.

But there was no time to worry about that now, because Archibald had started swirling his tongue faster, which felt *so good*, which felt like *magic* and *rainbows* and *perfection*, and she was going to… She was going to… *Oh, God,* she was going to…

That was when everything shattered.

CHAPTER 15

"I am terribly sorry about the vase, and I hope you will allow me to replace it."

Izzie watched Archibald, who was speaking to her mother, with dazed eyes. In retrospect, the thing that had shattered had been a gold and white porcelain vase that, up until a few minutes ago, had been adorning the console table running along the back of the sofa. It had apparently fallen victim to a flailing arm in the moment she found her ecstasy.

The sound of Messrs. Spode's handiwork missing the Axminster carpet by several inches and breaking into pieces upon the hardwood floor had drawn not merely her mother but all her siblings, their spouses, and family friends, including the Duke of Trevissick, Samuel Branton, a barrister who worked closely with the Ladies' Society and who was assisting with the search for whoever was trying to kill her, and Harrington's particular friend, Peter Ferguson.

Izzie made a valiant and probably fruitless effort to compose her features and pretend that Archibald had not just shifted the earth upon its axis, that what had passed between them had been a routine proposal of marriage, and that nothing improper had taken place. She had been useless, unable to recover a scintilla of composure, ever since Archibald initiated her into the world of bliss. He had been the one to restore her garments to rights and sit her up on the sofa, all while calling out to her mother that he was "Coming" as she frantically banged on the door and shouted for someone to fetch the spare key.

In spite of Archibald's best efforts, Lucy was giving her an arch look, a look that said *I am expecting a _full_ report*, but that was different. Lucy was her twin. She had expected Lucy to be able to read her.

But the possibility that *everyone* could guess what they had been up to was slightly horrifying.

"Please," her mother said, gesturing to the shards of porcelain scattered across the floor, "think nothing of it." She turned to face Izzie. Like everyone else in the room, she seemed determined to ignore the considerable evidence that significant improprieties had taken place during Archibald's 'offer of marriage.' "Have you accepted Mr. Nettlethorpe-Ogilvy's proposal, Isabella?"

"I have," Izzie said, her voice sounding dazed to her own ears. She cleared her throat, trying not to give the impression that she was swimming drunkenly through an ocean of pleasure. "I do believe that Mr. Nettlethorpe-Ogilvy and I will suit."

"Hmmm..." Her mother narrowed her eyes, then turned to Archibald. "If you will excuse us for a moment, I would like to confer with my daughter."

As her sisters flocked around Izzie, Archibald crossed to the far side of the room, where the men had gathered.

Izzie's eldest brother, Edward, poured a round of drinks. "To my future brother-in-law," he said, raising his glass.

A chorus of *hear, hear*s broke out.

Archibald could hear Izzie conversing with her mother across the room. "I know everything has happened very suddenly, but I am not displeased about the match. Quite the opposite."

Beside him, Morsley said, "You'll be good for Izzie. She wouldn't do well with some high stickler."

Her brother Harrington snorted. "Lord, is that the truth. If you were the type to throw a fit every time she bent one of society's rules, you'd find yourself in a never-ending fit for the next fifty years."

"Perfect," Archibald said. "I'm scarcely aware of society's rules. We'll rub along splendidly."

Across the room, he saw Izzie roll her eyes. "Yes, Mama. I know that I don't *have* to marry him. It happens that I *want* to…"

"The challenge," Harrington said, "will be getting Izzie safely inside your house. But I've got an idea how we can go about it." He gestured to the circle of men. "I'll need all of your help."

"What do you have in mind?" Morsley asked.

While Harrington described his plan, the Duke of Trevissick sidled up to Archibald. Leaning in, he whispered, "I agree with your assessment that you and Lady Isabella will rub along splendidly. Indeed, it seems that you're *rubbing along* splendidly already."

Archibald gave him a disbelieving look.

Across the room, Izzie raised her voice. "I will not even consider marrying anyone other than Mr. Nettlethorpe-Ogilvy!"

The duke glanced Archibald up and down. "*Impressive,*" he stage-whispered.

"*Shut it,*" Archibald hissed.

Trevissick flicked his wrist toward the section of the room where a pair of maids were sweeping up the last few porcelain shards. "Don't be so prickly," he whispered. "I'm sure everyone observed that your proposal was rather *explosive* in nature."

Archibald's voice was tight. "I kissed her. *Not* that it's any of your affair. But I am given to understand that sharing a kiss is considered to be acceptable after issuing a proposal of marriage."

"Hmm." The duke sounded baldly skeptical. "Where, exactly, did you kiss her?"

It was a good thing that Morsley was the one who happened to glance over just then. No one else in the room would've had a prayer of restraining Archibald as he lunged for the duke's throat.

"Very well, then," Lady Cheltenham said, rising from the sofa. "I suppose we will be having another wedding just as soon as it can be arranged."

That was probably the only sentence that could have made him forget his plans to strangle the Duke of Trevissick. Pure, unadulterated joy washed over Archibald. *He* was going to marry Izzie.

He couldn't believe it. Two days ago, he'd been unsure if she even knew his name.

Now, through some miracle, she was going to be his *bride.*

"Tomorrow," Archibald said, not wanting to give her time to change her mind. "I will secure a special license this afternoon."

Everyone murmured their agreement.

Samuel Branton stepped forward. "You'll need a marriage contract. If you'll tell me the basic points you want included, I can draw something up tonight."

"I would appreciate that," Archibald said.

Lady Morsley ushered Mr. Branton over to the writing desk in the corner and set him up with paper and quill. Archibald rubbed his chin. He didn't really know much about how these things worked. His grandfather's will called for Nettlethorpe Iron to go directly to him, skipping over his father.

In other words, Archibald would soon officially be one of the richest men in all of England.

"Let's see, Izzie will need... pin money." Archibald screwed up his face. How much pin money did one give one's wife? He had no idea. "Would ten thousand a year suffice?"

"*No*," Lord Thetford groaned in the same breath that his wife cried, "*Yes!*"

Archibald glanced around the room. "Is that not enough? If it's not enough, how about—"

"It's more than enough," Mr. Branton reassured him. "In fact, it is rather excessive."

"You're making the rest of us look *extremely* bad," Thetford explained.

Across the room, Izzie was peering at him, confused. "Archibald, are... are you rich?"

He told her his annual income.

The duke scowled. "That's more than I made last year!"

Archibald couldn't help it. He smirked.

Lady Cheltenham massaged her brow. "Izzie, how is it possible you did not know that Mr. Nettlethorpe-Ogilvy is one of the wealthiest men in Europe?"

She shrugged a negligent shoulder. "I thought he was some sort of blacksmith."

"Blacksmiths aren't usually invited to balls, dear," Lady Thetford noted.

Izzie tilted her head as if this was occurring to her for the first time. "Oh! I suppose that's true."

Her mother cast her eyes toward the elaborate

plasterwork scrolls adorning the ceiling. "I have long suspected that you do not listen to a word I say. This confirms it."

Although Lady Cheltenham was shaking her head in despair, Archibald felt a warm glow in the center of his chest.

He had always expected that some young lady would marry him for his money, in spite of despising everything else about him.

But Izzie wasn't even aware that he *had* a fortune.

He didn't pretend that she was marrying him because she liked *him*. But she did like the way he kissed her and the pleasure he'd given her a few moments ago.

That was a far cry better than being married for his money.

And, considering he would get to have the young lady he would have chosen above all others as his bride, the situation was more than satisfactory.

Morsley clamped one of his huge hands on Archibald's shoulder. "Branton also drew up my marriage contract with Anne, so he'll have a copy on file. Why not follow our provisions on pin money and what not? You know I will have been extremely generous as far as that is concerned."

Archibald knew Morsley to be head over heels in love with his wife. "That's a good suggestion." He turned back to Mr. Branton and listed off a handful of properties and assets to be transferred into Izzie's name should anything happen to him.

"... and Trelystan Castle," he concluded.

"You own a *castle*?" Izzie asked, looking adorably befuddled.

"Hmm? Oh, yes. Three of them, actually." He stroked his chin, considering. "Of the three, I think you would like Trelystan the best. It's a Welsh castle, like the one in your book. It's been fully restored and is quite comfortable, but it's"—he waved a hand, searching for the right word—"atmospheric." He ducked his chin, realizing that everyone was staring at him. Rubbing the back of his head, he added, "Perhaps, when it's safe, we could go there for a bridal trip."

This was the first time Archibald had seen Izzie rendered speechless. Mr. Branton scratched out a few final notes. "Perfect. I'll have something finished by the end of the day."

"Thank you." Archibald crossed the room to stand before Izzie. She rose from the sofa, and he took her hand.

How he wished they were alone so he could kiss her. His house was only half a mile to the north, but it would be a dangerous business, moving her there. He knew her family would take every conceivable precaution.

But still, he didn't like it, and he would not be able to relax until she was safely ensconced in his family's fortress-like townhouse.

"I'd better go and get the special license," he said. "What time should I expect you?"

"Half three," Harrington called.

Archibald nodded. "Half three it is." He pressed a kiss against her knuckles. "I'll be waiting by the door." He dropped his voice to a murmur. "Don't worry. I would never let anything happen to you."

"I know that," she whispered.

"Until this afternoon, then."

He pressed her hand one last time, then forced himself to leave.

CHAPTER 16

If anyone had been watching Astley House at a quarter past three, they would have seen Harrington Astley's tiger, a skinny boy dressed in a groom's attire of breeches, boots, tailcoat, and top hat, bringing Harrington's curricle around to the curb.

Harrington emerged from the house, carrying the case containing his dueling pistols. He was careful to look nonchalant as he climbed into the curricle and stashed his pistols beneath the seat.

Once his tiger had taken his place on the tiny jump seat behind him, Harrington set a course south toward the shooting gallery run by Joseph Manton, the famous gunsmith. This was one of his regular haunts, as he was a marksman of some repute.

But he didn't stop at the shooting gallery on Davies Street. Instead, he drove past it, then turned, plotting a circuitous route north.

Along the way, he caught glimpses of his brother Edward and his friends Thetford and Ferguson on horseback. They all pretended not to see one another.

An unmarked carriage pulled alongside them. He spied his sister Anne and her husband Morsley through the window. They had a half-dozen firearms laid out on the seats beside them, and… was that a *battle-axe*? Harrington was fairly certain that was the battle-axe that had recently been hanging above the mantelpiece of the first-floor parlor at Cranfield House.

He couldn't help but roll his eyes. *Subtle, Morsley. Very subtle.*

Anne and Morsley's carriage turned off, keeping up the illusion that these were chance meetings, just as they had planned. Another carriage took its place, this one bearing a grey-haired woman with a fierce expression holding a blunderbuss at the ready. She was accompanied by a half-dozen brown and white speckled dogs. Good old Aunt Griselda.

His plan appeared to be working because they weren't being followed, so far as he could tell, and none of the riders had dropped their hats, which was the designated distress signal. Twenty minutes after his original departure, he drove past the last of the older, more venerable squares of Mayfair and entered the area where the nouveau riche had built their mansions.

Most of the townhouses on the square where Nettlethorpe-Ogilvy lived were owned by rich industrialists like Harrington's future brother-in-law. But there were a few families who were considered to be good *ton*. Caleb Stanhope, the second son of the Earl Stanhope and a preeminent barrister, had a house here. So did Andrew Milner, a prominent M.P.

Harrington drew his curricle to a halt in front of the Gothic monstrosity that was the Nettlethorpe-Ogilvy townhouse and waited for his tiger to climb down.

At this point, his actual tiger, who had walked over an

hour earlier, came scrambling up the stairs that led to the coal vault and took hold of the horses.

This was fortunate because his other tiger was standing slack-jawed in the middle of the pavement, staring at the Nettlethorpe-Ogilvy manse with its crenelated walls, arched windows, and turreted towers.

"This is it?" the "boy" said, entranced. "I get to live *here*?"

"Only if you survive long enough to get inside," Harrington said, grabbing his sister beneath the arms and hauling her up the six stone steps.

Izzie tried to twist out of his grip. "I just want to see—"

"You'll have the rest of your life to look at it. Let's make sure it lasts longer than three minutes, shall we? Don't worry, I'm sure the inside is just as tawdry."

Harrington wasn't sure if the alacrity with which his sister hurried inside was a mark of how much she valued his sage advice or if she merely wanted to see if the house's interior could possibly be as ostentatious as its façade.

He rather suspected the latter.

For the last half hour, Archibald had been pacing the foyer of his family's home like the caged bear in the Tower menagerie and snarling a similar amount. He'd brought four dozen men over from Nettlethorpe Iron to serve as guards, and ten of them were stationed with him at the front door. By now they'd all given up on trying to offer him a reassuring word.

Jimmy Isaacs, one of the sharp-eyed apprentice boys he'd assigned to keep watch from the roof, came flying into the room, breathing hard from having run down four flights of stairs. "Curricle, coming up to the house, boss. Pulled by a pair of blood bays, just like you said."

Archibald peered through the narrow window next to the

door. Seeing Harrington Astley climbing down, he quickly unlocked the door and swung it open.

"Where is she?" he said tightly, seeing no one but Astley and his tiger.

"Right here," Astley said, giving his tiger a push through the door.

That was the moment that Archibald noticed that the tiger had rose-pink lips, delicate features, and huge blue eyes.

Time slowed down as he drank in the sight of Isabella in boy's clothing. Her long, slender legs encased in skin-tight breeches made his mouth go dry, but it was about to get a thousand times worse, because at that moment, she removed her hat and began pulling pins from her hair.

"Ugh, my maid had to pin it *so tightly* to get it under this hat," she explained, then groaned with relief as the whole mass came tumbling down her back in mahogany waves. She closed her eyes as she combed her fingers through her hair, massaging her scalp. "That's *much* better."

His men were as thunderstricken as he was. Who knew how long they would have all stood gaping in the foyer had his parents not scurried into the room.

"You must be Lady Isabella!" his mother cried, seizing her hands.

"We're so delighted that you're marrying our Archie!" his father added.

This was a significant understatement. The news that Archibald was going to marry not just the daughter of an earl but a member of the influential Astley family had sent his parents into paroxysms of delight.

The fact that an unknown group of criminals was trying to kidnap or possibly kill her and that he would be bringing this danger to their door was dismissed with a wave. "That'll all blow over in the next few days," his father had said.

"But you'll be married forever!" his mother exclaimed.

"Just think… Lady Isabella Nettlethorpe-Ogilvy! Now, Archie, you mustn't do anything that might cause Lady Isabella to change her mind."

"Best not to mention anything about the ironworks," his father agreed.

As if he needed to be reminded. Trying to court a highborn bride had been a never-ending series of humiliations. Over the past few years, he had been introduced to dozens, if not hundreds, of young ladies. Every single one, save Cecilia Chenoweth, had seemed to regard the prospect of being courted by a trumped-up blacksmith with horror. He'd had young ladies decline to dance with him on account of having turned their ankle, only to see that they had made a miraculous recovery by the next set. He'd had dining partners give him their back for the entirety of a meal, so much did they dread the possibility that he might attempt to speak with them.

And if he had a shilling for every time he'd overheard a young lady say something disparaging about him behind his back, he'd have… well, probably not even a whole pound.

But it would be close, a fact that was alarming in and of itself.

Izzie had never treated him this way, but he feared this was only because she didn't truly understand what he did. Her notion of a "blacksmith" was the version of Archibald she saw at balls and parties, once he had been thoroughly scrubbed and stuffed into an expensive suit. What she didn't realize was that he wasn't merely in trade. He was in a filthy trade that involved hard manual labor and getting his hands dirty.

The key was, therefore, to prevent her from finding out, certainly before the wedding and for as long as possible afterward. It was a daunting enough task at a ball or rout.

But it would be ten times harder now that she was living

inside his house. To make matters worse, he'd had no time to prepare and plan. Things had happened so quickly. When he left for Astley House that morning, he'd had no notion that his next stop would be Doctor's Commons to purchase a special license. Not that he had any regrets. As unexpected as this turn of events was, the question of whether he wanted to marry Isabella Astley did not require even a second's thought. The important thing was to seize the opportunity. He would just have to figure the rest out as he went.

He wouldn't be able to maintain the façade he was determined to construct forever. Eventually, she would realize what he was really like, and she would come to despise him, as every other member of the *haute ton* did. Of that, he had no doubt. But perhaps if he hid the awful truth, he could delay her disdain and enjoy a few weeks of newlywedded bliss.

His parents were fawning over Izzie as if she were a visiting queen, but she didn't seem bothered by their overly effusive display. Indeed, she hardly seemed to notice it. She was busy gazing around the foyer in awe. "You have the most *beautiful* home."

This sent his mother into a frenzy. "I am so pleased to hear you say so! Some people have had the nerve to imply that it is overly dramatic."

"Not at all," Izzie said, her gaze sweeping the vaulted ceiling before landing upon one of the twelve suits of armor lining the walls. "It's *perfect!*"

His mother actually squealed. "How delightful that my son has chosen a bride who has a sense of fashion. It pains me to think how few people do."

"Oh, my dove," his father said, "you mustn't let those people bother you. You know they're just jealous that they could never afford to do the same."

Harrington Astley squeezed his shoulder. "I've got to

head over to Manton's to keep up the ruse. I also need to give Edward the signal that Izzie made it in all right so he can let everyone know. Poor Lucy was frantic when I left, and my mother wasn't doing much better."

Archibald shook himself out of his stupor and offered his hand. "Of course. Thank you so much for bringing her."

"Thank you for taking her on." He laughed. "You're going to have your hands full with Izzie."

He gazed at Izzie, who was busy exclaiming over the pair of dramatic floor candelabras flanking the doorway. "I look forward to it."

His mother hurried over. "Oh, Lieutenant Astley, do you have to go? How dearly we would love for you to stay and dine with us."

"I do," Harrington confirmed. "I need to let everyone know that Izzie is safe. But I'll be back tomorrow for the ceremony, and my mother will arrive in an hour or so to chaperone her overnight."

"*The countess is coming!*" his mother screeched. "Lady Cheltenham, staying at *my* house! Oh, this is wonderful, absolutely wonderful!" She turned to her husband. "We must make sure everything is perfect!"

"She must have the best bedroom," his father said. "What do you think, the gold room?"

"The gold room?" His mother was already rushing toward the stairs, with his father close on her heels. "Are you sure, my darling? I was thinking perhaps the Emerald Suite…"

Archibald saw Harrington out, then locked the door behind him.

He offered Izzie his arm. "Would you like to see the rest of the house?" This seemed like a good place to start, as she seemed to like his mother's overwrought Gothic décor.

She squeezed his arm with both hands. "Yes, please!"

As he studied her enraptured face, suddenly Archibald

didn't mind so much that every room, including the closet that housed his chamber pot, was elaborately decorated with arches and spires, trefoils and crockets. He'd mostly grown inured to his mother's lurid taste, but using that particular room always made him feel strangely guilty, as if he were shitting in Westminster Abbey.

But if it made Izzie happy, that was all that mattered.

CHAPTER 17

*I*zzie could not believe her luck. Not only would she get to marry Archibald, but she would also get to live in this *marvelous* house. She had begged her father for years to let her add some Gothic touches to her bedroom, but he had always refused, on the grounds that they were "gauche" and "melodramatic."

Well, "gauche and melodramatic" more or less described her personality. And as far as she was concerned, the Nettlethorpe-Ogilvy manse was *perfect*.

All the rooms were tawdry in the best possible way, and Izzie exclaimed over each and every one. The dining room was in the style of a medieval great hall, complete with tapestries and a huge fireplace, and the parlor Archibald showed her could have passed for the interior of a cathedral but for the plush velvet sofas.

The only room that was a disappointment was the library, not because of the design, but because it didn't contain a single Gothic novel. It was all expensive antiques and first editions. As Izzie remarked to Archibald, they were, "the type of books that everyone admires but no one actually reads."

Archibald frowned, studying her face. "Don't worry. We'll get you copies of all your favorites. You can build your own collection."

Izzie eyed the packed shelves. "I don't think there's room."

"There will be," he muttered.

"There will? How?"

Suddenly, his brown eyes were bright with excitement. "An idea just came to me. It'll be better if I show you. Come, the room is on the first floor."

He led her toward the stairs. As they passed through the foyer, Izzie was distracted by the black stone statue at the foot of the stairs. She paused to peer at it. Was it possible that she was mistaken? Or did the Nettlethorpe-Ogilvys have a statue of a man's rear end adorning their entryway?

Archibald cleared his throat. "Please pardon the statue of the, er…"

"Man's fundament," she supplied. He seemed so horrified she couldn't resist teasing him. "You should see your ears. They've gone crimson. Why are you so embarrassed? Did you perchance serve as the model?"

"No." He ran a hand over his eyes. "It's Egyptian and predates me by a few millennia. It's of Anubis."

"The Arse of Anubis," Izzie breathed.

Archibald glanced at her, surprised. "That's how I think of it as well."

"Naturally."

His face was pinched. "It's tasteless and absurd."

"Yes," Izzie agreed solemnly, circling the statue to examine it from another angle. "I do believe that's what I love about it."

A smile broke over his face. He studied her for a beat, his eyes warm. "Come. There's something I should probably show you."

He led her not up the stairs but toward the back of the

ground floor. He glanced around as if to make sure they were alone, then dropped his voice low. "My parents are the ones who purchased the Arse of Anubis. They paid more than a thousand pounds for it. If you're going to be living under the same roof as them, you should be forewarned."

"Forewarned? They seem kindhearted," Izzie noted as he led her into the music room.

"They are," he agreed. "I don't mean to complain, but, well. The easiest way for me to explain is by showing you this."

He pulled out a huge case in dark brown leather. It was almost as long as Izzie was tall. It looked heavy and exceptionally unwieldy to Izzie's eyes, but he placed it on a glossy rosewood table as easily as if it were a flute or violin.

"This," he said, snapping open the metal buckles, "is a contrabassoon."

The instrument was enormous. Gleaming brown wood covered with delicate silver keys curved around in loop after loop.

"I don't believe I've ever seen a contrabassoon," Izzie noted, gently pressing a key.

"And that is why they purchased it," Archibald noted cheerlessly. "Not because any of our guests might wish to play it. Trust me, they don't know how. But because nobody else has one, and it's as expensive as one of our carriages. They had this notion that having such an instrument in our music room would be a good way to show off how very wealthy we are."

Izzie cringed. "It seems a shame. To have such a beautiful instrument, and for nobody to play it."

"Exactly." Relief flooded his eyes. "That's actually why I decided to learn to play it myself. Because it seemed like such a waste. But then…"

She nudged him with her elbow. "But then?"

He cringed. "That was around the time my parents started urging me to start looking for a wife. And they had this idea that my serenading young ladies on the contrabassoon would be the perfect means to subtly show off how wealthy we are."

Izzie bit her lip at the image because, as absurd as the idea of a romantic bassoon serenade seemed, she didn't want Archibald to feel that she was laughing at him.

He noticed her struggle. "It's all right. You can laugh. Goodness knows everyone else did. What made it even more ridiculous was the fact that I'd just started to play, and I was absolutely atrocious. But they thought it a marvelous idea, and I couldn't find a way to tell them they were wrong without hurting their feelings. And I would never want to do that."

Izzie's heart squeezed. This man who was to be her husband, who had beaten a swarm of attackers senseless as easily as she might lift her teacup, had a heart as squishy as a sponge cake inside his hulking exterior. This, she decided, was a good thing.

Something else occurred to her. "I also noticed that your parents call you Archie." She might be mistaken, but she thought she had detected a pained look in his eyes when they'd used the nickname.

He grimaced, confirming her suspicions. "Yes. They do."

She gave him a speaking look. "I take it that you do not wish for me to call you Archie, too?"

He sighed. "I must confess, I've never felt like much of an *Archie*. Not even when I was six years old. But *Archie* is"—he waved a hand, struggling to explain—"the son they want. A young Corinthian. A man-about-town."

"*Archie* is a fashionable nickname," she mused. "And your parents seem to like things that are fashionable."

"Lord, is that the truth," he muttered.

She tapped a slender finger against her lip. "What if we could come up with something even more fashionable?"

He chuckled but looked down. "I don't think anyone would describe me as fashionable."

Fashionable probably wasn't the right word. Archibald was never going to be one of those men who spent hours practicing the art of handling their walking stick in the mirror so that everyone would exclaim over the way he sauntered down St. James's Street on the way to his club.

But he had a timeless masculine appeal that Izzie preferred.

Much preferred, if she was being honest.

She circled him, studying his profile. "I think you're right about *Archie*, in any case. As an author, I can say that if I was writing you as a character in my book, I would never call you *Archie*."

He snorted. "I doubt very much that any author would name a character Archibald Nettlethorpe-Ogilvy."

"Indeed, what sort of idiotic author would give their character such a name? Only imagine how her hand would cramp each time she had to write out *Mister Nettlethorpe-Ogilvy* for the simplest piece of dialogue attribution. No"— she tapped her lip, considering—"were I to give you a nickname, I think it would be... Thorpe."

"Thorpe?" He looked up, startled.

"Thorpe," she repeated. It was simple. Unpretentious.

Masculine.

Just like him.

"Thorpe," he said again as if testing the way it felt on his tongue. "Thorpe. I... I like that. Quite a lot, actually. I doubt my parents would use it, though. I don't even know how I would go about asking them. They've been calling me Archie my whole life, and as I said"—he dropped his voice low—"I would never want to hurt their feelings."

Her lips twisted into a wry smile. Already a plan was forming in her mind. "Leave everything to me. That is, if you're sure you like it. If we're going to convince your parents to call you something else, it's important that it feels like the real you."

"No, I'm sure. *Thorpe* feels much more like the real me."

Izzie nudged him with her elbow. "Speaking of the real you, I know shockingly little about you, especially considering that we're to be married tomorrow. Won't you tell me more about yourself? Perhaps about your work at Nettlethorpe Iron?"

Izzie had asked some shocking questions in her day, but she hadn't thought this was one of them. Yet Archibald flinched as if she'd delivered a withering set-down.

"Archibald?" she asked. "Is everything all right?"

"Of course," he said hastily. "I, uh… Why don't I show you the upstairs?"

He was already towing her through the door and toward the red-carpeted stairs.

"Are you certain nothing is the matter?" It was a good thing she was wearing boots and trousers. Otherwise, she wouldn't have been able to keep up with his brisk stride. "I have an appalling tendency to say precisely what springs into my mind. I hope I did not speak out of turn." Although, thinking about what she had just said, Izzie was struggling to grasp how she might have given offense…

"You didn't." His eyes were sincere. Beseeching, even. He gestured toward the upper floors, seeming eager to change the subject. "You remarked upon the lack of Gothic novels in the library. It occurred to me that you might like to choose a room for yourself. Not as your bedroom. I mean"—his ears turned red—"you'll have one of those t-too, of course, but… um…"

She squeezed his arm, unable to resist teasing him. "Will I be needing my own bedroom? Perhaps we'll want to share."

Now his entire face was scarlet. "I, uh... I wouldn't mind. But maybe you would. We'll figure that out after the... the wedding." He cleared his throat. "But I thought you might like to have a study. Or a library, or office... whatever you want to call it. You can keep all your books in there, and we'll also get you a nice desk, so you'll have a place to work on your writing."

A place to work on her writing! An image sprang to mind of the library of her daydreams, with tall windows and floor-to-ceiling bookshelves covering every wall...

She tamped down her excitement. Archibald probably had something much more modest in mind. And really, it would be such a luxury to have any room for her own use. The notion of a snug writing nook held tremendous appeal.

"I would love that, Archibald." She felt tears pricking. "What a thoughtful suggestion."

"There's a particular room I have in mind," Archibald said as they reached the top of the stairs. "Let's see what you think of it."

He led her halfway down the red-carpeted corridor. The door he tried proved to be locked, so he asked the footman positioned at the top of the stairs to run and fetch the key from the butler, Giddings.

While they waited, Izzie looked around. She noticed that the wall at the end of the hallway was curved and recalled that from the outside, the house had had round towers on each corner. "Oh! Is this one of the towers?"

"It is," he confirmed.

"I thought they were just a façade. I didn't realize there were tower rooms!"

The footman had returned with a ring of keys. Archibald was flipping through them, looking for the right one.

Izzie gazed longingly at the arched wooden door that led into the tower room. She wondered what it looked like on the inside. A castle tower—the very notion seemed inherently romantic!

Archibald was still busy with the keys. Maybe she would just have a quick peek…

She was just poking her head through the door when Archibald hissed, "Izzie! Wait!"

CHAPTER 18

s Archibald watched Izzie stride through the tower room door where his grandfather lay resting, his heart flew and his throat constricted. Was this it, the moment that his fragile dream of having Izzie as his wife came crashing down around him?

Thanks to his parents' influence, Archibald could perform a somewhat convincing pantomime of being a gentleman. But there was no such hope for John Nettlethorpe. He had an East London accent and the colorful vocabulary that went with it. Archibald's grandfather drank gin, not brandy, and his favorite sport was cockfighting, not horseracing. The second he opened his mouth, Izzie would understand precisely what kind of family she, the daughter of an earl, was marrying into.

Heart in his throat, Archibald peered around the door. His body sagged with relief when he saw that his grandfather was asleep.

Shame immediately coursed through him. He *loved* his grandfather. His grandfather understood him a thousand times better than his parents ever would. He was the one who had provided him with the means to escape the stultifying life his parents had planned for him.

But he couldn't take the chance that Izzie would be put off by his common roots, not until their marriage was signed, sealed, and consummated. He wanted Izzie for his wife with a clawing sort of desperation. He was pathetically in love with this woman, had been from the moment he clapped eyes on her. He knew their marriage was going to go to pot eventually. It wasn't as if he could prevent her from meeting his grandfather now that they would be living in the same house.

But it was imperative that he hide the awful truth for as long as he could.

Izzie stood framed in the doorway, looking not inside the tower room but up at Archibald with wide eyes.

He came up to stand beside her. "We need to be quiet," he whispered, gesturing toward the bed. "See?"

Izzie squinted as she turned her gaze toward the darkened room. Her gasp marked the moment she noted his grandfather lying still on the bed.

Archibald gently took her elbow and led her out into the corridor, shutting the door behind them.

"I'm so sorry," she said softly. "I didn't realize—"

He immediately felt bad. "It's all right. You didn't know."

She bit her lip. "Who is that? If you don't mind my asking."

He swallowed. She was going to be living here. There was no sense trying to keep it from her. "That is my grandfather, John Nettlethorpe. He had a tumor." Archibald rubbed a spot on his chest, just to the side of his heart. "They were able to cut it out, but he's not improving. The doctors think he has a few weeks."

Her eyes were full of distress as she clasped his hand in both of hers. "Oh, Archibald, I'm so sorry."

He nodded sadly. "As am I. He's been sleeping more and more. I don't know if he'll be able to attend the ceremony tomorrow."

"I hope he will," she said, staring forlornly at the door. "I would very much like to meet him."

Archibald's feelings about Izzie meeting his grandfather were more fraught, but he nodded. "Hopefully soon." He placed his hand on the small of her back, shepherding her toward the adjoining room. "Come, let me show you the room I had in mind for your library."

Izzie cringed as Archibald led her down the corridor. Of course, the room had turned out to be his dying grandfather's bedchamber. And there she'd gone, barging in!

Leap before you look—that should be her motto. If she ever decided to make an effort at her needlework, she would embroider it on a cushion.

She couldn't *believe* she had been so thoughtless. Well... she could believe it. This was what came of drifting through life, not paying attention to the world that surrounded her. But her horrible mistake had certainly alerted her to the perils of behaving in such a heedless fashion. Thank God that through some miracle, Mr. Nettlethorpe had managed to sleep through her disruption.

She peered up at Archibald, wondering if his good opinion of her had just been destroyed. His expression was carefully blank. Unreadable.

What if he didn't want to marry her anymore? She bit her lip. Just when she finally found a man she really, truly liked, a man she thought she might even be able to love, she managed to go and ruin everything. *Typical, Isabella. So typical!*

Archibald cleared his throat as he twisted the knob of the room next door. "See what you think."

Izzie gasped. The room had high ceilings and a trio of tall, arched windows that let in a good amount of light. Its design was similar to the dining room, more of a medieval Gothic, with a vaulted ceiling and flagstones on the floor.

She peered at Archibald, disbelieving. Surely he couldn't intend this magnificent room for *her*.

He didn't look angry with her. He had wandered over to stand before the central window, which, upon closer inspection, proved to be a bay window. "I was thinking this would make a nice spot to install a window seat."

Izzie's eyes went wide. "A window seat?" She had always wanted a window seat!

He turned to face the room, eyes shining. "Your desk could go here. That way you'll get a good amount of natural light." He gestured to the walls. "Then I thought we could add a gallery halfway up the wall, with a spiral staircase in each corner. That way you could have bookcases running all the way from floor to ceiling."

Floor-to-ceiling bookcases! She had dreamed about having a library with floor-to-ceiling bookcases for as long as she could remember.

She couldn't believe he was talking about building her floor-to-ceiling bookcases when she had just gone and behaved so atrociously.

Maybe... maybe he didn't hate her after all. Her impression of him was that he was exceptionally patient. Forgiving.

Just what you need, Isabella...

Tears pricked in the corners of her eyes. But he didn't seem to notice that she was overcome, because he continued talking, as if everything was normal and he was not making one of her fondest, most impossible dreams come true. "We'll have the bookcases custom-made so they fit perfectly. And I'll build you a rail running around each level, and we can attach some ladders on wheels. That way, when you need to get a book down, you'll have a ladder readily at hand."

She managed to form the words, "Could you really build something like that?"

He laughed. "Of course. Something like that would be easy. You should see the things I usually...ahem." He broke off suddenly, rubbing the back of his head.

She gazed about the room, picturing it. This would truly be her dream library.

But the thing that had her turning as mushy as a blancmange wasn't how magnificent the room would look when it was finished. It was the fact that Archibald had thought of it at all. That he cared so much about her being happy in this, her new home.

He also thought that her writing was important enough to have its own space. He didn't expect her to squeeze a tiny desk into her dressing room, or work on it in the morning room with a parade of visitors streaming in and out around her.

She felt a tear slip down her cheek and wiped it away with her thumb. She couldn't *believe* her good fortune. Not only was Archibald not furious with her, but he was also building her this wonderful library.

How had she been so ridiculously lucky, that she got to marry this man?

Archibald frowned. "I should say that these are only suggestions. This is to be your room, and if you would prefer something else—"

"No," Izzie sniffed. "I would not prefer something else. I would prefer exactly what you just described."

She threw her arms around his neck.

CHAPTER 19

*A*rchibald was stunned insensible as Izzie threw herself into his arms. Which was more or less how he always felt when he found himself in close proximity with her.

But today, it was particularly hard to think about anything other than touching her, with her delicate curves outlined by her borrowed breeches and her hair tumbling down her back in raven-dark waves.

His frazzled brain registered that she was speaking. "This is the kindest, the most thoughtful... the absolute best present anyone has ever given me." She pulled back enough that he could see her face, and although her eyes were damp, she was smiling. "I've always dreamed of having a library just like this. Thank you."

"Good," he said gruffly. "And you're very welcome."

So, they were happy tears. He'd been worried for a second there.

God, but it was gratifying to have done something right, for once, where a woman was concerned.

Izzie kissed him on the cheek, then skipped out of his

embrace. It seemed that the crying spell had passed. She tipped her head back to the vaulted ceiling and twirled in a circle.

He wanted to take her shopping for the books she would need to fill her floor-to-ceiling bookshelves personally, especially if there was any chance she would look at him like *that* again…

He cleared his throat. "I'll bring an architect in to start working on the gallery. And whenever you're ready, we can go to Chippendale's, or any cabinet maker you prefer, and you can select the designs you'd like for the furniture."

He'd expected her to be excited at the prospect, but her face fell. "I would love that, but I'm not sure I can go. Leastwise, not until they catch whoever's trying to kill me."

Well done, Archibald. Just when she was feeling happy again, you had to go and remind her about her problems.

He rubbed the back of his head. "Hopefully that situation will be resolved in the next few days. And if it's not, the furniture makers can come here with their design books."

"I'm sure you're right." She laughed. "I'm just eager to get started. It's going to be *perfect*."

Archibald smiled, relieved. "Almost perfect. It might be a little loud."

She tilted her head. "I haven't noticed any noise."

"Not right now, no. But seeing as my workshop is across the hall—"

"Your workshop?" She grabbed his hand and towed him toward the door. "I can't wait to see it!"

Shit. Why had he gone and said that? The last thing he could let her do was see his workshop. For one, he was supposed to be concealing the grimy nature of his work. But what was even worse, it would all be over if Izzie discovered that his notion of a passion project involved making *screws*.

"You wouldn't want to go in there," he said as they

stepped into the hall. He saw that the door was standing ajar. *Perfect.*

"Of course, I would." Her smile was dazzling. "I'm eager to see all of your machines."

He managed to slip in front of her and block the doorframe. "There isn't much to see," he said, reaching behind him for the knob. "Besides, it's"—he cast about for an excuse—"very dirty."

She laughed. "Then today is the perfect day for me to go in," she said, gesturing to the boys' clothing she still wore.

"Umm." He managed to lay his groping hand upon the knob and pulled the door shut behind him. "There isn't really that much to see. My main machine shop is over at Nettlethorpe Iron. So that's where I do most of my building. This is just a hodgepodge."

This wasn't strictly true. The reason Archibald had a workshop at home was so he could put things together whenever inspiration struck. And it happened that he had an advanced prototype of his screw-cutting lathe on the other side of that door.

Not that he was about to let Izzie see it.

Pulling the ring of keys the footman had brought him earlier from his pocket, he turned and hastily locked the door. "I'll take you to my proper workshop sometime."

Sometime in the *distant* future, he added silently.

He turned to face her. Izzie looked... crestfallen. *Damn it.* He knew he had just disappointed her, but if ever there was a critical moment, this was it. He couldn't take the chance that anything he showed her today might put her off from marrying him.

He could tell she was trying to tamp down her disappointment. "When will I be able to visit your other workshop?"

"That depends on when it's safe."

She blew out a frustrated breath. "I hope it will only take a few days, but what if it's longer?" She leaned around him to gaze longingly at the door to his workshop. "Could I not just—"

It was time for another diversion. Offering to build her a personal library had been an inspired thought when she'd started to ask about his work. He wasn't going to come up with something better than *that*.

But maybe he could try something similar…

"There's something you need to do," he said, taking her hand and tugging her gently but firmly down the hall.

"Can it wait?" she asked, looking over her shoulder. "I would very much like to—"

"Your bedroom," Archibald said in what he hoped was an enticing voice, leading Izzie to the stairs and climbing toward the second floor. "You need to pick which one you'd like."

She squeezed her eyes shut. "Surely that will keep for ten minutes. We still need to discuss… Oh!"

Having reached the second floor, Archibald pushed open the door leading to the first bedroom, which was salmon pink with Gothic motifs outlined on the walls in crisp white plasterwork.

She swallowed as she drank in the room. "This… this is lovely," she said reluctantly.

God bless his mother and her florid taste. Izzie wandered, entranced, over to the mantelpiece, her request to see his workshop momentarily forgotten.

Archibald was breathing a sigh of relief when Rory McPherson, the office manager at Nettlethorpe Iron, stuck his head in the door.

Archibald frowned. McPherson wasn't one of the men he'd brought over to guard the house. "What are you doing here, McPherson?"

McPherson clutched his hat in front of his stomach. "Apologies, Mr. Nettlethorpe-Ogilvy, sir. But could I have a quick word?"

He nodded, holding up a finger for McPherson to wait, then crossed the room in three strides. "Izzie. Izzie!" He jiggled her arm until she glanced up at him, dazed. "The two rooms at the far end of the east wing belong to my parents. But any of the others, you could have. All right?"

"Not the two at the end of the hall," she repeated. "Very well."

"I have some business to attend to. Have a look around. I'll join you momentarily."

"All right," she said, then squealed as she spotted an elaborately carved mirror.

Archibald stepped out of the room and walked up to his office manager. "What is it?"

It turned out that the King of Salaria had turned up at the forge today. They had signed a contract with the former monarch, his brother Charles Frederick IV, for the delivery of fifty cannons last month and another fifty come spring.

Now that he had seen the quality of the cannons, the new king was demanding delivery of the additional fifty his brother had ordered, effective immediately.

"Well, he can't have them now," Archibald explained. "We're fully booked working on orders for other customers. They'll be ready when the contract says they'll be ready, and likely not a minute before."

"That's what I tried to tell him," McPherson said, twisting his hat. "He, uh… he didn't like that answer very much. He's been asking to speak with you."

Archibald suppressed a groan. "Did you tell him that I'm dealing with an emergency? That someone tried to *kill* my betrothed?"

"I did."

"And that I'm getting married tomorrow?"

"I told him that as well. But you know how it is—royalty doesn't like to wait."

Archibald scrubbed a hand over his face. "I'll meet with him just as soon as I'm back at work."

Hope flared in McPherson's blue eyes. "When will that be, sir?"

Archibald had hoped to take a few days to enjoy his status as a newly married man. If things went well, he was hoping he wouldn't be leaving whichever of these bedrooms Izzie selected for several days.

"I don't know," he answered honestly. "It could be a few days."

McPherson's brow creased. "But Mr. Nettlethorpe-Ogilvy, sir—"

Archibald reached out and squeezed McPherson's shoulder. "Put him off as best you can."

McPherson nodded, swallowing thickly. "I'll do my best, boss."

CHAPTER 20

*A*fter McPherson left, Archibald wandered down the hall, looking for Izzie. He found a half-dozen doors standing ajar, suggesting that she had visited the rooms but no sign of his bride-to-be.

At last, he made his way to his own room. The sight that met him inside robbed him of his breath.

Her boots lay in a heap on the floor, and the borrowed jacket, waistcoat, and cravat she'd had on had been tossed haphazardly upon a chair. Izzie lay upon the enormous bed —*his* bed—clad only in a white linen shirt, skin-tight breeches, and stockings, dark hair falling loose around her, gazing dreamily up at the carved black wooden canopy.

A guttural sound rose from his throat. Izzie looked up and smiled, seeing him framed in the doorway.

"Oh, Archibald—this is the one I want! Just look at this magnificent bed." She ran her arms down the red silk counterpane, luxuriating, and Archibald's cock went from half-mast to hard as granite.

Izzie hadn't seemed to notice what was going on beneath the falls of his trousers, because she continued in a dreamy voice, "Could we spend our wedding night here? It would be my every fantasy come true for my first time to be in this *gorgeous* bed."

Archibald's feet had carried him into the room unbidden. His mouth had gone as dry as the Arabian desert. Isabella Astley wanted to lose her virginity in his bed? He would be more than happy to accommodate her, although he wasn't sure they were going to make it to the wedding night.

She lifted her head to look at him, her smile fading as she registered the heat of his gaze. "What is it?"

He peeled off his jacket. "This is my room."

"It is?" She glanced around, startled. "I'm sorry. I didn't realize. You don't have many personal effects. I assumed this was a guest room."

He kicked off his boots. "I don't spend much time here. Mostly I'm in, er…" It was on the tip of his tongue to say *my workshop*, but he stopped himself just in time. "Other rooms."

He climbed on the bed, knees straddling her slender legs, then placed his hands on either side of her shoulders, so he was looming above her. He brought his face just a few inches from her neck and caught a hint of the cherry-sweet scent of her lips. "But, in answer to your question…"

He couldn't stop himself from pressing a kiss against her exposed neck and was gratified when she shuddered beneath him.

"Y-yes?" she gasped.

His voice was pitched an octave lower than usual as he said, "You can spend as much time in this bed as you want."

Then they were kissing, if this feverish clash of tongues and lips could be considered a kiss. Archibald was so desperate for her he used no finesse, none at all, but Izzie didn't seem to mind if the way she was clinging to his neck was any indication.

His rough hand cupped one of her delicate breasts

through the linen of her shirt, and he groaned into her mouth. Much to his shock, instead of pulling away, she arched into his touch, then reached up and began yanking at the knot of his cravat.

The cravat gave way, as did his waistcoat. Izzie must've done it. Archibald had no idea when or how. He was lost, lost in her, unaware of anything but the sweet sensation of Izzie's lips on his and the pleasure of her body shuddering as he caressed her in places he had never dreamed he would be permitted to touch.

She urged him to sit up, and he thought she was pushing him off. But it was only so she could peel his shirt over his head.

"Archibald," she breathed, her delicate hands tracing over his chest. "*My God.*"

Her gaze was transfixed on his thick arms. He knew his working-man's build made him look like a great boor. "I'm afraid you're marrying a big, hulking brute."

"You are better than anything I could have imagined." Her voice was full of awe as she traced her hands reverently across his shoulders. "And I have a *very* active imagination."

He had to kiss her again after that, and it was a thousand times better because, by some miracle, Izzie seemed to actually *like* his burly form and proceeded to touch him all over with her soft, sweet hands.

But it was also a thousand times worse, because if he had thought his cock was desperate before, it was nothing next to how he felt now, with her lips hungry on his and her hands all over his famished skin.

Suddenly, she slid her hands lower, digging her nails into his buttocks and pulling him down so he was lying on top of her. He was so startled that he let her do it, and the feeling of Isabella Astley beneath him on a bed, her delicate thighs falling open to cradle his hips, felt so indescribably wonderful that he had to struggle not to spend himself in his trousers.

He started to press himself up again, because *God*, he must be crushing her, but she clung to his shoulders. "No, Archibald! No, don't leave! Stay right there. That feels… That feels…"

He was breathing hard, as if he'd just gone three rounds in the boxing ring. "I *love* having you beneath me, Izzie. I love it too much. I… I'm losing control. I should probably stop now before—"

"Please, don't stop!" she gasped, grinding her hips against his and making a desperate whimpering sound. "Please, I want to feel it again. What you did to me this morning. I… I need it!"

He swept her hair back from where it clung to her sweaty brow. "Shh, it's all right. I'll give that to you, Izzie. You'll have it as often as you need it."

He kissed her neck and was reaching down to fumble with the buttons of her borrowed trousers when the sound of someone clearing their throat came from the doorway.

"Mr. Nettlethorpe-Ogilvy, how kind of you to once again assist my daughter in 'disentangling her hair from the branches of a tree.'"

"Mama!" Izzie shrieked as Archibald buried his face in the pillow, mortified.

"I see that I arrived just in time." Lady Cheltenham strolled into the room. "It's a good thing you two already had plans to marry tomorrow."

Izzie covered her shirt, which was gaping open, with a pillow. "Could you possibly give us a moment of privacy?"

The countess arched a brow. "I think you have had enough moments of privacy, at least, until the vicar has done his work. And really, darling—if you wanted to be left alone, you might have shut the door."

Archibald groaned. Lady Cheltenham was correct. He hadn't even closed the door. That's how far gone he had been, seeing Izzie sprawled out on his bed.

"Oh, don't be so embarrassed," the countess said. "You're getting married tomorrow. Paradoxically, a part of me is pleased by this development. Any mother would be concerned to see her daughter forced into such a hasty wedding. But it seems that you both have considerable enthusiasm about the prospect. That's not a bad thing. Now come, Izzie. We had best put you back into a dress."

Archibald reluctantly rolled off her. He sat on the side of the bed, facing the far wall, with his elbows on his knees and his face buried in his hands. It was bad enough that his future mother-in-law had walked in on him pawing her daughter without so much as a shirt on. She didn't need to see the way his cock was tenting his trousers.

He heard Izzie scramble off the bed and slip on her discarded clothing. After a moment, Lady Cheltenham called out that they would see him at supper. Archibald mumbled something in response, then came the click of the door.

He rubbed his brow. He was trying to summon the will to go to the washstand so he could splash himself down with cold water when the door to his dressing room swung open.

His valet, Jack, strode into the room. "How in the name of Satan's sweaty ball sack did *you* convince the likes of *her* to marry you?"

Archibald glowered. "You were watching us? That's—"

Jack held up a finger. "I ain't no peeping Tom. As soon as I saw her ladyship come through the door, I scurried into your dressing room so as not to alarm her. So I didn't see nothing." He gave Archibald a shrewd look. "Although I *heard* a fair bit."

Archibald ran a hand over his face. "I need a moment."

"Damn right, you do." Jack crossed to the washstand and

made a show of filling the basin. "There's some nice *cold* water for you, as I'm sure you'll want to be saving that"—he cast a significant look toward Archibald's groin—"for your wedding night."

Archibald doubted it would be an issue. He didn't think he was going to have any trouble maintaining a cock-stand so long as Izzie was in his bed.

Getting his prick to go down for two fucking minutes when it came time to take a piss, that was going to be the trick.

Jack was bustling around the room. "Well? You still haven't told me how you convinced her."

"She was desperate," Archibald muttered.

"She certainly sounded *desperate*," Jack retorted.

"You are speaking about my future wife!" Archibald snapped. "Leave, before I dismiss you."

Jack drew himself up, feigning outrage as he headed toward the door. "Look who's in a foul mood! Can't say that I blame you. I wager you'll be in a *much* better mood by this time tomorrow."

As eager as he was to rid himself of his valet's unwanted commentary, something occurred to Archibald. "Jack. Wait."

His valet paused in the doorframe. If he had been expecting an apology, he was doomed to disappointment. Archibald was still trying to tamp down the urge to throw the bowl that held his shaving soap at Jack's head.

"I need a ring to give Izzie tomorrow, but I don't want to leave her alone in the house. Go down to Rundell and Bridge and arrange for them to send someone over with a few choices."

Jack huffed. "Oh, I see. Now you want me to be your errand boy."

"What do you think I'm paying you for?" Archibald snapped. "Believe me, it's not for the conversation."

Jack muttered the rest of the way out the door. But at last, the bloody man was gone.

Archibald glanced at the clock on the mantelpiece. It was a few minutes to five. The wedding would take place tomorrow at ten, so he only had seventeen hours before Izzie would become his wife.

He was fairly certain they were going to be the longest seventeen hours of his life.

CHAPTER 21

*A*rchibald rose the following morning at six o'clock, having tossed and turned imagining Izzie beside him in his bed and managed little in the way of sleep.

Jack was already bustling around the room. "You're up early."

"Thought I might as well get up," Archibald mumbled. "I wasn't getting much sleep, anyway."

"Well, now, don't worry. I'll wager tonight, your new bride will have you sleeping like a baby."

Archibald ran a hand over his face. "One of these days I'm going to strangle you. You know that, don't you?"

"Yes. Most probably, I'll deserve it," Jack agreed.

Seeing the plain grey suit Jack had laid out for him, Archibald frowned. "Is this what Bastian says I'm to wear at my wedding?"

Jack snorted. "Don't be daft. This is what you're wearing to breakfast. Bastian is coming over personally to get you ready for the wedding."

Archibald groaned. *"Delightful."*

A half-hour later, Archibald made his way down to breakfast. He was surprised to see his parents up and about, as they usually didn't rise until noon.

He sniffed the air tentatively. The smell he detected was definitely new. It didn't smell bad, precisely. It was clearly some sort of flower.

But whatever it was, it was *extremely* strong.

He wandered over to the parlor where his parents had determined the ceremony would take place. The smell grew stronger with each passing step.

"Another vase of them over here on the mantelpiece, Phillip!" his mother said to a footman struggling to lift a large urn of white flowers while gasping for breath.

"Better yet," his father said, "let's have *two* vases on the mantelpiece. One on each side!"

"Oh, yes, my dove!" his mother exclaimed. "You always have the *best* ideas! Oh, good morning, Archie."

"There's the bridegroom!" his father said, jogging over. "What do you think, Archie, my boy? Aren't they marvelous?"

He made a sweeping gesture to the twenty-some-odd urns of white flowers that covered every available surface. The smell was sweet but so potent it made Archibald's eyes water.

"They're called gardenias," his mother said. "They come from the Far East."

"*Very* expensive," his father added, sounding inordinately pleased about it. "But of course, we wanted to do something spectacular for our only son's wedding!"

Archibald could scarcely breathe. "They're lovely. But is the smell not a bit strong?"

"Not at all!" his father crowed. "We want everyone to notice them, after all."

"Yes," his mother agreed. "It's important that we make a statement, especially with the Duke of Trevissick coming!"

Predictably, his parents had been over the moon last night when they learned that the Duke and Duchess of Trevissick would be in attendance at the wedding ceremony.

"That's just it," Archibald improvised. "It's about... the duchess."

His mother's gaze snapped to him, her eyes keen. "What about the duchess?"

"It's, uh... it's not an allergy, precisely. But strong smells give her, a, um... a headache."

This, of course, was a lie. But Archibald knew Ceci would go along with it, and he figured the Good Lord would forgive him for trying to spare his mother's feelings.

"Oh, dear!" his mother cried. "Whatever are we to do? We cannot risk offending the duchess!"

"I have an idea," Archibald said. "We will have two urns of flowers here in the room. That will be enough for everyone to... enjoy. We'll move the rest of them to the back garden, and then after the wedding breakfast, we can give them out as gifts to each of our guests."

"By Jove, Archie!" his father exclaimed. "That's a splendid idea!"

"Our guests will be so impressed to receive such an expensive gift," his mother added, beaming.

Phillip the footman cast him a grateful look. "I'll just start moving a few of these to the back garden, shall I, Mrs. Nettlethorpe-Ogilvy?"

Archibald fled the pungent parlor and headed toward the breakfast room. As he crossed through the foyer, he was surprised to see Izzie coming down the stairs.

Her eyes were red, and her cheeks were blotchy.

She had been crying. Panic flared in his chest. He *hated* the fact that she was upset and anxious that he might be unable to mend whatever was causing her distress. He rushed across the room and took her hand. "Izzie, what's wrong?"

She looked at him, and her face crumpled. "I'm so sorry, Archibald. But I cannot marry you."

CHAPTER 22

$\mathcal{A}$rchibald led Izzie into the library, the one full of expensive books that no one read. At least here they would be able to speak in private.

He should have known this would happen, should have known that *he* would never get to marry the likes of *Isabella Astley*, even for one night. He wondered what it was that had given him away? A stray word from a servant, perhaps, about their master's strange fervor for making screws?

He shut the door behind them and seated her on the gold satin chaise longue. He wanted to comfort her, but considering what she had just said, he could only assume she would not welcome his touch.

"I'm so, so sorry," Izzie said tearfully. "I don't know why it didn't occur to me sooner. But if we marry, I'm likely to find myself... you know. In the family way."

That did seem exceedingly likely, given what Archibald had in mind. He was far too devastated to form actual words, but he made what he hoped was a soothing sound.

"I just sold my first book to The Minerva Press," Izzie continued. "They've offered me a five-book contract. If there's any hope of me becoming one of their regular writers, I must show them that I'm reliable. I must turn my next book in on time. And if I should conceive right now, there's no way I'll be able to balance writing with motherhood."

"Wait." Archibald blinked, confused. "That's the reason? Because you don't want to get pregnant?"

"That's right." Izzie dabbed at her eyes with a handkerchief. "I feel like, once I've completed this contract, once they've come to know me, perhaps they would be a bit more flexible. But the timing is just wretched."

Archibald peered at her, sure his ears were deceiving him. "Is that the only reason you don't want to marry me?"

"Yes, that's the only reason. And I wish you wouldn't phrase it that way. I *do* want to marry you. I know things have happened quickly, but I'm not unhappy about it. It almost feels like… like fate," she said, looking down at her hands.

His heart couldn't help but thrum, hearing her say those words. He knew she would take them all back as soon as she learned the first thing about him. He wasn't so lucky as to be destined for a life with Isabella Astley, however much he longed for it.

But an idea was forming in his head. Maybe he could salvage this after all.

"Do you want to have children?" he asked.

"I do," she said swiftly, then bit her lip. "But…"

"But?" he asked gently.

"But my mother bore *eight* children," she said in a rush. "Even with a flock of nursemaids, it left her little time to do anything else. And women talk, you know. Carrying baby after baby, year after year, takes a heavy toll on your body."

"In an ideal world, how many would you like to have?" Archibald asked.

She screwed up her face. "I don't know. Maybe… two?"

Archibald nodded. He did want to have children of his own.

But he found he didn't particularly care about the number. Two sounded… fine.

And he could understand Izzie's logic. As much as he wanted to marry her, he would be devastated if doing so meant he had to give up his work as an engineer. It was only logical that she would feel the same way about her writing. And, given that she was the one who would have to carry and bear any children they did have, it struck him that there was much more at stake for her than for him, and perhaps she should have some say on how many children they ultimately had.

He took her hand in his. "I have a proposal for you. What if we were to take precautionary measures?"

Izzie blinked up at Archibald, certain she had misheard.

"Precautionary measures?" she asked, unsure.

"Precautionary measures," he said firmly. "There are things we could do that would dramatically reduce the chances of conception. I could use something called a sheath, for example."

Archibald had misunderstood—Izzie knew what a sheath was, and she was familiar with a variety of precautionary measures. She'd spent most of her life listening with eager ears for any information she could ferret out about intimate relations. In particular, when she first got her courses, her sister Caro's lady's maid, Fanny, had explained that there was a way to count the days around her menses and how to figure out which days she would be most likely to conceive.

So, it wasn't that Izzie needed an explanation of what precautionary measures were. She'd asked her question because she couldn't believe Archibald was willing to consider them.

Most men considered the number of children they had to be a mark of their virility. Izzie had a distinct memory from when she was around twelve of listening at the door to the morning room with Lucy while her mother's friends gossiped about how Lord Such-and-Such ought to leave his poor wife alone. She had borne him ten babes in twelve years, they had noted, and it wasn't as if he didn't have a mistress to satisfy his urges. Yet there was his wife, expecting again.

It was also accepted as fact that the purpose of lovemaking was procreation, and any attempt to subvert procreation was sacrilegious. What Archibald had suggested was beyond scandalous.

Not that Izzie was offended by his suggestion. *Scandalous* was practically her middle name.

And if he was willing to do this, maybe…

Maybe they could still wed.

Hope flared in her heart, a fragile thing with butterfly wings. Because she hadn't been lying when she said that she wanted to marry Archibald. She didn't know him as well as she'd like, but everything she did know about him seemed wonderful.

She felt more convinced than ever that marrying this man was not a mistake.

"I won't lie to you," Archibald continued. "The precautions to which I refer are not foolproof. There is a chance that they could fail and that you could find yourself with child before you're ready. That, even if we agree to try for two children, we could wind up with three, or even four. The only guarantee is abstinence, and"—he laughed darkly —"given what happened yesterday afternoon, I do not think it realistic to imagine that we could live under the same roof and keep our hands off one another. But were we to take these precautions, I think we could do fairly well. I certainly don't think we would wind up with eight children."

Izzie gave him a watery smile. "You would be willing to do that for me?"

He glanced at her, incredulous. "Of course. If it means having you as my wife..." He cleared his throat, looking away. "Besides, I can see your point. I would be devastated if someone told me I had to give up my engineering work just because I was married. It's easy to understand why you would feel the same way."

She threw her arms around his neck. Tears pricked at her eyes as she hugged him tightly. She was so, so lucky to be marrying this man, who thought her dreams were important, too.

"Is the wedding back on, then?" Archibald asked.

"It is." Izzie drew back so she could give him a watery smile. "Thank you *so much*. It didn't even occur to me to ask if you would be willing to do that for me." She paused as something occurred to her. "Assuming we succeed, there will likely be gossip."

Archibald, whose body had sagged as soon as she confirmed they were getting married, after all, opened his eyes, unconcerned. "Gossip?"

"About us," she clarified. "If we marry, and I don't fall pregnant in the first few years, people will probably say nasty things about us. That one or both of us are lacking in, er... *fecundity*."

Izzie wasn't sure what response she had expected to this line of thought, but it wasn't laughter. "Izzie," he said, shaking his head, "do you have *any idea* what people say about me right now?"

She frowned. "What do they say?"

"They call me a blacksmith."

She drew herself up. "What's wrong with being a blacksmith?"

He gave her a strange look. "It's not a very elegant profession."

Suddenly, she felt irate on his behalf. "But you build cannons! How do they imagine our glorious navy would fare against the French without cannons?" She huffed. "I should like to see any of those pompous fools do something a tenth as useful."

She noticed Archibald smiling as he rubbed his eye with the heel of his hand.

"What?" she asked.

"Nothing," he said quickly. "It's just—you're very different from anyone I've ever met."

"Well, I should hope so. I would never do something so boring and trite as being like everyone else."

He chuckled. "Of course you wouldn't. Please, don't change. I like you just as you are."

This statement caused Izzie's heart to trip in her chest. Because she'd scarcely dared to dream she would find a man who liked her just the way she was. Men generally considered her to be shrewish, strident, and far too prone to stating her own opinions.

But not Archibald. She knew it was a foolish notion, considering they had spoken to each other for the first time just four days ago, but Archibald really did seem perfect for her...

"Come," he said, squeezing her hand, "let's go and get some breakfast."

"Wait!" she cried, pulling him back down on the chaise. "Regarding those precautionary measures you mentioned earlier."

Heat flared in his eyes. "Yes?"

"I know of one," she said quickly. "One of our maids told

me how to count the days." She couldn't quite bring herself to add *between my courses*, but comprehension flared in Archibald's eyes. "So, we could use that, too." She cleared her throat. "It happens that the next few days should be safe. So, we shouldn't have to use the… the sheath."

"Thank God for that," he muttered. At her quizzical look, he added, "I don't have any sheaths lying around, and I doubt I'll have time to go out and get one, considering the wedding's at ten." He raked a hand through his hair. "I'm going to regret saying this. But on those days when the chances of conception are high, if you would prefer to sleep apart, I mean… You're always welcome to sleep wherever you want. I would never force myself on you, Izzie."

Her heart melted all over again. "I appreciate that. But I don't think it will be necessary to sleep apart." She dropped her voice down to a whisper. "I have a plan, you see—on those days when I'm likely to conceive, we can perform unnatural acts upon each other."

His face froze in shock. "Unnatural… Dear God, how do you even *know* about unnatural acts?"

"My brother, Harrington, has this book he keeps hidden beneath his mattress—"

He held up a hand. "Say no more."

"Don't you want to know what kind of book it is?"

"I have a fair idea," he muttered.

Izzie laughed at his discomfiture. "I didn't think I would shock you. After all, was that not an unnatural act you performed upon me yesterday in my parents' drawing room?"

His ears had gone red. "Do not mistake me—we are going to perform… perhaps not *every* act in that book. Some of those books are a bit, um…"

"I know what you mean," Izzie said quickly. "For example, the page my brother has dog-eared shows—"

He cut her off with a strangled sound. "I don't need to know that about your brother."

"But your point is well taken," Izzie continued. "Although I would be extremely eager for us to try most of the plates together, there are a few where I fail to grasp the appeal."

Archibald buried his head in his hands. "Oh, my God. We need to stop talking about this."

Izzie frowned. "But you just said that you are eager to participate in many of the acts depicted on those plates."

"That's the problem, all right. In three hours, I have to stand up in front of the vicar, my parents, and everyone I know." He gestured vaguely to the front of his trousers. "I don't need to be picturing you snooping through your brother's book of naughty prints or us performing unnatural acts when I do it."

Izzie giggled. "I'm causing you all sorts of trouble, aren't I?"

"The very best kind of trouble." He pressed a kiss against her temple, then put his hands on his knees and pushed himself to his feet. "Now, breakfast."

"Are you *sure* you don't want to stay here a little longer?" Izzie asked, voice teasing.

Archibald groaned. "I do. But we both know that as soon as things get interesting, your mother will walk in on us. *Again.*"

They were both laughing as they headed, arm-in-arm, to breakfast.

CHAPTER 23

Three hours later, Archibald stood in the foyer, helping his parents greet their guests. As threatened, Bastian had been by earlier and had insisted upon giving Archibald's hair a fresh trim before wedging him into a skintight coat of dark blue superfine, along with a cream waistcoat and breeches.

The clerk from Rundell and Bridge had arrived as Bastian was finishing up with him, which was probably for the best. Archibald didn't know much about jewelry, and so Bastian had helped him select a ring. In spite of his grumbling, Jack had done an excellent job, even borrowing one of Izzie's rings from her lady's maid so that every ring the clerk had brought over was sized perfectly for her hand.

Coincidentally, the ring Bastian had insisted Izzie would like best was the one Archibald had been drawn to from the start.

"The Duke and Duchess of Trevissick," Giddings announced, recalling Archibald to the foyer. "Lady Griselda Saxe-Mecklenburg, and Lady Diana Latimer."

Archibald hurried over and bowed over Ceci's hand,

whispering, "Should my parents ask, strong floral scents give you headaches."

Comprehension flared in her eyes, which was unsurprising. They were friends, so she knew what his parents were like. Plus, the smell of the two remaining vases of gardenias was discernable even from three rooms away. "They absolutely do, and how thoughtful of you to have remembered it," Ceci replied.

"Thank you," he murmured.

She squeezed his arm and leaned up to whisper in his ear, "I am *so* happy for you."

Archibald gave her a sheepish smile. Ceci had picked up on his infatuation with Izzie after she caught him staring at her at a ball. It had been an embarrassing turn of events, especially as Archibald had ostensibly been courting Ceci at the time.

"Thank you. I'm happy for you, too," he said, nodding toward Ceci's new husband, the duke, who was speaking to Izzie's brother, Edward.

Ceci's brown eyes sparkled as she said, "I think everything has worked out for the best."

Archibald nodded, and Ceci drifted off to join her husband. The Trevissick party was the final group to arrive, so Archibald went over to instruct one of his men to lock the door and admit no one without consulting him first.

He glanced around the foyer. His mother was beside herself with glee as she welcomed the Duke and Duchess of Trevissick into *her* home. Lord and Lady Thetford were laughingly admiring the Arse of Anubis, which was apropos, as they had been the ones to saddle him with it.

Perhaps he would give it back to them. It would make a lovely Christmas present.

Archibald's father crept up behind him. "This is the best thing you've ever done, Archie."

Archibald privately agreed, although not for the reasons his father had in mind—the connections they were forging by marrying the daughter of an influential family.

He would've wanted to marry Izzie if she were a dairymaid.

But he settled for saying, "Thank you, Father. I'm glad to have your approval."

Across the room, his mother clapped her hands. "Shall we all head to the parlor where the ceremony is to take place?"

Archibald joined the procession and took his place at the front of the room. His only disappointment was that his grandfather had been asleep when he looked in on him a half-hour ago. He had been hoping that, if his grandfather was awake and feeling up to it, Archibald could carry him downstairs so he could be there for the ceremony. But it wasn't meant to be.

Glancing around the room, he saw that his grandfather wasn't the only person who was missing.

"Where is Izzie?" her twin sister Lucy asked, craning her neck to look around the room.

Archibald's throat tightened. God, he hoped she hadn't changed her mind again. He'd thought that they had worked through her concerns during their conversation that morning. What if she was having cold feet?

Just when he was starting to panic, Izzie appeared in the frame of the doorway. She looked heart-stoppingly beautiful in a gown of rich purple silk. "There you are! Oh, dear—did I keep everyone waiting?" She hurried over to Archibald, seizing his hands. "I just had to check one more time. And you'll never believe it—he's awake!"

Archibald's mind was still reeling at the notion that in a few scant minutes, this gorgeous woman was going to marry *him*. He shook his head, struggling to focus. "He's awake... do you mean—"

Izzie squeezed his hands. "Your grandfather! If we hurry, he can see us wed."

Out of the corner of his eye, Archibald saw his mother give a violent shudder. She sidled over to the writing desk in the corner, slid open a drawer, and pulled out some smelling salts.

Izzie did not seem to have noticed. Her eyes held nothing but excitement. "I'm afraid I had to introduce myself rather hastily. But he seemed to take the news that you were marrying some strange girl he'd never clapped eyes on in stride. I asked how he would feel about us invading his bedchamber so he could be present for the ceremony, and he said, 'Go on, then.'"

The corner of Archibald's mouth twisted up at Izzie's impression of his grandfather's east London accent.

His father, on the other hand, buried his face in his hands.

Izzie swept the room with her gaze, eyes entreating, until she found his mother. "You don't mind, do you, Mrs. Nettlethorpe-Ogilvy? I know you've gone to so much trouble to prepare these beautiful decorations. But if it means that Mr. Nettlethorpe will be able to watch Archibald wed..."

"Oh, er..." Archibald could tell his mother was casting about for an excuse that wouldn't sound coldhearted.

"And that room will be lovely for the ceremony," Izzie continued. "It's in one of the corner towers, and it has stained-glass windows. It even feels like you're in a chapel."

"We wouldn't want to tire him out," Archibald's father noted.

"To tire him out!" Archibald's mother exclaimed. "That's just it. It will be rather too much for him, don't you think, Archie?"

A touch of worry came into Izzie's blue eyes. "What would you like?"

Archibald found he didn't need time to consider the

question. His parents might be horrified, but Izzie didn't seem put off by her brief introduction to his grandfather. And he couldn't imagine marrying without one of the most important people in his life present.

He pressed Izzie's hand. "Although it probably will tire him, I know Grandfather would wish to see me wed, regardless." He brought Izzie's knuckles to his lips, then dropped his voice low. "This means a great deal to me. Thank you."

She beamed at him. "You're very welcome."

Archibald and Izzie led the procession to his grandfather's tower room. His parents appeared to be on the verge of an apoplexy, but Lady Thetford helped him by looping one arm through his mother's and the other through his father's and distracting them with fawning compliments about their striking décor all the way up the stairs.

When he opened the door to the tower room, Archibald found that someone had propped his grandfather up on a stack of pillows and helped him slip a dressing gown over his nightshirt.

"This young lady informs me yer getting married today," his grandfather said, East London accent on full display for the sundry dukes and earls streaming into the room. Out of the corner of his eye, he saw his father cover his eyes, and his mother press the back of her wrist to her forehead.

"Yes, Grandfather," Archibald said. "I'm sorry I didn't tell you earlier. Things happened rather quickly, and—"

He held up a hand. "That's all right. Now, hurry up and marry yer gal before I nod off."

"Yes, Grandfather."

The vicar had positioned himself beneath the stained-glass window. Izzie tugged his hand, leading him into their positions. The dappled light sparkling through the stained glass fell on her face, and suddenly, the moment was overwhelming. He was marrying the woman of his dreams, and not only that, she had made the extra effort to make sure his grandfather could witness the ceremony. She didn't seem the least bit put off by his grandfather's humble accent. Much to the contrary, she seemed delighted that John Nettlethorpe was present.

It gave him a faint, flickering hope that maybe, just *maybe*, she could love someone like him.

How Archibald got through his vows without his voice quavering, he would never know. But it was no great sacrifice for him to promise to love and cherish Isabella Astley, 'til death did they part. He would love and cherish her for the rest of his life regardless of whether they were man and wife, so he was merely speaking the truth.

Then it was time for him to give her the ring he had selected that morning. It was a simple design—a heart-shaped ruby with a tiny diamond flanking it on either side, set in a plain gold band. It was an antique, which was unsurprising, as heart-shaped stones had been more fashionable for wedding rings during the previous two centuries than this one. His parents had despaired when he showed them his choice because the gem was neither large nor particularly costly. But from the second he saw it, Archibald could picture the delicate ring on Izzie's slim finger. He had a feeling she would like it, an opinion both Bastian and Jack had seconded.

Judging by the tremulous smile she gave him after he slipped it on her finger, he had chosen well. He said nothing as he completed the ancient ritual, but if he'd had the courage to tell her the truth, he would have said, *"You already have my heart, so all I can give you is this."*

Then it was done, and, in an inconceivable turn of events, Isabella Astley was his wife.

No. Make that Isabella Nettlethorpe-Ogilvy.

They left his grandfather to rest and repaired to the dining room, where a wedding breakfast had been laid out. His parents had been in rare form, even for them, when selecting the menu. It was a good thing they would have four dozen men from Nettlethorpe Iron watching the house around the clock because otherwise, Archibald had no idea what they would have done with all the leftovers. They started with turtle soup and moved on to caviar, lobster, and veal in truffle sauce. There was saffron rice and asparagus dressed with lemon. Archibald wasn't sure that the flavors went well together, but the foods were united by a common theme—they were all very, very expensive, so no one missed the fact that the Nettlethorpe-Ogilvys could afford them.

As the third course was being laid out, Izzie leaned close and whispered, "Do we have to stay for all of this?"

"I believe so, as we are the guests of honor," he returned in a hushed voice. "Why do you ask?"

She heaved a petulant sigh. "I was hoping we could go upstairs and consummate the marriage."

Archibald's cock twitched eagerly at this suggestion. "Although I would like that above all things, I think we have to stay. *Soon*, though."

Archibald's hopes that the meal would conclude quickly proved fruitless, unlike the dessert course, which was finally brought out an hour and a half later. Its theme seemed to be *pineapple*. After sampling a spread of pineapple cakes, pineapple ices, and pineapple tarts, the interminable breakfast finally concluded.

Finally, the time came to move to the foyer to see their guests off. Izzie was chatting with her sister, Lucy, and her friend, Diana Latimer.

"Thorpe is going to build me my own library. It's going to have floor-to-ceiling bookcases!"

While Lady Lucy and Lady Diana were busy squealing over the prospect of floor-to-ceiling bookcases, his friend, Morsley, sidled over. "Are you going by Thorpe now?"

Archibald considered his response. "Izzie thought it up the other day. I do like it. We'll see if it catches on."

"It's just that"—Morsley dropped his voice low, so the ladies wouldn't overhear—"it's actually quite a mouthful to say, 'Damn it, Nettlethorpe-Ogilvy.' Especially when you've just punched me in the jaw."

The corner of Archibald's mouth twitched. "Feel free to use it, then, because I plan on landing quite a few blows to your jaw."

"We'll see about that, Thorpe."

The Duke of Trevissick, who had just approached, scowled. "What's this? Why was I not informed that I had the option of calling you Thorpe?"

"I only started using it recently." *Recently*, in this case, meaning thirty seconds ago. "Why do you ask?"

The duke curled his nose. "I have probably devoted days of my life to pronouncing the extraneous number of syllables in your last name. *Thorpe* is a thousand times better."

"I am sorry to have wasted so much of your time," Archibald muttered.

"Yes, well." The duke pulled a folded sheet of paper from his pocket and offered it to Archibald. "I received this report from the Bow Street Runner I hired to look into the incident in Hyde Park. I imagine you will be interested in its contents, seeing as—"

Diana Latimer came up and elbowed her brother in the ribs. "Seeing as you were *wrong*, and the target of the attack was Izzie and not me. As *someone* tried to tell you," she added, glowering up at the duke.

Trevissick pinched the bridge of his nose. "Once again, I am sorry. I will admit a tendency to be overly vigilant where you are concerned. Now that our father is dead, I am trying to change my ways, but it will not happen overnight."

The duke was referring to the fact that their father, who was recently deceased, had been physically abusive toward his wife and daughter, a matter which had become public knowledge when the present duke was called to testify at a recent trial involving the family's long-serving butler.

Diana was not in a forgiving mood. "Well, you need to try harder. *You* were the one who convinced Lady Cheltenham that I was the true target, and that is the reason Izzie was at Lady Waldegrave's rout. If you hadn't bowled over the rest of us, as you always do, Lady Cheltenham would have heeded Aunt Griselda's warning and kept Izzie safe at home."

"At home, where she was an easy mark," the duke countered. "As it was, she was in the company of Thorpe, here, when the kidnappers struck. Which proved the best place she could have possibly been."

"That was a lucky coincidence," Diana countered.

While the siblings bickered, Archibald unfolded the papers, eager to see if the Runner had discovered anything of import. He started scanning the first of three pages.

"I can save you some time," the duke said. "There's not much of note in there. Our footmen were found bound and gagged. One of them sustained a blow to the head, from which he is recovering. They were both taken from behind unawares and didn't have any material information about the men who attacked them. The report that will be of real interest will be the one regarding Lady Waldegrave's rout, as they were able to detain those four men."

"Did your Runner give any hint as to what that report will contain?" Archibald asked.

The duke shook his head. "When this was delivered, they

had not yet been able to question them. It seems that all four of them sustained particularly nasty concussions."

Archibald couldn't say it in front of Lady Diana, but he shot the duke a look that said, *damn right, they did.*

The duke smirked. "We will be staying in town for a few weeks to purchase Cecilia a wardrobe befitting her new station as a duchess. I understand that Lady Isabella will not be able to move about freely until the issue with her attackers has been resolved. But perhaps Diana could call upon her here."

"Oh!" Diana brightened. "I would like that. Could I come tomorrow?"

Archibald was spared from having to answer this awkward question by the duke. "*No.*"

"But Marcus—"

"Thorpe will let us know when he and his wife are receiving visitors," the duke said firmly, shooting Archibald a lurid look.

"I know Izzie would like to see you." Archibald could feel his ears reddening. "We will send you a note just as soon as she is, er, settled in."

Comprehension flared in Lady Diana's pale blue eyes. "I would appreciate that," she said in a clipped voice before excusing herself.

Their guests were starting to leave. Archibald positioned himself next to Izzie, shaking hands, accepting well wishes, and trying not to cringe as his parents foisted urns of gardenias on each departing guest. The Astleys accepted this unusual offering with good grace, even the bachelor brother, Harrington, who said he would take his down to the barracks of his new regiment. "Trust me," he said solemnly, "could you but get a whiff of the men of the 95th Rifles, you would understand how badly I need these."

Finally, the only guests left were Lady Cheltenham and Lady Lucy, who was openly crying.

Izzie pulled her twin into a tight hug.

"I'm sorry," Lucy gasped. "I've always known this day would come. That one of us would eventually marry and move away. I just… everything happened so quickly, I… I thought we had more time…"

"There, there, darling," Lady Cheltenham said, patting her daughter's shoulder. "We won't be leaving London until the threat against Izzie has been resolved. So, you'll be able to visit her. That will give you a chance to get used to the situation."

"Could we come tomorrow?" Lucy sniffed.

"No, darling," the countess said firmly. "We need to give Izzie and Thorpe a few days."

Lucy nodded sadly, then stepped back. "I'm happy for you. I truly am. I know I don't look it." She gave Archibald a miserable smile. "I am sincerely glad my sister is married to such a fine gentleman as yourself."

Archibald bowed over her hand. "Thank you."

"Come," Lady Cheltenham said, then put an arm around her daughter's shoulders and steered her out the door.

At last, he was alone with Izzie. She wasn't crying, as her sister had been, but her eyes were moist and her cheeks were red. Archibald wasn't sure what to say, so he settled for squeezing her hand. She glanced up and gave him a tiny smile that did not reach her eyes.

Just then, his parents hurried into the foyer, followed by a trio of footmen bearing urns of gardenias. "Has Lieutenant Astley left?" his mother asked, breathless.

"He has," Archibald confirmed. "Why do you—"

"Quickly!" his father shouted. "Perhaps his carriage has not yet drawn away from the curb."

"He'll be wanting these," his mother called over her shoulder. "For his regiment!"

Archibald groaned, rubbing his eyes as his parents sailed out the front door in a cloud of floral perfume. Beside him, Izzie giggled.

"I'm sorry about my parents," he said. "They're a bit, er…"

"They're really not so bad," Izzie mused. "Other than their misguided response to the prospect of your grandfather attending the wedding."

Archibald grunted. So, she had noticed that.

"What your parents need," Izzie continued, "is *managing*."

Archibald shook his head. "Believe me, I've tried. They're impervious to management."

Izzie drew herself up, affronted. "I see that you have forgotten to whom you are speaking. I am the daughter of Georgiana Astley. Being managing is my *birthright*."

Archibald chuckled. "You're more than welcome to try." Something occurred to him. "Does that mean you'll be managing me, as well?"

She tapped her lip as if deep in thought. "Let's see, over the course of our short acquaintance, you have rescued me from both Tristan Bassingthwaighte and an entire gang of kidnappers, then offered to build me my own library." She looped her arms around his neck, smiling brightly. "You're doing quite well on your own. I can't wait to see what you come up with next."

He released a breath he hadn't realized he'd been holding as he raised his hands to her waist. "Good."

"Speaking of which"—she twined her fingers in his hair at the nape of his neck—"is it *finally* time to consummate this marriage?"

Without warning, Archibald scooped her into his arms. "*Yes*. It is."

CHAPTER 24

Izzie squealed and tightened her grip on Archibald's neck as he charged up the red-carpeted stairs with her in his arms. Not that she was complaining. She'd always dreamed of being carried up the stairs by a big, strong man, just like this. Besides, Archibald was going faster than she could possibly manage in skirts, and she was eager to reach their destination.

Izzie had been impatiently awaiting this moment for years. As Archibald bore her to their marriage bed, her toes curled in her slippers, because *at last*, she was going to find out what the fuss was all about.

Archibald carried her across the threshold of his bedroom, kissing her forehead as he deposited her gently on the bed. But instead of joining her on the plush mattress, he jogged back to the door.

"Archibald?" she asked, sitting up. "You're not leaving?"

"No," he said, pulling a key from his pocket and locking the door. Before she could blink, he was back across the room, pinning her to the mattress with his hips. "Most people know better than to interrupt a newlywed couple, but you've met my parents. They're impervious to social cues. And my valet is even worse. He knows certain things are unacceptable, but he couldn't care less."

He lowered his lips to her neck and pressed kisses against the sensitive skin of her throat. When he spoke, his voice was deep. "And this time, *nothing* is going to interrupt us."

Izzie liked the sound of that. And, as her husband claimed her lips, she reflected upon how much she liked this new version of Archibald, Married Archibald. To be sure, she had liked the old Archibald, Determined-to-Do-the-Right-Thing Archibald, as well. It had been especially diverting, trying to tempt Determined-to-Do-the-Right-Thing Archibald into doing the *wrong* thing, such as touching her in a way he clearly wanted, but mistakenly believed was too forward.

But Married Archibald had no such compunctions. Married Archibald was undressing her with those marvelously big, warm, strong hands of his. And she *loved* it!

"God, Izzie," he murmured as her clavicle came into view. He lowered his lips there, muttering, "So beautiful," between kisses.

She squirmed upon the bed, kicking off her slippers, and curled a stockinged foot around the back of his calf muscle. It was as big around as her head and flexed deliciously beneath her curious toes.

Izzie's motion caused her thighs to fall wider open, which had the splendid effect of allowing the swollen ridge beneath the placket of his breeches to settle against her core. *That* reminded her of the delicious things he'd done to that particular part of her anatomy yesterday in her parents' drawing room, and she circled her hips against him, forcing him to break off his kiss with a groan.

This also reminded her that things were not yet equal between them. While most of her body had been bared to his gaze at one time or another, she had yet to see anything below his waist, which seemed patently unfair.

She yanked at his beautiful blue jacket. There was the sound of a seam ripping, but Archibald did not appear to care. He tossed it to the floor in an inglorious heap, then busied himself shoving her dress down.

They tumbled around the bed, panting between kisses and clawing at one another's garments until she was down to her shift, and he wore nothing but his breeches. Izzie reached eagerly for the buttons on his falls, behind which there was a familiar bulge, but Archibald clamped his hand around her wrist.

"Wait," he said, breathing hard.

"Name six good reasons why I should," Izzie countered. "I, for one, am extremely eager to see what you've been hiding under here."

"Don't want to... alarm you," Archibald said through gritted teeth.

"Happily for you, I am not the easily alarmed sort."

He released her wrist, and her curious fingers began tracing his shape through the fabric. More eager than ever, she began undoing his buttons with one hand while continuing to explore him with the other. His head lolled back, and he groaned.

Izzie was enjoying driving him out of his mind, possibly a little too much. She managed to undo enough buttons that his falls sagged open, and she eagerly reached inside his breeches to take him out.

She had no trouble locating his man-part; indeed, the words *impossible to miss* came to mind. The moment she grew concerned was when her fingers failed to meet when she attempted to wrap her hand around it.

"Archibald!" she exclaimed as she brought it out for her examination. Although she was an innocent, she had wormed information out of a housemaid *and* made a detailed study of her brother's book of scandalous prints. She had thought herself relatively well-prepared for this moment.

But nothing she had learned up until that point had suggested that he would be so *thick*. She knew where Archibald's shaft was supposed to go, and this was not going to work.

"It is going to work," Archibald insisted. Apparently, she had spoken that last bit out loud.

Izzie considered him from another angle. "I don't believe it is."

Archibald kissed the top of her head, then pulled her into his lap. "This is what I was trying to avoid. I will admit, we may have a rough time of it on our first go. That's true no matter what, though. But just as my body swells and changes when *I* grow aroused, your body will respond in kind when *you* become aroused. You may not think it will fit now. But if I pleasure you enough, it will."

"That doesn't sound entirely bad," Izzie conceded. Well, there was nothing for it. A bride wasn't permitted to inspect her husband's intimate bits before the ceremony. You got the husband you got, and she'd managed to marry the one who was part Clydesdale. "I suppose let's give it a try."

Archibald kissed her deeply. Without warning, he tossed her back on the mattress. With a snarl, he seized the neckline of her chemise in both hands, then ripped it clean down the front, baring her body to his gaze.

Izzie whimpered, and something between her legs gave a damp pulse. Archibald was studying her, the corner of his mouth twitching. "I thought you would like that."

"I did," she gasped, shrugging off the remains of her shift.

He sat up so he could look at her. "God, Izzie. I've been dreaming about seeing you like this for so long."

"You have?" She had never been naked before a man prior

to this moment and had wondered if she would find it embarrassing. But there was nothing tawdry about the way Archibald was looking at her. His eyes were full of yearning, full of worship. Just when it occurred to Izzie to feel abashed about her meager bosom, Archibald reached out a hand, then paused as if he didn't dare touch her.

"What is it?" Izzie asked.

He swallowed thickly. "It's just… you're *perfect*. It's like touching a goddess. I feel so unworthy."

Well, if he liked her diminutive curves, who was she to go telling him he was wrong?

"Funny," she said, placing a hand on his firm chest and letting her fingertips trail lower across the sculpted muscles of his stomach, which flexed beneath her touch. "I think you're the one who looks like a god."

His breath had gone shallow. "Not a god. Just a blacksmith."

She traced one side of the vee where his hips met his abdomen. "Hephaestus, then." She began tugging at his breeches, which were sagging around his thighs.

He turned to sit on the side of the bed so he could pull them off. He didn't meet her eyes as he said, "Aphrodite despised Hephaestus. She would have been happier with Ares."

He made the remark with a forced lightness that made Izzie suspect it contained a kernel of truth, or at least, what *he* believed to be the truth. "That's because she was an idiot, as shallow as she was insipid. In fact, I refuse to assume the role of Aphrodite in this scenario. I think we can all agree that I have much more in common with Pandora."

That earned her a smile as he tossed his breeches aside. "But Pandora didn't marry Hephaestus."

She forced herself to tamp down her curiosity and keep her eyes on his face as he turned toward her, fully nude, as she sensed this conversation was more important than he was letting on. "She did this time. That's the best part about being the author—you get to write the ending any way you want. And include as many guard bears and naked pirate swordfights as you wish."

Archibald paused in the act of reaching for her. "Wait—are you referring to your book?" At her nod, he continued, "So, you're saying you wrote a scene where naked pirates, er... cross swords?"

"My goodness, it sounds tawdry when you phrase it that way! Of course, there is. Just the regular kind of swordplay, mind you. But my point is, *we* are the authors of this story. And I say things would have worked out splendidly for Hephaestus had he married someone worthy of him."

"Hmm." He didn't look convinced. "What happens next in our story?"

"This." Without warning, she pushed his chest with both hands.

Archibald did not budge so much as an inch. He sat there blinking at her, confused, before comprehension dawned in his eyes, and he obligingly fell back on the bed.

She threw a knee across his torso to straddle him, placing her hands on his chest. "I've got you now, Archibald Nettlethorpe-Ogilvy!"

"I surrender," he groaned as she lowered herself to lie on top of him.

She had intended to kiss him, but the second every inch of her skin came into contact with his big, warm, firm body, her brain guttered and went out.

"Ar... Archi-*ohmygod*," she moaned. "N-need a minute. Can't think. My *God*, that feels so good!"

His strong arms stole around her, which did nothing to restore her composure as she was exposed to the exquisite sensation of even more of his skin caressing hers. "It really does, doesn't it?" his deep voice rumbled beneath her ear.

"Why do people ever leave their beds?" Izzie asked, rubbing herself against him like a cat.

He chuckled. "And we haven't even come to the good part yet."

"Are you sure?" Izzie gasped. "I can't imagine it getting better than this."

"Let me show you."

Then he was kissing her, and the combination of Archibald's hungry mouth on hers and his gorgeous body laid out beneath her made her feel drunk with pleasure. His hands were everywhere, which was exactly where she wanted them. Her hands seemed to explore his body of their own accord, enjoying the hard ridges of his stomach, the little dimple behind his hipbone, and the gasping breath he took as she traced the shape of his flat, brown nipples.

Abruptly, he sat her up, spreading her legs so she straddled him. He aligned her damp core with his man-part, which was pointing all the way up, flat against his stomach. He bent his head and caught one of her nipples in his mouth, giving her a deep pull. Her whole body hitched as she cried out, which had the effect of rubbing that magical spot he had pleasured with his tongue the previous day against the thickness of his cock.

"That's it," he encouraged, flexing his hips to slide back and forth against her. "Use me to take your pleasure."

She couldn't seem to stop herself from doing just that. Everything Archibald was doing to her felt *so good*, and after yesterday, she knew enough to realize that she was building toward another one of those glorious explosions.

After a few minutes of pleasuring her breasts, Archibald suddenly grabbed her, flipping her over and reversing their positions. He started kissing his way down her stomach, and

Izzie spread her legs, hoping he might kiss her again on that place that was now pulsing like a heartbeat.

He didn't disappoint her. "So beautiful," he groaned, kissing the inside of her thigh. "God, how I've longed to kiss you here."

"Please, Archibald. Please!"

He buried his face between her legs with a moan. This time, Izzie was even more aroused than she had been in the drawing room, and the pleasure came upon her immediately.

"Please don't stop!" she cried. "You're going to make me come!"

Archibald didn't stop. But just when Izzie thought she was going to tumble over the peak, he slid one of his fingers into her passage. It went in up to his middle knuckle, but then met resistance.

Izzie froze, distracted from her pleasurable daze. It didn't feel bad so much as *tight*. Which was unsurprising. Archibald's fingers were as beefy as the rest of him.

"Shh," he said, pressing a kiss against her thigh as he gently slid his finger in and out. "You just need a moment to get used to me. It'll be all right."

He resumed stroking her with his tongue, and she willed herself to relax. Indeed, with each passing minute, the feeling of being stretched grew less and less, until he was able to slide his finger all the way in without any discomfort at all.

She was again making progress in that indelible climb toward her peak when he added a second finger, and she came screeching to a halt.

He groaned, pressing his forehead against her stomach. "I know it's hard, but try to relax," he said, kissing a trail down the place where her leg met her torso. "You're doing marvelously. And after today, it will never hurt again."

He settled once more between her thighs, his mouth finding that little nub between her legs where it felt so good to be fondled. He began stroking it in earnest with the flat of his tongue, and the pleasure was so staggering that she almost forgot the uncomfortable sensation of being stretched.

He soon added a third finger, which put her right back to where she'd started. But she couldn't deny that she was making progress. When her thighs began to twitch, and she felt sick with the need to climax, she tugged at Archibald's shoulders.

Archibald glanced up at her, studying her reaction. He repositioned his mouth over that bud between her legs and started to suck.

Izzie started to babble aloud. "Oh, Archibald! That feels so good! I'm... I'm going to... Oh. Oh, my *God*. Archi... Archiba... *Oh, my God!*"

There were no more words after that, just cries of pleasure as she exploded like one of the cannons her husband was so good at making. Her back arched off the bed, and her legs shook uncontrollably on either side of his head. Archibald stayed with her the whole while, drawing out her pleasure and then gentling his strokes just as the sensation became too much.

He slid up the bed and pulled her into his arms. She was sweating and panting, but he didn't seem to mind.

She framed his beautiful face, pressing kisses everywhere. "You're *wonderful*. The best husband in the world."

He laughed bleakly. "I hope you still feel that way ten minutes from now."

"Ten minutes?" she asked. "Is that how long it's going to take?"

He nodded tightly, veins standing out in his neck. "Probably less. I want you too much. But it's probably not a bad thing for your first time to be quick."

"All right." She pulled him on top of her, and he came willingly. "I'm as ready as I'm going to be."

His entire body was tense. "I'm afraid this still might hurt."

"It probably will." She pressed a kiss against the column of his neck. "But that's all right. I'll get through it."

He nodded, then reached down to position himself at her entrance. She immediately felt pressure as he started to slide forward. She took a shaky breath and reminded herself to relax.

A look that bespoke the best kind of agony stole across Archibald's face. "Oh, God, Izzie. You feel *so good*."

It helped to have something to concentrate on other than her own discomfort. This was a special moment for Archibald, too, and she wanted to make it good for him.

She began tracing shapes across the smooth skin of his back with the pads of her fingers. "That's it. You can keep going."

His eyes were squeezed shut. "I can't believe this is happening. I can't believe I got to marry you. I'm the luckiest man in the world!"

That made her heart glow. The tension between her legs eased a fraction.

He opened his eyes, his brow creased with concern. "Is it too painful?"

"It's not," she hastened to reassure him. "It feels… snug. Very snug, but I wouldn't call it painful."

His face remained skeptical. "If you're sure…"

"I am." She tightened her grip on his shoulders.

"All right, then." Tentatively, he pressed forward. Much to her surprise, his cock slid into her unimpeded until he was buried to the hilt.

His eyes rolled back in his head. "Iz… Izzie.. Oh, my… my… Guh. So guh…"

A giggle rippled out of her, seeing her normally precise husband incoherent with pleasure.

His gaze snapped back into focus. His forehead was knotted with consternation. "Izzie, I—I'm sorry. I didn't mean to go so fast, it just—"

"It's all right." She stroked her hands across his shoulders. "It didn't hurt."

"R-really? Then I can…"

She kissed his cheek. "Go ahead."

Studying her face, he slowly withdrew then pushed forward again. It felt strange but not painful.

Seeming to satisfy himself that he wasn't ripping her apart, Archibald's head lolled to the side and the tempo of his thrusts increased. "Oh, Izzie! That feels so good… *too* good. I'm not even going to last a full minute."

She didn't understand the reason for his rueful tone. "That's all right."

"D-do better… next time," he gasped.

Archibald was obviously overwhelmed. Izzie, on the other hand, wasn't feeling the same desperate sort of pleasurable sensations building within her. But she loved the feeling of Archibald, his weight upon her and his skin against hers. She loved seeing the pleasure on his face. And she especially loved this feeling of closeness that had blossomed between them.

His shoulders hardened to iron beneath her fingers. "Izzie!" he cried. "Izzie, I… I…"

His motions grew frantic, and she could tell his crisis was upon him. She clung to him as tightly as he was clinging to her and murmured soothing sounds in his ear as he cried out her name. Then he gave a great shudder before collapsing on top of her, eyes closed, head next to hers on the pillow.

After a moment, his eyes opened. He looked dazed. "Izzie." He brought a hand up to trace the outline of her cheek. "I almost thought it was a dream. That was *amazing*. Thank you."

He kissed her, but only briefly before rolling onto his back, cradling her against him. "I must be crushing you."

"It's all right." It was true, although Izzie had liked being crushed, at least a little bit. But it also felt nice lying snuggled up to Archibald with her head on his shoulder, so she didn't complain.

He drew the counterpane over their legs. His deep voice rumbled beneath her ear. "How do you feel?"

"Happy," she answered without thinking.

"Happy is good," he murmured.

They lapsed into a contented silence. Izzie found that she enjoyed having his big, muscular body at her disposal. Her hand traced across the flat planes of his chest, then the bulging muscles of his arm.

As she explored the tightly contoured ridges that crisscrossed his stomach, she noticed a tent forming in the bedclothes directly over his groin. Ducking her head, she grinned into his shoulder, then began stroking him with diabolical intention. She lingered over his flat nipples, enjoying his gasping breath. She scraped her nails gently up his side and was gratified by his shudder. She rubbed her own naked body against his like a cat, earning her a tiny moan, one she could tell he was trying to suppress.

But when her fingers stroked down past his stomach and slipped beneath the edge of the counterpane, she abruptly found her wrist seized in an iron grip. Suddenly, she was flat on her back, both of her hands held in place above her head and her husband's hips pinning her to the mattress.

Izzie's mouth went dry and the place between her legs went wet. As always, she *really* liked this position.

His eyes were slightly wild. "Unless you want me to fall on you like a rutting animal—"

"Yes, please," Izzie moaned. She couldn't help but roll her hips against the ridge of his hard cock.

He made a sound of despair. "You're not supposed to say *yes, please*. It hasn't even been five minutes since I took your maidenhead. I'm trying so hard to be good."

"I know. I would try the patience of a saint," Izzie agreed. "Do you have any idea how *gorgeous* your arms look when you hold them up over your head like that?"

"Gorgeous?" He gave her a strange look. "I'm not sure that a brutish, hulking blacksmith can be considered gorgeous."

"You do look like a blacksmith. But you would also make a good Viking. I was thinking—maybe sometime we could find some furs to spread out on top of the counterpane. Then you can carry me into the room, toss me on the bed, and *ravish* me."

His arms were shaking, and his voice when he answered was strained. "If that is something you would like, I would be glad—*more* than glad—to do it for you. But surely I need to be gentle with you for at least a few days."

Izzie wrapped her legs around his hips and started to rub her core against his swollen cock, back and forth and back and forth. "You want to do it again."

His eyes had gone hazy. "I… I…"

"You can't hide *this*," she said, grinding against him.

"Of course, I want to," he bit out. "But I wouldn't hurt you for the world."

"But it didn't hurt! That's the remarkable part. And…" She bit her lip, too shy to say the rest.

She got nothing past Archibald, who was studying her face intently. "And what?"

"Nothing." Seeing that he wasn't buying it, she sighed. "It's just… I did want another try at it. To see if I enjoy it more the second time around."

Archibald released her wrists and pulled her into his

arms. "You were perfect. I'm given to understand that few women truly enjoy their first time."

Izzie ducked her head into his neck. That wasn't what the housemaid she'd questioned had told her. She'd said that, although there would be a moment of pain when she lost her maidenhead, there would be nothing but pleasure after that.

Izzie hadn't felt that stab of pain. But the truth was, she hadn't felt the pleasure, either. Not the way she did when Archibald rubbed that little nub between her legs.

Archibald laughed ruefully. "And if you didn't find your pleasure, it was my fault. Don't worry. I'll last longer this time around."

Izzie was on the cusp of asking what the significance of how long he lasted was when his words washed over her. "This time around? You mean... we're doing it again?" she asked brightly.

He was really quite handsome when he smiled. "You've strong-armed me into it."

Izzie couldn't suppress a giggle at the notion that she could strong-arm this man into anything.

"But," he continued, flopping onto his back, "you have to take the lead. That way I'll know we're only doing things that feel good to you."

She sat up. There had been a picture like this in the book Harrington kept hidden under his mattress—of a man lying on his back with a woman astride him.

She had liked the way she felt when she looked at that picture...

She swung her leg over Archibald's torso so that her core was aligned with his. She had liked it when he loomed over her, holding her wrists. When she was entirely at his mercy.

She found that she liked having him at her mercy just as much.

"Oh, dear," he said, looking up at her. "I recognize that expression. You like this, don't you?"

"*Yes*," she breathed.

"Go on then," he said, flopping his head back against the pillow and raising his arms over his head. "Do your worst."

She did.

CHAPTER 25

*L*ying back on the bed, Archibald reminded himself that he was the luckiest man in all of England.

Even if he was currently in a state of agony.

His beautiful, delightful wife, who displayed every indication that she was going to drive him out of his goddamn mind, sat naked astride his torso, an excited gleam in her eyes. Archibald was coming to know her well enough to understand that this particular gleam foretold good things.

But only after she'd tortured him within an inch of his life.

Izzie smoothed her hands across the planes of his chest, making a sound of pleasure. He still couldn't believe that she liked his burly frame. It wasn't fashionable, as his tailor had made clear. But he no longer gave a damn, as apparently, it made his bride wish he would throw her on the bed and ravish her like a Viking, a request that would be extremely easy to grant, given that this was what he wanted to do every time he saw her.

He reminded himself that he had just pledged to lie back

and let Izzie do whatever she wanted. It was her turn to ravish him.

Eyes sparkling with mischief, she proceeded to stroke every inch of his torso and arms, cooing with delight and murmuring admiring words all the while. When she grazed the sensitive skin beneath his arms, he gave a ticklish flinch, and his cock brushed her core.

She seemed to take this as an excellent suggestion because she aligned her bud with the ridge of his cock and began rocking back and forth. Archibald groaned. She was hot and slick and what she was doing simultaneously felt so good, and not nearly good enough. He wanted to grab her by the hips and lower her sweet, tight cunny down onto his cock, but of course, he couldn't do that.

Izzie tried and failed to assume an innocent expression. "Is anything the matter, Archibald?"

"You're driving me mad, and you know it," he gasped.

She tutted. "Oh, no. I haven't even begun to drive you mad."

He was trying to decide whether this was a good thing or a bad thing when she slid down the bed, kneeling between his legs. She stroked her hands up and down his thighs. "There was a particular picture in that book my brother had. Would you like to know what it showed?"

"Oh, my *God*."

She let her hands drift up to his pelvis, framing the base of his cock, but not touching him where he needed it. "Would you like for me to give it a try?"

"*Yes*."

She laughed. "I haven't even told you what it is yet."

"Touch my cock," he begged. "*Please*, just touch my cock. I've dreamed about you doing this for so long."

She looked up, a smile curling the corners of her lips. "Have you?"

He was so far gone that he didn't care what he was admitting. "*Yes*."

"Well, since you asked so nicely."

She wrapped her hand around him—as far as it would go, in any case—and began a gentle exploration that was simultaneously heaven and hell. Her hands were *so soft* and felt *so good* on him. But if he had expected the orgasm he'd had ten minutes ago to take the edge off, he was doomed to disappointment, because he needed to come, needed to come *right now*. He couldn't decide whether he wanted her agonizingly soft caresses to go on forever, or to cover her sweet little hand with his own so he could show her how to jack him off in three strokes.

She came up to explore his head, where he was the most sensitive, and where a drop of moisture had formed right at his tip. "Oh!" she exclaimed upon discovering how slick it made him. "That's useful. Does that feel good?"

"*So* good needa come *please* Izzie," was the garbled string of babble that emerged from his mouth.

She laughed, delighted. Her expression was impish as she lowered herself down upon the bed. "Don't you want to know what *else* it showed on that print?"

He thought he had a fair idea, and, as much as he did want that, he recalled that her original purpose was for them to make love again so she could see if she found more pleasure in the act the second time around. "I do want that, but if you want to make love, perhaps we should save the other thing for next time. I'm liable to explode the second you put your lips on me."

"Let's just see, shall we?"

"Izzie, are you sure you want to—oh, *fuck*." His vision blurred as the indescribable pleasure of her soft, pink lips stroking the head of his cock washed over him. "I'm sorry!"

he said quickly. "I didn't mean to say... Oh, my *fucking God,* Izzie! That feels *so good!*"

All of his good intentions to apologize for his coarse language flew out the window as she started to use her tongue on him. If her giggle was any indication, she wasn't overly offended. She had both of her hands wrapped around his shaft, and next time, he would show her how to pump them up and down in concert with what she was doing with her mouth.

Next time. Because this time, he was seconds from flooding her mouth.

God, just the sight of her was almost enough to set him off. The vision of Isabella Astley, pink lips twisted into a smile even as they were wrapped around his cock, was something he had dreamed about a million times and never imagined he would actually get to see.

Suddenly, it was all too much. "Wait, Izzie, I'm... I'm going to... That's going to make me... Didn't you want to... to..."

She pulled her lips off him with a pop. "Oh, all right." She moved up the bed, throwing a knee on either side of him, and started aligning his cock with her entrance.

"Wait. Are you sure you're wet enough? Maybe I should—"

Izzie laughed. "Oh, I'm wet enough." She proceeded to prove it by sliding down onto his cock, taking him to the hilt in one smooth stroke.

"Izzie! God, that's so good! God, I—"

He cut himself off before he could utter the words *I love you,* because, as far as she knew, they'd only really met three days ago and were having a whirlwind courtship. Never mind that for him, this "whirlwind courtship" had started more than a year ago. But he didn't want to alarm her.

She didn't want his heart, after all. She wanted him to

protect her, and she wanted him to give her pleasure. She wanted to live with him in his Gothic mansion, and she wanted the extravagant library he was going to build for her.

That would have to be enough.

Speaking of making her come... Izzie was sliding tentatively up and down his length, a slight frown on her face. "Does it hurt?" he asked.

She blew out a frustrated breath. "No, it's not that."

It was plain as day that she wasn't enjoying herself nearly as much as he was. And, although he had vowed to lie back and let her take the lead, he couldn't let that stand.

So, he reached a hand between her legs, settling his thumb upon that little bud that was the secret to a woman's pleasure and began to rub. She was already nice and slick there.

The change was instantaneous. Izzie's back arched as she gasped. "Oh, Archibald! That feels..."

"Yes?" She was so distracted by his ministrations that she had forgotten to keep moving. But that wasn't a problem. He reached his other hand around to grasp her hip, sliding her up and down along his length, pleasuring himself while he was pleasuring her.

"It's so good!" she gasped.

"Touch your breasts," he suggested because she had seemed to like that quite a lot and because, as much as he would've liked to do it for her, his hands were fully occupied.

Surprise crossed her face for a second, but then she complied, and the look of pure, unadulterated bliss on her face was beautiful to behold. Her head tipped back, sending her dark hair trembling down her back in a shiny cascade. "Oh, Archibald!" Her thighs began to tremble. "I think I'm going to... going to..."

He circled his thumb as quickly as he could, and she cried out. And this was what he wanted, what he had dreamed about for so long—the pleasure on her face as he brought her to orgasm, the feeling of her passage convulsing around him, the desperate way her hands clung to him for purchase.

It drove him straight over the edge. He exploded inside her with a shout, his motions as frantic as hers and the pleasure purer than anything he had ever known.

She flopped forward onto his chest, and he wrapped his arms around her. God, but this felt perfect. Surely this was the best moment of his life.

He was going to *treasure* this woman…

Gently, he lifted her face to his so he could kiss her.

And saw that she was blinking back tears.

CHAPTER 26

"Izzie," Archibald said, his voice full of alarm, "what's wrong?"

She wished he wouldn't ask that question. "Nothing!" she lied.

His face was agonized. "Did I hurt you? Oh, God, Izzie—I'm so sorry, I—"

"It's not that," she bit out, then cringed because her phrasing implied that there *was* a problem; it just happened to be something else.

"Then what is it?" he asked gently. When she sat up, looking away, he sat up, too, and took her hand. "Izzie?"

"I'm just"—she cast about for the right word—"disappointed."

"I see." He fell silent a moment. "I apologize. I somehow formed the impression that you reached a similar level of satisfaction during our lovemaking as I did. Clearly, that was not the case, and I will set about rectifying it immedia—"

"That's not it," she groaned. Lord, but this was embarrassing. "It was very good for me. It could not have been better."

He waited for her to continue. When she didn't, he asked, "Then what has you feeling disappointed?"

"There's something the matter with me. I did enjoy it, but only when you started rubbing me at that spot between my legs. But I'm supposed to derive my pleasure from… from…" She blushed, looking away. "You know."

"From my cock?" he asked.

"Yes. That." Gracious, her cheeks were on fire. She might be bold, but she'd been a virgin a half-hour ago. "There's obviously something wrong with me, and I…" She trailed off, looking down.

When she chanced a glance up, Archibald was studying her. "This is all starting to make sense."

She laughed, incredulous. "It is? I'm glad one of us thinks so."

"Yes." He took her by the waist, hauling her into his lap. "Who says you're 'supposed to' reach your pleasure from just my cock?"

"Everyone," she answered immediately.

He shook his head. "No, not everyone. I don't say that. So, who told you that?"

"One of our housemaids," Izzie said in a rush. "When I was fourteen, I paid her a shilling to answer my questions, to explain what went on between a man and a woman."

"Ah. And this housemaid was your primary source of information, other than your brother's book, of course."

"That's correct."

"And she didn't say anything about that other spot? The one on the outside, where I touched you?"

"No. I was quite surprised when you started kissing me there in the drawing room. Although it worked remarkably well."

He rubbed her back. "So, that's why you were worried that you were frigid. When you experimented, you followed this maid's advice and touched yourself on the inside, but you didn't even know about your clitoris."

Izzie was too startled to feel embarrassed about the fact that he had guessed exactly what she'd been doing—or at least, attempting to do—alone in her bed at night. "My... what's it called? Cli...?"

"The clitoris. The spot that is the center of most women's pleasure."

Izzie frowned. "The maid I asked didn't mention anything about that."

He shrugged. "I don't think your maid lied to you. I think she told you what *she* likes. But that doesn't mean it's what most women like, and it certainly doesn't have to be what *you* like."

Izzie peered at him. "How do you know all this?"

He ran a hand over his face. "Not by sleeping with dozens of women, believe me. Although I will admit to not being a virgin. Prior to you, I had slept with precisely two women. But, as a general rule, I like to understand how things work. So, I asked questions. Lots and lots of questions."

Izzie shrugged. "It's probably for the best that one of us knows what they're doing. But..." She bit her lip. "Did they truly say that? That *most* women prefer the... the clitoris?"

His ears had gone pink. "The question I asked was how best to please a woman. They both directed me to attend to that spot. The first time, I was surprised and asked if women would not derive pleasure from... well. Doing what pleased *me*. She told me that some would, but not all, and that if I *really* wanted to make a woman happy, I would fondle her clitoris."

Izzie raked a strand of hair out of her face. "I wish I numbered amongst those who enjoy both. I can't help but feel like it's extra work for you."

"You could just as easily consider the things that bring me

to climax to be the 'extra work,' and the things you enjoy to be fundamental to the act," he countered.

She blew out a frustrated huff. "Nobody would consider *your* acts to be the superfluous ones. Your acts are necessary for procreation."

His chest shook with laughter. "We are specifically trying *not* to procreate!"

She narrowed her eyes at him. "Must you be so contrary? You're not one of those men who cannot bear for anyone else to win an argument, are you?"

Eyes tender, he brushed a strand of hair behind her ear. "You are one of the most intelligent people I've ever met, so I'm sure you will win a good many arguments. Just not when the point you're trying to make is that something is wrong with you. Because that position is indefensible."

Izzie felt her insides turn to mush. He was slightly wonderful, this new husband of hers. "Still, it seems like a lot of extra trouble for you, especially if you add those minutes up over time."

"Izzie," he laughed, "the minutes I spend making love to you are the best minutes of my day. Do you really think I'm going to complain that I get a few more of them?"

"I suppose not. Still—eeyah!" She shrieked as Archibald seized her about the waist, rolling them back onto the mattress. "What are you doing?"

His voice was full of humor. "This morning, you implied that there would be more unnatural acts and fewer arguments about whether one or both of us are reaching orgasm the wrong way. Which is a nonsensical question. The wrong kind of orgasm—now there's an oxymoron if ever I've heard one."

Izzie recognized this as the distraction it was. But it was a *good* distraction, and she found herself asking, "Was there a particular unnatural act you were hoping to try?"

"It happens that there is. Was there a picture in your brother's book of a man lying on his back and the woman sitting on his face?"

"There was. I wasn't quite sure what they were—eek!"

He had lifted her as easily as if she were a rag doll, spreading her legs and settling her above him. She felt everything between her legs give a throb.

He smiled up at her. "I believe a demonstration is in order."

Afterward, Izzie had to own that Archibald did not, in fact, seem to mind going to the extra trouble of bringing her to satisfaction. In fact, he seemed to have a particular enthusiasm for the task. And as she settled her head on his shoulder and allowed her eyes to drift shut, she mused that this hasty marriage just might work.

CHAPTER 27

$\mathcal{M}$uch to Archibald's gratification, they did not emerge from their bedchamber for three days.

A few times a day, maids would enter, bearing some combination of food, fresh linens for the bed, or cans of hot water for the bath. Archibald gave Izzie one of his dressing gowns, an ostentatious burgundy velvet garment that had made him feel ridiculous both times he'd attempted to wear it, for her to wrap herself in while the maids went about their work. It was huge on her, but he quite liked the sight of her wearing it at the table by the window, a quiet acknowledgment that she was his.

But other than those brief intrusions, it was just the two of them. They would make love when they awoke, then have a leisurely breakfast together, make love again, then talk about nothing and everything until it was time for luncheon. Izzie had her maid fetch the manuscript for her book, and they read it together, lying side by side on the bed, waiting for the other to finish before turning the page. Archibald managed to laugh in all the right places, and although it was one of those rare instances when Izzie was bashful, she seemed genuinely pleased by how much he enjoyed it.

On the afternoon of their third day as husband and wife, Archibald was reflecting that the past three days had been the happiest of his life when the knock came at the door.

Izzie had fallen asleep after their latest bout of lovemaking. Archibald had been heading in that direction, but he gently extracted his arm from beneath her head, replaced it with a pillow, then pulled on a shirt and trousers and padded over to the door.

It proved to be his office manager, McPherson, clutching his hat in front of him. "A thousand apologies, Mr. Nettlethorpe-Ogilvy, sir. But might I have a quick word?"

Archibald stepped out into the hallway. It turned out that the King of Salaria had not proven understanding regarding Nettlethorpe Iron's inability to deliver his order of cannons earlier than promised.

"I've been trying to put him off. But he shows up every day with his entourage, shouting and complaining. Today, he threatened to go to the king."

"King George?" Archibald raked a hand through his hair. "I would think the king would take our side, considering the British Army's orders would be the ones pushed back were we to expedite those of Salaria."

Still, he didn't want the hassle of royal attention. "Tell the king I'll meet with him tomorrow."

McPherson's eyes shone with relief. "Thanks, boss."

It occurred to Archibald that this was not the only matter he had been neglecting. "And arrange meetings with my contact over at the Office of Ordnance and with the Bow Street Runner who's investigating the threats against my wife. Have them come to Nettlethorpe Iron if at all possible."

McPherson bowed his head. "Yes, sir. I'll send a letter

with the meeting times as soon as I have everything arranged."

"Thank you."

Archibald slipped back into the room and found Izzie sitting up in bed, the sheet clutched to her chest. "What was that about?"

He came and sat next to her on the bed. "I'm afraid I have to go to Nettlethorpe Iron tomorrow. The King of Salaria is demanding to jump up the queue and have his order of cannons delivered earlier than promised. I have to inform His Majesty that he's going to have to wait his turn."

"The King of Salaria!" Izzie made a show of looking impressed. "Such lofty company!"

He flopped onto his back beside her. "Everyone wants cannons when there's a war on. Not that these kings and princes are excited to make my acquaintance. He'd probably cut me dead if he saw me in the street."

Wrapping her arms around his chest, she kissed his cheek. "Well, I think you're worth a hundred of him."

He slipped his arm around her, enjoying the feel of her head pillowed on his shoulder. "I feel bad about leaving you alone here."

"I'll be all right. You have plenty of guards in place."

"I worry not so much about your safety as that you'll feel confined."

"Oh." She chewed her lip, thinking. "I might if this stretches on too long. But I know you can't stay away from Nettlethorpe Iron forever. You have a business to run and an important one at that."

He ran his fingers through her silky, dark hair. It still felt unreal that he was permitted to touch her like this. "Would you like to invite someone to come here? Maybe your sister, or Lady Diana?"

"That's a splendid idea. Having some visitors will cheer me considerably."

"I'll also be meeting with Bow Street and my contact over at Ordnance. So, hopefully, I'll have some good news regarding the investigation."

"Let's hope so." Izzie pressed a trail of kisses up his jawline. "Do you know what seems truly unfair?"

"What?" he asked, his breath starting to quicken.

She nipped at his ear. "That you're wearing all of these clothes while I'm lying here naked."

He turned on his side, pulling her flush against his chest. "How thoughtless of me. Allow me to remedy this oversight…"

So it was that the following morning, Archibald and Izzie did something slightly unfamiliar.

They dressed and came downstairs for breakfast.

His parents were already there, helping themselves to the usual spread that would've been better suited for a family of twenty. At least with dozens of his men coming over to guard the house in shifts, the food wouldn't go to waste.

Izzie smiled at his mother as she settled in with a plate of toast and a poached egg. "Mrs. Nettlethorpe-Ogilvy, have you heard the latest gossip?"

If it occurred to his mother to wonder how he and Izzie would know any of the latest gossip, considering they had not emerged from his room for three days, she gave no sign of it. She leaned forward, her eyes keen. "No! Do tell."

Izzie glanced around as if she were about to reveal a great secret. "Your son has a new nickname."

"A new nickname!" In an instant, his mother was all aflutter. "Oh, my gracious heavens. I hadn't even heard!"

His father perked up, as eager for the gossip as his wife. "What is it?"

"Thorpe. It's terribly fashionable." Izzie looked up from spreading marmalade on her toast and gave a little wiggle to convey that she was now coming to the most exciting part. "The Duke of Trevissick is using it."

"The *Duke of Trevissick!*" his mother gasped, hands flying to her heart.

"By Jove!" his father exclaimed, looking equally impressed.

His new wife was a genius. Archibald had known that since the day he met her, but this confirmed it.

Her tactics were brilliant, and he could see that her carefully aimed shot had found its mark. There was naked longing on his mother's face, warring with just a trace of uncertainty.

The longing won out. "Archie?" she asked. "Would you mind terribly if I used your new nickname? I mean... I hate to ask, as I know you *prefer* to go by Archie—"

Across the table, Izzie made a strangled sound, but she managed to hold her expression neutral. Gesturing to her throat, she covered it by taking a sip of her cocoa.

"—but if the *Duke of Trevissick* is using it, maybe I should too," his mother concluded.

Archibald swallowed a mouthful of coffee and set his cup down. "I don't mind at all. In fact, I rather like it. I feel like it suits me."

His father grinned as he gestured for a footman to refill his cocoa. "Well, if the Duke of Trevissick likes it, that's good enough for me!"

"Thorpe," his mother said to herself. "Thorpe. Thorpe. It may take a few days to accustom myself to using it, but it must be done. How I should hate to appear out of fashion!"

"I daresay you'll master the trick of it faster than you

think, my dove," his father said. "Thorpe. Has a nice ring to it. Thorpe."

Across the table, Izzie winked at him. Archibald raised his coffee cup in a subtle salute before taking a sip.

He was going to enjoy being married to this woman. He was going to enjoy it very much.

CHAPTER 28

Upon arriving at Nettlethorpe Iron, Archibald learned that the Bow Street Runner, Mr. Thomas Daubney, was waiting in his office.

Unfortunately, Mr. Daubney hadn't had much in the way of news to impart.

"Three out of the four men you incapacitated have come around," Mr. Daubney said, nodding his thanks as he accepted a glass of port. He gave Archibald a wry look. "The fourth remains disoriented. Just how hard did you hit him?"

Archibald bristled. "Not half as hard as he deserved. They were trying to kidnap my wife! Or possibly"—it was difficult to say the word—"kill her."

The Runner set his glass on the desk. "At least I can shed some light upon the question of their goal—kidnapping versus murder."

"And?" Archibald's heart was in his throat, dreading the answer.

"All three men confirmed that they were directed to kidnap Lady Isabella if possible but kill her if necessary."

Archibald surged to his feet. "Kill her?" Darkness swam

around the edges of his vision. "They'd better stay the hell away. If they lay so much as a fingernail on my wife, I will tear them limb from limb!"

"You certainly seem qualified to do the job," Mr. Daubney mused.

Archibald stalked across the room, unable to sit calmly with fury coursing through his veins. "Who is behind this?"

"That, we do not know. The four men we brought in are well known to their local magistrates. Petty criminals with a reputation for running with the wrong crowd, willing to do all sorts of things for the right price."

"Then why were they at liberty to roam the streets and threaten my wife?" Archibald snapped.

The Runner held his hands up. "They hadn't done anything this serious before. Or at least, the charges hadn't stuck. But they'll get transportation this time, at the very least."

"Good," Archibald muttered, pacing back over to his desk.

"All four said they heard about the job from one of the other men there that night. Hugh Jacoby, the one whose wrist you broke. He's of the same ilk as the others—a common street ruffian. I doubt he's the mastermind behind this, but it appears he might have made contact with that person."

"And do you have this Jacoby in custody?"

Mr. Daubney shook his head. "He's gone to ground. We're looking for him," he added when Archibald growled.

"Spare no expense. He must be captured, and I will pay whatever is necessary to see it done." He pulled out a sheet of paper and a quill. "And write down everything you know about him. Lady Morsley will have contacts in the neighborhoods he frequents. Perhaps she can dig something up. My wife is her little sister, you know."

Mr. Daubney took up the quill. "Her contacts will be as good as ours. It's certainly worth a try."

Once the Runner had left, Archibald tried to sort through the mound of paperwork that had accumulated in his absence. But he couldn't concentrate on a damn thing.

Those bastards would have *killed* Izzie. They'd better hope they got sent to New South Wales. It was in their own best interest to put as much distance between themselves and him as possible because if he ever got his hands on them…

Suffice it to say, when McPherson knocked on his door a quarter of an hour later and announced the King of Salaria, Archibald was not in the absolute best mood for receiving visitors.

King Charles Filiberto had a long, thin nose and bulging eyes. He was taller than Archibald by several inches but probably weighed five stone less. He was dressed in full military regalia, which Archibald found ironic—although his island nation had a navy of some repute in spite of its small size, their king had never led it into battle.

The king minced into the room, wrinkling his nose at Archibald's plainly furnished office. "Mr. Nettlethorpe-Ogilvy, it is about time, yes? I have called five times. Five times, and only now do you deign to receive me! You must think very highly of your cannons to keep a king wait—"

This was the moment the king turned and beheld the dark scowl upon Archibald's face. He recoiled, his expression a mix of alarm and offense.

"I believe you were informed that my wedding occurred three days ago? Your Majesty," Archibald remembered to add.

The king drew himself up. "I was told."

"And that someone has been trying to *kill my wife*?" Archibald was unable to keep his voice from shaking with rage as he uttered those words.

"They did say something about your troubles, yes."

Archibald's voice emerged as a low growl. "As sorry as I am to have kept Your Majesty waiting, perhaps you can appreciate that these are exceptional circumstances."

The king looked affronted at the notion that he should be expected to appreciate anything. "Exceptional circumstances or not, royalty should not be kept waiting. Now, regarding my order of cannons. I do not wish to wait six months."

Archibald had reached the limit of his patience. "I understand completely. I will, therefore, be more than willing to cancel Your Majesty's order and refund their full purchase price."

"Cancel?" The king bristled. "I do not wish to cancel! I insist that the full fifty cannons be delivered immediately!"

"Well, they can't be delivered immediately. *Your Majesty.*" Archibald drew in a breath. He couldn't be rude to a king, even if he was a self-important boor. "I'm afraid the cannons we are making today have already been spoken for. Your choices are to wait your turn or not to receive any cannons at all." It was all Archibald could do to stop himself from adding, *as my office manager told you four times.*

The king raised his nose in the air. "I see it is no use speaking to you. You are as bad as the other man. You leave me no choice—I shall go to your king!"

Archibald nodded gravely. "Please do. Tell him of your desire to jump the queue. Assuming he agrees to push back the delivery date on the order we are currently working on, which is for the British Royal Navy, then I suppose we can accommodate you."

The king's eyes darted around. Archibald knew damn well he wasn't going to demand that the King of England push back his own country's order of cannons, and he was trying to come up with some other card that he could play.

There was a knock at the door. McPherson poked his

head in. "Robert Smalley from the Office of Ordnance is here to see you, Mr. Nettlethorpe-Ogilvy, sir."

"Excellent." Smalley entered, and Archibald ushered the king toward the door. "This is in regard to my wife. I did mention that someone is trying to murder her?"

"Yes, b-but—"

"And, of course, I would never dream of detaining Your Majesty. You're on your way to speak to the king." Archibald bowed deeply. "Do let me know what he says."

It was unthinkably rude to shut the door in a ruling monarch's face.

Archibald did it anyway. He was that eager to find out what Smalley had learned.

In defiance of his name, Smalley was a bear of a man with a stocky frame from days spent inspecting cannons and moving them around, with pale blue eyes and a ginger beard.

"Well?" Archibald asked, too eager to bother with pleasantries. "What have you learned?"

Smalley held up both hands as if not wanting to get Archibald's hopes up. "I *think* we have him."

Archibald collapsed in his chair, relief washing over him. He gestured for Smalley to take the seat across the desk. "Who is it? How did you catch him?"

"There are four warehouses in the London area where small arms are stored. I had to hire enough men to watch all four of them. I hope you don't mind if I send the bill to you. You did say no expense was too great—"

"I'll pay it. What did you find?"

"Last night, one of my men saw him. There's a small storehouse down at the Royal Dockyards… thank you," Smalley said, accepting the glass of port Archibald had handed him. "One of the overseers, a man by the name of Roderick MacDonald, came back to the storehouse just after midnight and unlocked the building. Had a pair of men with him. They loaded three crates onto a cart, then the men and the cart went one way, and MacDonald went the other. That has to be him."

Archibald slumped back in his chair. "It certainly looks suspicious."

"It does." Smalley leaned forward. "I went over the books, and MacDonald has marked a suspiciously high number of guns as damaged upon receipt. But only one hundred in the last week. I think you mentioned his contact was expecting two hundred."

"That's correct."

Smalley nodded. "I've arranged it with the local constable—he and I are going to keep watch for the next few nights. See if we can catch him in the act and make the arrest."

"Good, good. I'll advise the Bow Street Runner working the case. He'll likely want to be on the scene as well. And I'm going to send some men from Nettlethorpe Iron to fan out through the neighborhood. I don't want to give them any chance to escape."

"We could use the extra muscle, I'm sure. There's an inn on High Street where we can meet. The Brown Bear. Say at ten o'clock?"

"Ten o'clock." Archibald stood and offered his hand. "I'll arrange it."

After he left, Archibald asked McPherson to recruit a few dozen men to reinforce Smalley that night, offering a generous bonus to volunteers, as there was some degree of danger associated with the task.

Archibald had hoped he could make today's visit quick so Izzie wouldn't be alone at the house all day. But as soon as he emerged from his office, Draycott, the foreman who oversaw the blast furnaces, waylaid him.

"Beg pardon, Mr. Nettlethorpe-Ogilvy, sir."

Archibald carefully kept his face neutral. "What is it, Draycott?"

Archibald could tell by Draycott's cringing expression that he was aware that his employer had somewhere he would rather be. "We've been having problems with one of the blast furnaces. I'm sorry. I've tried everything I could think of. Would you mind taking a quick look?"

Archibald nodded. "Of course."

It took him a half-hour to diagnose the blast furnace. After that, a veritable parade of men requested "just five minutes" of his time. Of course, most of the requests took more than five minutes, but none of them were unreasonable. He'd been away from the forge entirely for four days. Problems were bound to have arisen in that interval.

By the time he finally managed to get away, the shadows were growing long. He hurried out to his waiting carriage, wondering how Izzie had fared on her own.

CHAPTER 29

*A*rchibald didn't realize his mistake until he was halfway home.

He usually bathed and changed clothes as soon as he arrived home. The problem was, he was now sharing a bedroom with Izzie. This meant that if he continued his previous routine, she would see him in all his dirt, not only looking but smelling like a blacksmith.

It was crucial that she never see him this way. Izzie seemed to have romanticized the idea of him being a blacksmith, but she had only ever seen him when he was washed up and dressed in fine clothes to attend some *ton* entertainment. Were she to see him coated in coal soot and smelling like he'd been lifting cannons all day, she would realize what a terrible mistake her marriage had been. Hell, it was considered déclassé for the daughter of an earl to marry a banker or a barrister. But to marry a man who worked at an iron forge? Not merely running the business side of things but supervising the heavy, filthy work that took place on the factory floor? It was absolutely unthinkable, and it did not matter one iota how rich this work had made him. He was a thousand miles beneath her.

Archibald had, therefore, brought a change of clothes with him to Nettlethorpe Iron that morning, resolving to wash up in his office and return home in his finery. He only had a wash stand and basin there, but he was just going to have to make it work.

Unfortunately, old habits were difficult to break, and at the end of the day, he had climbed into the carriage the same way he had for years without remembering to perform his ablutions first.

Stepping into the foyer, Archibald peered around nervously as he took off his hat and handed it to Giddings. He did not see any sign of his wife.

Striving for an air of normalcy, he asked Giddings, "Were there any attacks on the house today?"

"None, sir."

"Good. How is Lady Isabella?"

"Well, sir, so far as I can tell. She had a number of callers this morning who stayed through luncheon—her mother and sister, Lady Lucy, as well as Lady Diana Latimer and Lady Griselda Saxe-Mecklenburg."

That was good. Archibald was glad she hadn't been alone all day. "And, uh… where is she now?" he asked, trying to sound nonchalant.

"Last I saw, she was visiting Mr. Nettlethorpe."

Archibald looked up sharply, dread pooling in his stomach. "With Grandfather?"

As usual, Giddings' expression was completely neutral. "Yes, sir."

"Thank you," Archibald muttered, already turning toward the stairs.

He took them two at a time. Now, he had two things to

worry about. What would Izzie think about his low-born grandfather? Even worse, what might his grandfather be telling Izzie about him at this very moment? His grandfather was one of the few people who actually understood the engineering projects about which Izzie seemed strangely curious. Not that John Nettlethorpe was the loquacious sort, but if Izzie peppered him with questions, who knew what he might reveal?

What does my grandson do in his workshop all day? Oh, yes— he makes screws. 'Tis his proudest achievement and life purpose— making screws.

He hurried into his bedroom. "Jack!" he boomed. "Where are you?"

His valet strolled leisurely out of Archibald's dressing room, shoe-brush in one hand and a tin of boot blacking in the other. "Well, would you look who's chosen to grace us with his presence?"

Glad to see the tub was full and waiting, Archibald all but tore off his jacket and shirt. "I need a clean change of clothes."

"You certainly do." Jack wrinkled his nose as he retreated into the dressing room.

Archibald spent the next ten minutes washing with all possible haste, ignoring Jack's mutterings about how he'd been unable to perform his job for the past three days on account of being locked out of the room. "Although I suppose there wasn't much to do," Jack added waspishly. "Doesn't seem you were wearing much in the way of clothes."

Finally, he was clean. He had managed to dodge disaster today, but he must remember to get cleaned up at Nettlethorpe Iron from now on.

Having made it out of the frying pan, it was time to leap into the fire. He hurried down one floor to his grandfather's tower room to try to avert the next crisis. He knocked softly at the door before pushing it open.

The first thing he noticed was that his grandfather was asleep. The next thing was Izzie, seated at a small writing desk someone had moved into the room. She perked up as he entered and began gathering the papers she'd been working on in silence.

Archibald rubbed the back of his head as they slipped into the hallway. "How was your day?" he asked, because that seemed like a more normal greeting than, *"Just how much did he tell you about the screws?"*

She smiled up at him. "It was nice. Lucy and Diana came over this morning, along with my mother and Lady Griselda, and they all stayed through luncheon. After they left, I decided to look in on your grandfather, and he was awake!"

Cold sweat broke out on the back of Archibald's neck. "And how did that go?"

He had tried to make his voice nonchalant, but some strain must have showed on his face, because Izzie laughed. "We got along swimmingly. We chatted for a few minutes, and he mentioned that the worst part about dying was that it was so dull. I offered to read him my book, and he accepted."

Archibald was struggling to wrap his head around the image of his plainspoken grandfather listening to a story about a duke living at the bottom of a well, pretending to be a ghost, while naked pirates fenced in the background. "How did he like it?"

"Fairly well, I think. He was chuckling."

That was high praise, indeed. His grandfather wasn't much of a chuckler. Archibald tugged at his neckcloth, trying to sound casual. "And did you discuss anything else?"

"No. He told me to stop after an hour as he was starting to nod off. I asked him whether he minded if I wrote in his room while he slept, as it was hard to find a quiet spot around the house. He replied, *'Lord, is that the truth,'* and told me to go ahead."

Archibald couldn't hold in a smile. He knew his grandfather was referring to his parents, who could talk the ear off a brass monkey. John Nettlethorpe had never understood his own son and was equally baffled by Archibald's mother.

"It's true that I need a quiet place to write," Izzie continued. "And I figured that if I use his room, I'll be on hand when he awakens to keep him company."

"I appreciate that," Archibald said, meaning it. To be honest, his grandfather's remark that dying was dull stung. He felt bad about leaving his grandfather alone for such long stretches, but when he had offered to spend more time at home, his grandfather had replied that it would be a greater comfort if Archibald made sure the business he'd worked all his life to build didn't founder.

John Nettlethorpe did not find the company of his son or daughter-in-law soothing, and when Archibald had tried to hire a nurse to sit with him, he'd complained that he didn't want people fussing over him. He was perfectly capable of ringing for a footman if he needed something. But, in spite of his bluster, Archibald wasn't surprised his grandfather was bored and lonely.

He seemed to like Izzie, though—goodness only knew that John Nettlethorpe would have banished her from his room had he found her annoying—and even if this development was unexpected, Archibald was grateful for it.

"Well, I'm glad you found a good place to write." He offered her his arm. "Dinner will start in about an hour. Why don't we—"

She seized his arm rather than looping hers through it. "Wait. While we're here"—she smiled brightly, gesturing to the locked door before them—"perhaps you could show me your workshop!"

Archibald's heart tripped. "My... my workshop?" He tried

to chuckle, but it emerged sounding forced. "You wouldn't want to see that."

"I assure you, I would." She laughed, and unlike the strangled sound he had made, hers was bright and sparkling. "As much as I've enjoyed discovering the house's Gothic flourishes, I think I'm even more curious to see what you're hiding on the other side of that door."

Screws. Mostly just screws. "Oh, er… There's nothing very interesting in there. Just a few odds and ends. You wouldn't want to see it."

She frowned. "If there's nothing much to see, why not just show it to me? It won't take a minute, and it will assuage my curiosity." She squeezed his forearm, her lips twisting upwards. "I'm Pandora, remember?"

Oh, he remembered, all right. The problem was the metaphor was a little too apt. Just like Pandora's Box, he would never be able to shut the door again once Izzie learned what a dull fellow he really was.

A drip of sweat had just started to make its way across his brow when the solution came to him in a flash. "I had some news today. About the men who tried to kidnap you. An arrest could be made as soon as tonight."

She gasped. "Tonight? Truly?" She gave a shaky breath at his nod. "I hadn't even dared to hope."

"Yes, it's wonderful news." Placing a hand on the small of her back, Archibald guided her toward the stairs. "Let's go somewhere so I can tell you everything."

He brought her to their bedroom, where they sat facing each other on the bed. Archibald related everything he had learned in his meetings that morning.

"MacDonald," Izzie said. "I think that was it—the name I heard in the dark walks. Do you really think he could be arrested tonight?"

"It all depends on when he decides to transfer the next

shipment of guns. They want to catch him in the act, if possible. I've arranged to have significant manpower watching the dockyards. I want to make sure he doesn't slip through our fingers."

"Significant manpower." Izzie gave him a wry look. "That you're paying for, I imagine."

"Of course." He studied her a beat. She looked… frustrated. "What of it?"

She blew out a breath. "I feel like I've caused you a lot of trouble."

He made an incredulous sound. To be fair, depending on how long this stretched on, it was conceivable that he might wind up spending hundreds of pounds on guards for the house.

But in exchange, he got Izzie as his *wife*.

It was the bargain of the century, as far as Archibald was concerned.

He touched her cheek. "I would pay a lot more than that to secure your safety. And you're not trouble. You're…"

It was on the tip of his tongue to say *the best thing that's ever happened to me*, but he couldn't quite bring himself to utter the words. He thought that maybe, just maybe, he and Izzie were headed toward a place where she would welcome such a declaration from him. But whatever this was that was blossoming between them still felt fragile, and he didn't want to risk crushing it by asking for too much too soon.

"Not trouble?" The indignation in Izzie's voice was offset by the corner of her mouth, which was twitching, and the way she looped her arms around his neck as she crawled into his lap. "I will have you know that I am a *tremendous* amount of trouble," she said, pushing him back on the bed.

His last words before her lips descended on his were, "I daresay I could use more trouble in my life."

They were late to dinner.

CHAPTER 30

No arrest was made that night, nor the following one.

But on the third night, Roderick MacDonald fell into their trap.

Izzie had been on tenterhooks the entire time, sleeping poorly at night and unable to concentrate by day. She had resolved to try to work on her latest manuscript, as fruitless as the effort seemed, and was heading down the hall toward John Nettlethorpe's chamber when she heard Archibald call her name.

"Archibald?" Confused, she blinked at her husband, who was jogging up the stairs. He had left for Nettlethorpe Iron only an hour earlier. "What are you—"

"They got him," he said without preamble.

Her heart skipped a beat. "Got him? Do… do you mean—"

"Roderick MacDonald. As well as William Cooper—"

"I *knew* his name was Cooper!"

Archibald reached her, and she threw herself into his arms. He hugged her close, cradling her against his chest.

"You were right. They nabbed MacDonald, Cooper, and a half-dozen of their henchmen."

"Do they know who Cooper was working for?"

Archibald shook his head. "Bow Street is questioning him right now. I don't have much in the way of details. But I thought you would want to know."

"I do. Thank you for coming to tell me right away." She felt tears pricking. She truly had the most wonderful husband.

She brushed her damp eyes with the back of her hand. "I can't believe it's over."

"I believe and hope it probably is. But, considering the lengths these men were going to kill you, we should still proceed cautiously. I wouldn't just walk out the front door."

"You're right, of course." Izzie sighed. "And I'll be fine. Lucy and Diana are coming to keep me company this afternoon. I can manage a few more days cooped up inside."

Archibald's eyes were sympathetic. "I don't even know that it needs to be a few days. But let's confirm they have the right men. Then we can formulate a plan. I want to be there the first time you venture out, along with a good-sized group of my men. Assuming that goes well, we can adjust the level of precautions accordingly."

"That sounds reasonable."

He brushed his lips across hers. "I have to get back to the forge. We'll talk more tonight."

"Yes. Tonight."

That evening, Izzie left the Nettlethorpe-Ogilvy mansion for the first time in a week. In addition to the half-dozen men riding on the outside of the carriage she and Archibald took, they were accompanied by an escort of three carriages stuffed with ironworkers ready to come to her aid if there was any trouble.

But the ride was uneventful. With a dozen of his men standing guard, Archibald swept Izzie into the Bow Street Offices.

They were greeted by Thomas Daubney, the Runner who had been assigned to the case. He led them toward the back of the offices.

"The men are about to be questioned," Mr. Daubney explained. "We need you to confirm if they're the same pair you overheard in Vauxhall." He opened the door to a dark, empty room. "If you'll wait in here, you can watch as I lead them by, and hopefully, you'll be able to see them without them spotting you."

Izzie agreed, and she and Archibald settled down to wait in the shadows. After a few minutes, Mr. Daubney walked by, followed by two men being escorted by guards.

Izzie held her breath as they passed in front of the open door. "That's them," she whispered to Archibald once they were gone. "I'm sure of it."

She told Mr. Daubney the same thing, then climbed back into the carriage and was whisked back to the Nettlethorpe-Ogilvy mansion less than an hour after she had stepped outside.

Buoyed by the success of the excursion and their growing confidence that the men responsible for the attempts on Izzie's life had been arrested, she and Archibald decided to try again the following day. That morning, Archibald accompanied her for a stroll about the green. The walk only lasted ten minutes, and three dozen of his men were fanned out around the square, looking out for any sign of trouble.

It was entirely uneventful, and Izzie started to believe

that she was finally waking from this nightmare. They repeated the exercise the following morning and slowly started reducing the number of men guarding the house around the clock. Archibald also brought in an architect he'd worked with before to start planning the modifications that would be necessary to build Izzie's library.

On the third day, they ventured out once more, this time to The Temple of the Muses, the largest bookstore in all of England. Archibald had arranged for the store to stay open after its usual closing time so they wouldn't have to worry about potential assassins lurking behind every shelf.

It was Izzie's every fantasy come true. Archibald told her to buy as many books as she wanted and to get copies of all her favorites. "We need to fill those floor-to-ceiling bookshelves, after all."

He proceeded to follow her around the store, carrying her books for her while she browsed. Well, that wasn't quite true. No one man was capable of carrying the number of books she selected. But he carried them for her until one of the clerks came scurrying up the stairs to convey them to the main sales counter below.

Izzie even had the delightful experience of finding her own book in stock in the section dedicated to Gothic novels. Archibald tried to buy all seven copies, but Izzie stopped him. "How will new readers discover my book if it isn't in stock?"

Archibald sulked but settled for buying three and placing an order for an additional twenty.

Izzie was reaching for a book on a high shelf in the history section when she noticed how dark it was outside. "What time is it?" she asked Archibald.

He consulted his pocket watch. "Half eight."

She blanched. "Half eight!"

She peered at her husband. His expression seemed almost… jovial.

That didn't make any sense. She'd been shopping for more than two hours! Surely, he was bored to tears. "I'm terribly sorry," she said, climbing down from the stepladder she had been using.

"Sorry?" Archibald's brow creased. "Why are you sorry?"

"I didn't realize how long I'd been browsing. I'm sure you must be finding this dreadfully dull."

"Not at all," Archibald said gallantly. At her skeptical look, he added, "No, really. You looked so happy." He rubbed the back of his head, staring at the floorboards. "I like seeing you happy."

He stood there holding a stack of books, ears turning pink, and Izzie marveled at the fact that she had only spoken to this man for the first time two weeks ago.

And here she was, falling in love with him.

Because she was certain that the champagne-bubble sensation arising in the general vicinity of her heart was love, not dyspepsia. And really, how could she resist this man? He kissed her like the world was about to end, he threw himself at knife-wielding villains to save her, and then he declared that her florid Gothic novel was the most marvelous thing he'd ever read.

He was building her dream library for her. He even followed her around the bookstore for hours on end, smiling softly and carrying her books!

Really, what chance did a girl stand?

"Well," Izzie said, blinking back the tears that were suddenly pricking in her eyes, "I'm sure the salesclerks are ready to head home to their supper. Shall we do the same?"

"As you like." Archibald shifted the stack of books to one arm so he could offer her his other one.

Downstairs, Izzie felt bashful as she noted just how many crates it had taken to hold all the books she had selected. Archibald was speaking in hushed whispers to the store manager. Izzie couldn't make out all that they said, but she did catch the words, "—hundred pounds."

"Oh, dear," she said as Archibald ushered her out to the waiting carriage. "How much did all of this cost?"

He handed her up. Once they were alone inside, he answered, "Less than a tenth of the sum my father has spent commissioning statues of himself as Alexander the Great if it makes you feel better."

That startled a giggle out of her. She had seen his father's new statue, after all.

Still… "You don't think I spent too much?"

"Izzie." He squeezed her hand. "I was prepared to give you ten thousand pounds a year in pin money. I truly don't want you to worry about this. What I want is for you to be happy"—he looked down, ears reddening, and added softly —"with me."

Izzie crawled into his lap and looped her arms around his neck. "I am *very* happy with you." She pressed her lips to his.

When she pulled back, he was looking down. "Because I'm so—"

"Thoughtful," she supplied as he uttered the word "rich."

Archibald looked up, startled. "Thoughtful?"

She trailed kisses across his jawline toward his lips. "Thoughtful. Kind. Supportive."

He still looked befuddled. "Me? Thoughtful? Real—"

Her lips claimed his then, and there was no more conversation for some time.

The carriage ride was not long enough for them to finish what they started.

No matter. Archibald carried her up the stairs again, and they made good use of the hulking canopied bed.

Afterward, as she drifted off to sleep, Izzie smiled, glad that the danger had finally passed and her life could return to normal.

But she was wrong.

CHAPTER 31

The following morning, Archibald was just heading down to breakfast when Izzie emerged from the bedroom next door, which she had been using to dress, wearing a midnight blue traveling costume trimmed in silver.

He kissed her hand. "You look beautiful this morning."

She smiled at him as she twirled a little hat that matched her outfit. "Thank you."

"Are you going out today, then?"

She bit her lip. "I was thinking that I might. It seems that the danger has passed. Do you agree?"

Archibald had been thinking the same thing. It wasn't reasonable to expect Izzie to remain cooped up in the house forever or only to leave in his company. "I do. Perhaps you could bring some guards with you?"

"That's what I was thinking," she said in a rush. "And I won't go wandering about town. I have a very specific location I'd like to visit. One that's extremely secure."

Archibald grinned. "Let me guess—you're going to Latimer House to visit Lady Diana." The duke's home was a detached mansion surrounded by walls on all sides. It would be the ideal place for Izzie's first excursion.

"Not Latimer House," she said.

"Hmm. Your parents' house, then?" Astley House was less secure than Latimer House, as it opened directly to the street. But Archibald didn't think it was an unreasonable choice.

"Not Astley House, either." She gave him a teasing smile. "See if you can guess—it's a place I've been terribly eager to visit."

"Let's see… back to The Temple of the Muses? You're welcome to go there, of course, but I must confess, I was hoping to accompany you on your next excursion. I enjoy watching you shop for books."

"Not The Temple of the Muses. I quite enjoyed shopping for books with you, too." She caressed his bicep. "It's useful having a big, strong man to carry my books for me."

That made Archibald's heart swell. He enjoyed being useful to her, and it was gratifying to hear that she liked having him around.

Another possibility occurred to him. "You're meeting your friends at Gunther's for ices."

"Not Gunther's."

"Umm…" He wracked his brain, trying to imagine where else she might want to go. "Perhaps Lady Diana has secured tickets to the British Museum?"

"No!" She laughed. "I can't believe you haven't guessed already. I've been talking about visiting this place all week."

Archibald was having trouble thinking of possibilities. "Maybe the dressmaker's?" Although he couldn't recall her mentioning the dressmaker's, not even once.

"Not the dressmaker's."

"Hyde Park?"

"Not Hyde Park. As I said, it's a place that's very secure."

She laughed. "It's probably more secure than even being here at the house."

It occurred to him in a flash. "The Tower of London! You're meeting Lucy and Diana to see the animals."

"No!" She laughed. "Try again."

He hadn't managed to guess by the time they entered the breakfast room, where his mother interrupted his speculation. "Oh, Thorpe, Lady Isabella! I'm so glad you're here. I've been waiting to show you this!"

She pulled out a swatch of brocaded silk in a particularly virulent shade of chartreuse. "What do you think?"

The vein behind Archibald's left eye gave a throb. The poison green color was so bright it was difficult to look directly at it. "It's, uh… It's really…"

Izzie seemed to sense he was at a loss for words. "How bold," she offered as she helped herself to a poached egg.

"Bold!" his mother cried. "That is precisely the word!"

"And it's the most fashionable color right now," his father noted. "The designer was raving about it."

Archibald shot Izzie a look. He hadn't seen anyone else using that color.

Izzie gave him the tiniest of nods. Her expression said, *don't worry. I'll handle it.*

Taking a seat at the table, Izzie took up her knife and began to butter her toast. "Where were you thinking to use it?"

"The front parlor," his mother said. "We'll have the color everywhere! The walls, the cushions… we're even having a new rug made up."

"It's badly overdue for a change," his father explained. "The room hasn't been redecorated in eighteen months."

Archibald was scrambling to figure out how to explain that redecorating the entire parlor in the color of vomit was not, in fact, the height of fashion without hurting his parents' feelings when Izzie lowered her knife. "Oh, dear."

"Whatever is the matter, dear?" his mother asked.

Izzie's face was crestfallen. "It's just… I was speaking to my mother the other day. And to my sister, Lady Thetford."

His mother leaned forward eagerly. Lady Cheltenham and Lady Thetford were two of the leading tastemakers of the *ton*. "What did they say?"

"Although you are absolutely correct, and that shade of green is the peak of fashion *at the moment*, my mother and sister are convinced that its reign will be… short-lived."

"Short-lived?" His mother's eyes went wide as guineas.

"You don't say!" his father exclaimed.

Izzie took up her teacup, her expression one of regret. "I fear so. And, because a full redecoration, with a new rug and reupholstering all of the furniture, will take time, I dread the possibility that, at the very moment your new parlor is complete, the color will become *passé*."

"*Passé!*" his mother gasped. "The horror!"

"Whatever shall we do?" his father cried.

Izzie's eyes went wide as if the solution had just occurred to her. "Although a room takes considerable time to make over, I'm sure your modiste could have a spencer made up for you in this shade in a matter of days, Mrs. Nettlethorpe-Ogilvy. And perhaps a waistcoat for you, sir."

"A spencer!" his mother exclaimed. "In velvet, I think."

"It will be the perfect thing for the crisp autumn weather," his father noted.

"Just so," Izzie agreed. "And then, you can have the room made over in what my mother and sister assure me will be the *next* fashionable color…"

His parents both leaned forward, holding their breath.

Izzie paused for dramatic effect, then said, "Pale blue."

"Pale blue!" his mother cried. "But of course!"

"Very elegant," his father added. "What do you think, Thorpe?"

He swallowed a bite of eggs. "I don't pretend to be a great arbiter of fashion. But if Lady Cheltenham and Lady Thetford recommend pale blue, I do not think you could do better."

"Just so," his mother agreed. "When the designer comes today, we will tell him we have changed our minds and insist upon pale blue…"

Across the table, Izzie caught his eye, the corner of her mouth curving up a fraction.

He saluted her with his coffee cup. God, he loved his wife.

CHAPTER 32

wo hours later, Izzie settled into one of the Nettlethorpe-Ogilvys' plush carriages. Instead of footmen, two guards from Nettlethorpe Iron mounted the steps on the back, and another took a seat next to the coachman. An additional coach followed, filled with more guards, including her husband's valet, Jack Rattigan. She should be safe, indeed, as she made her way across town.

Izzie leaned back against the red velvet squabs. She couldn't believe Archibald hadn't guessed her destination, which was, of course, Nettlethorpe Iron. Had she not been begging to see his workshop all week?

Today, she finally would—his real one, where he kept all his most advanced machines. She couldn't wait to see the look on his face when she walked through the door!

Ten minutes later, Izzie was trying to imagine what the process of making a cannon might entail when she heard the coachman shout, "Hey! Watch where yer going!"

Suddenly, there were hoofbeats all around them, which wasn't entirely unusual, but for the fact that they sounded much too close.

Then, the shouting began.

Izzie peered out the window. A horse's head was mere inches from the glass pane. She tried to peer back at its rider. She didn't have a very good angle, but the man's arm was outstretched toward the guard who had taken up the position on the rear step usually reserved for footmen. They appeared to be scrapping.

Abruptly, the rider pulled wide of the carriage. Izzie shrieked as her guard went tumbling off the step, landing in the cobblestone street and rolling several times before coming to a stop.

She scooted to the opposite window and saw that the other guards were similarly engaged. Izzie's heart thundered in her chest. Looking down, she was alarmed to see how far they had veered to the left.

Before she had time to cry out a warning, one of the wheels smashed into the curb. A sharp crack filled the air and the coach tilted off balance, which surely meant they had broken a wheel.

Terror-stricken, Izzie watched as someone wrenched the door open. A man leaned in. He didn't look like a common criminal. His dark hair was neatly combed and held in place with pomade, and he was simply but neatly dressed.

"Lady Isabella." He gave a malicious smile. "We meet at last."

He reached in and grabbed her by the arm. Izzie screamed and kicked him in the chest. The man scowled but didn't let her go.

"Fine, then," he snapped. "We'll do it the hard way."

He grabbed her by the hair, dragging her out of the carriage. Izzie cried out at the sharp stab of pain and struggled to twist out of his grip. Out of the corner of her eye, she saw her three guards, including the man who had taken such a nasty fall, brawling with a swarm of men. They were struggling valiantly but were outnumbered three to one.

The dark-haired man forced her toward an unmarked black carriage. She clawed at his face and he slapped her so hard her vision momentarily went cloudy.

She regained her senses just in time to see the carriage looming before her. Her abductor climbed inside, trying to pull her in after him. She braced her hands against the doorframe, stiffening her arms. "Help!" she shouted. "Someone help me! Please!"

Just then, the Nettlethorpe-Ogilvys' second carriage, the one filled with Archibald's men, drew up behind them. How it had become separated from the first vehicle, Izzie had no idea, but she caught the eye of one of the two men hanging off the back steps—her husband's valet, Jack.

"Jack!" she cried desperately. "Jack, help!"

His eyes flared with recognition. He leaped from the step, barreling through the swarm of attackers, shouting curses as he swung his good arm. He managed to break through and grab Izzie by the back of her coat. She heard the fabric of her traveling costume rending, but Jack was able to hold her back from the gaping door, and that was the only thing that mattered.

The dark-haired man pulled a knife from his boot, brandishing it with his free arm in an underhanded grip. Snarling, he raised it for the strike. Jack's good arm was already occupied in the life-or-death tug-of-war match in which Izzie was the rope, so all he could do was step forward, shielding her with his body. He grunted as the knife came down on the back of his shoulder.

"Jack!" Izzie screamed.

Just then, another one of her ironworker guards arrived, lunging at her attacker's throat. Blanching, the dark-haired man released her arm and scrambled back inside the black carriage, shouting for the driver to flee. The horses leapt forward, and the carriage took off down the street with the door flapping open.

Izzie glanced around. Even with the men who had poured out of the second carriage, they were still outnumbered. But Archibald's men were significantly bigger and stronger than their opponents, and one by one, the would-be kidnappers started to flee. After a minute of scuffling, all the miscreants had made their escape, save for three who had been captured by Archibald's men.

"Get her in that carriage," the coachman shouted. "Wheel's broken on this one."

"You heard the man," Jack said, seizing her upper arm and hustling her toward the second carriage.

She blanched at the damp red stain on the sleeve of his coat. "You're bleeding."

He wrinkled his nose in dismissal. "Eh. That arm wasn't good for nothing, anyway."

"But what if it becomes infected, or—"

He snorted as he hoisted her into the carriage. "We Rattigans are hard to kill. Yer husband won't be rid of me so easy."

He started to back away, but Izzie grabbed his wrist. "You must come too, Jack. And anyone else who was injured."

Jack tried to object. "'Tis nothing—"

"I insist," Izzie said.

"Get in," one of the other men said, shoving him from behind. "Yer wasting time."

A few men climbed into the carriage, and two more climbed up on the back. Izzie pressed her handkerchief against Jack's shoulder. "Where are we going?"

"Nettlethorpe Iron," Jack said. "It's naught but a quarter mile from here."

Surely enough, within minutes, they pulled up to a

hulking brick building. Izzie thought the bricks might have once been red, but they had been stained black by years of smoke. At a shout from the coachman, two huge wooden doors were pulled open, and the carriage drove right inside.

Disembarking from the carriage, Izzie stepped down onto a packed dirt floor. The warehouse was huge, probably fifty yards long and half again as wide. There was a metallic grinding sound coming from the far end of the factory, deafening even over a distance, but it stopped after a few seconds. Light so bright it was almost blinding poured out of what she supposed must be a furnace, and a thin stream of molten metal flowed through a carefully carved trench into bar-shaped molds. Men in heavy leather aprons stood around with rakes and shovels, carefully minding the liquid metal's progress.

Most of the ironworkers were peering at them, curious to see the reason for this interruption. At last, she spotted Archibald in the crowd. He looked... different. He was wearing a coarse linen shirt with the sleeves rolled up to his elbows, topped by a waistcoat of plain grey wool. She supposed that made sense. Of course, he wouldn't wear the same clothes he wore to attend a ball on the floor of a forge. He was... She blinked, certain her eyes were deceiving her, but no, he was holding a *cannon*, which he appeared to be inspecting. To be sure, it wasn't a *particularly large* cannon. But still, it was a *cannon*! It had to be tremendously heavy, yet he handled it as easily as if it were a child's toy.

Someone said something to him, and he looked up. At first, his expression was merely confused, as if he could not understand why she was here. But she marked the moment he noticed some combination of her ruined hair, crushed hat, and torn dress. His face went white, and his eyes filled with distress.

"Izzie!" he cried. Without looking, he handed the cannon

to the man standing next to him, who staggered and would've fallen had two of his fellows not rushed up to help him bear the weight. Oblivious, Archibald hurried across the packed dirt floor. "What's going on? Are you hurt?"

"I'm all right," she hastened to say. "Really, I'm—" She promptly ruined her attempt to reassure him by bursting into tears.

He scooped her up in his arms as he turned to one of the men who accompanied her. "What happened?"

"Ambush on the carriages, boss. Five riders descended on us. They forced us into the curb, and the wheel broke."

"The carriage with most of the guards got separated," another man added. "A wagon pulled out in front of us in the middle of a junction. The driver claimed his horse wouldn't move." He laughed blackly. "I bet that wasn't no accident. By the time we caught up, they'd pulled Lady Isabella out and were trying to get her into another carriage."

Archibald's arms turned to steel around her. "They almost took her?"

"They would've," the first man said, "if it wasn't for Rattigan. He went charging in after her."

Izzie managed to find her voice. "Jack was injured. After he pulled me back, the man trying to abduct me pulled out a knife. Jack stepped in front of me and was stabbed in the shoulder."

"Summon the surgeon," Archibald said.

Jack waved this off. "It's naught but a scratch."

Archibald's jaw clenched, his voice brooking no argument. "I want it looked at by a surgeon, and any other injuries that were sustained as well." He caught Jack's eyes and held them. "Thank you, Jack."

"Eh." Jack rolled his eyes. "There'd have been no living with you if I'd let them take her."

Archibald grunted in response. He was already carrying Izzie toward the far end of the warehouse.

Most of Nettlethorpe Iron seemed to consist of a huge, open room with a ceiling three stories high. But she could see rooms with windows lining the far wall. She took it these were the offices.

Archibald carried her up a flight of stairs into an open room full of desks. A dozen clerks looked up at their entrance, their eyes full of concern. A man she recognized as his office manager, Mr. McPherson, hurried over. "I heard about the attack, sir. Is Lady Isabella all right?"

"I am," Izzie said. "A little shaken is all."

"She would've been kidnapped were it not for Jack Rattigan, who suffered a knife wound," Archibald said. "He is to receive a reward of one thousand pounds."

Mr. McPherson blanched. "One—did you say one *thousand*, sir?" At Archibald's nod, Mr. McPherson laughed nervously. "Is that not a bit excessive?"

Archibald was already halfway across the room. "He stepped in front of a knife to save my wife. I don't find it excessive at all. See that it's done."

He shifted Izzie to one arm so he could open a door, then closed it behind them. They were alone.

She expected him to hold her close, to offer her the comfort of his arms. Instead, he deposited her on top of the desk at the center of the room and hurried over to the washstand. Filling the basin with fresh water, he took up a bar of soap and began scrubbing his hands with furious intensity.

"Archibald?" she asked, peering at him. "Can that not wait?"

He snorted. "You obviously didn't see how filthy I am. I'm sorry, Izzie. I didn't mean for you to see me like this, and I certainly didn't mean to touch you when I'm covered in grime."

"It's all right." She made a bleak sound as she unpinned her jaunty little hat. As she suspected, it was crushed. "I suspect I'm not looking my most elegant, either."

His only response was a grunt. She took the opportunity to look around his office. It was a plain room with whitewashed walls and bare boards on the floor. There were a pair of windows overlooking the factory floor, but they were situated at either end of the room, and Izzie couldn't see out of them from this angle.

Archibald's desk was not particularly neat. As he was still scrubbing his hands, she took the liberty of straightening a few stacks of papers and placing them out of the way so she wasn't sitting on his things. She moved an inkwell back out of the way and almost dropped it. That was when she noticed that her fingers were trembling.

It was probably shock setting in. "Archibald?" she called, trying to keep her voice from shaking. "Are you almost done over there?"

He had taken up a brush and was scrubbing his nails. "Not yet," he grunted.

"Please hurry." A tear streaked across her cheek.

A minute passed, and he was still scrubbing. Her shoulders began to shake, and she wrapped her arms around her midsection, trying to hold herself together as best she could. "Have you finished yet?"

He held his hand up to the light, inspecting it. Izzie couldn't see a single speck of dirt. "I don't want to come to you in all my dirt. It's bad enough that I got that smear of grease on your cheek."

Izzie frowned. "My cheek?" She didn't recall him touching her cheek. She raised a hand to her face. She couldn't feel any grease or grit, but the spot over her cheekbone was exquisitely tender.

"Oh! That wasn't you, and it isn't dirt. I think a bruise must be forming. That's where my would-be kidnapper slapped me."

The scrubbing brush clattered to the floor. Izzie glanced up and found Archibald bent over the washstand, head lowered, gripping its sides with white knuckles. "Someone slapped you?" he asked in a quiet voice that was ten times more frightening than a bellow.

"Y-yes."

Archibald said nothing, but if Izzie were a betting woman, she would have wagered all her new books that the thought going through his head was, *that man will die.*

His expression dark, he began washing his forearms almost violently.

Izzie had had enough. "I'm sure you must be very clean by now."

"Not clean enough to touch you," he muttered.

She tried again. "Believe me, a slight smear of dirt will be far from the worst thing that's happened to me today."

"Humph," was his only response.

"Archibald!" she cried, and at least this had the effect of causing him to look at her. He seemed to notice for the first time that she was in distress.

She swallowed, trying to compose herself, but felt a tear trickle down her cheek. "I do not need for your hands to be perfectly clean. I do, however, need for you to hold me."

He crossed the room in three strides, not even bothering to dry his hands.

CHAPTER 33

*A*rchibald cursed himself for a fool as he scooped Izzie off the desk and into his arms. He couldn't do anything right. For starters, he'd failed to keep her safe and had obviously failed to catch whoever it was who had designs upon her life.

Then he'd let her see him looking like a common blacksmith. So much for his carefully constructed façade of being a gentleman. She knew the awful truth now.

Then, he'd been in such a panic upon learning that she'd been attacked, he'd gone and made things ten times worse by grabbing her with his grubby hands and pressing her against his soot-stained work clothes. By the time they reached his office, he'd calmed down enough to realize his mistake.

But then, he'd taken too long about it and failed to comfort her.

He felt worse than useless. But much to his surprise, Izzie wasn't shouting and upbraiding him. As he settled on the desk in the place she'd just been occupying with her in his lap, she made a sound of relief, wrapping her arms around his shoulders and burying her face in his sweaty neck.

"I'm sorry," he said because he was fairly certain he wasn't smelling like a rose.

"This is so much better," Izzie whispered. "Please, just hold me. I always feel so safe when I'm with you."

Although he was sure she would come to regret it when she realized how grimy he was, he wasn't about to ignore a direct instruction, so he wrapped her firmly in his arms. She was trembling like a newborn fawn, which destroyed him, but he tried to stay calm, rubbing her back and murmuring that he would never let anything happen to her.

After a few minutes, she said in a small voice, "I thought it was over."

He could not bear the bleakness in her voice. "As did I."

She sniffed. "What do we do now?"

"Whatever we have to do," he said without thinking. "Anything it takes to keep you safe."

She sighed. "And at least we have the means to do it. I shouldn't complain. I know how fortunate I am. It's just… being the princess locked away in the tower sounds romantic in a fairy tale. But I must confess, I was looking forward to going back out into the world."

"Naturally so," Archibald said, holding her close.

"Staying locked away for two weeks isn't so bad. But I can't help but wonder how long this is going to last. A month? A year? The rest of my life?"

Archibald wished he had an answer. "We'll find whoever is behind this."

Izzie sat up, rubbing her eyes. "Your men did manage to capture three of the assailants today. Perhaps they'll reveal something upon questioning."

As she withdrew her hand from her face, Archibald saw with horror that her cheek was coated in a fine film of coal soot, transferred, no doubt, when she had pressed herself against his waistcoat. He had chosen its dark color specifically so it wouldn't show dirt, which meant he hadn't realized how filthy it was.

He began fumbling with the buttons. Izzie looked up at him, confused. "Archibald?"

"Sorry," he said, peeling off the offending garment and dropping it on the floor. "I—"

"*Yes*," she said, tugging his shirt from the waistband of his trousers. "This is what I need."

He frowned. "This is what you need? What do you—" The answer occurred to him when her hand stroked over the muscles in his stomach, and her lips found his jaw. "Izzie! I only meant to remove my soiled garments so as to make myself less offensive. I wasn't suggesting that we... that we..."

"Well, I am," she said, pushing his shirt up over his head and tossing it aside. She made a sound of approval, stroking her fingertips over the planes of his chest. "I want to forget about what just happened."

"But Izzie," he protested, "we can't make love on my desk!"

She was kissing his neck, which was not helping his resolve. She reached down and caressed the bulge that had unsurprisingly sprung up between his legs. "Are you sure?" she asked, voice full of mischief. "Because it seems like this could work."

He groaned, his head lolling back. *God*, that felt good, and of course, he *wanted* what she was suggesting. There was never a moment he didn't want to make love to this woman...

She giggled in his lap, then tugged her skirts up to her thighs so she could straddle him. Again, this did not help his sense of resolve.

She began unbuttoning the jacket of her traveling costume. "See? This will work splendidly."

He was struggling to come up with reasons why they shouldn't do the thing his cock was absolutely desperate to do. "What if… what if someone comes through the door?"

She tossed her jacket on the floor, then unbuttoned her skirt and peeled it off, leaving her in only her fine white chemise and stays. She bit his earlobe, which made him jolt with pleasure. "Do your employees normally come barging into your office without knocking?"

"No," he admitted. She scraped her nails gently across his nipples, and his whole body shuddered. It was impossible to think while she was doing this to him…

"What if… What if somebody hears us?" he managed.

Just then, the din of a cannon being bored out started up on the forge floor below. From this distance, the sound wasn't earsplitting, but it would certainly drown out whatever they were doing in the office.

She was undoing the buttons of his falls. Archibald made a final effort to be good. "I'll make a rumpled mess of you, and then everyone will know… will know…"

She wrapped her soft, sweet hand around his cock, and every thought fled his brain except getting inside of her. She began stroking him up and down, paying particular attention to the head of his cock, just the way he liked. "I'm already a rumpled mess," she whispered. "Take off my stays."

"I… I shouldn't."

She guided his hands to the ties in the back. "You know you want to," she teased.

He did want to, and his fingers were already fumbling with the ribbons. "I'm going to hell," he muttered, tossing her stays on the floor.

She giggled. "No, you're not. We're married, for goodness' sake." She reached down to push his trousers out of the way, and—God help him—he lifted his hips to assist her.

Pulling her chemise up and out of the way, she carefully

aligned herself so she could grind the little pearl between her legs against his cock. Her eyes went hazy with pleasure, a sight Archibald would never tire of seeing, not if they were married for ten thousand years.

"That's it, Izzie," he said. "Make yourself feel good." He began kissing his way up her neck. God, she looked beautiful in her snow-white shift. The teasing glimpses he got of her rosy nipples through the thin fabric were as tantalizing as seeing her naked.

"It does feel good," she gasped. A teasing gleam came into her eyes. "But what about you?"

"Don't worry about me." He wanted to make sure she found her pleasure. His could wait for afterward.

"Are you sure?" She reached down and massaged the head of his cock, wet with a clear liquid drop that had seeped out, and his vision scrambled. She laughed, delighted. "It seems to me that you could use some attention, too."

"I'm fi… fin…" The words died on his lips as Izzie rose up on her knees, brought him to her entrance, and slowly slid down over him. She was tight and wet and slick, and she felt like *heaven*. "Oh, my… *Fuck*, Izzie," he gasped. "That feels *so good*."

"Does it?" she asked breathlessly, sliding up and down his length.

"So g-good," was all he could manage to say, as his brain had turned to mush.

She proceeded to ride him. He tried to hold out, because the pleasure was exquisite, and he wanted this moment with her to last forever.

But the desperation soon overcame him. "Izzie," he gasped, "can I… do you mind if I—"

"Of course," she said without even knowing what he was asking.

Babbling incoherently, he stood, lifting her in his arms,

and reversed their position so she was seated on the desk and he was standing between the vee of her legs, his cock still thick inside of her. He started thrusting in her, fast and hard. "I want... I n-n-need..."

"Yes, Archibald," she said, caressing his shoulders. "*Yes.*"

He pounded into her, his climax building. He was worried he might be handling her too roughly, but she murmured nothing but encouraging words in his ear, and when she dug her nails into his buttocks, he exploded inside her with a cry.

It took a few minutes for the room to stop spinning. Archibald found he had slumped against the desk. He pushed himself up. "Sorry. I must be crushing you."

"I like being crushed by you," Izzie countered.

He leaned forward, kissing her deeply. "Your turn," he whispered, voice pitched low.

He proceeded to kiss his way down her partially clothed body, pausing to suckle her nipples through the thin fabric of her shift. By the time he knelt before her at the foot of the desk, her cheeks were glowing, and she was squirming with anticipation.

Pushing her shift out of the way, he pulled her up to the edge of the desk and eased her legs open. He pressed a trail of kisses up the inside of her thigh, but just when he almost reached her core, he pulled back to give her other leg the same treatment. Mewling with displeasure, Izzie wove her fingers into his hair and directed him to the spot she wanted to be kissed. Archibald's lips curved into a smile as he complied.

As Izzie had suspected after their wedding night, she didn't seem to reach her climax through penetration alone. Archibald didn't care. He genuinely liked doing this for her, kissing her in the little spot that gave her the most pleasure. They had also found some positions where it was easy for him to reach down and rub her while they were making love.

Those were also nice. He loved feeling her come apart when he was inside of her and having her tremble in his arms.

He was starting to figure out what pleased her the most, so he started off lightly, teasing her with the tip of his tongue. She was already fairly far along and soon began making blissful sounds. Flattening his tongue, he massaged her on that special spot, then glanced up to see her reaction.

Her gorgeous blue eyes were incoherent with the pleasure he was giving her. As he caressed her, her back arched and she began to babble, "Please, Archibald! Please, don't stop! I *need* to come!"

He redoubled his efforts. He knew he was on the right track when he felt her thighs tense beneath his fingers. Surely enough, the next instant, her legs began quaking around his head. He slid his hands around her hips, holding her in place so he could draw her pleasure out as much as possible. When her thighs clamped around his ears, he knew it was time to gentle his tongue.

As always, Izzie was boneless afterward. Archibald scooped her off his desk and took her place, depositing her in his lap. He kissed her temple. She lay her head upon his shoulder, still breathing hard, eyes closed and a look of contentment on her face.

After a moment, she opened her eyes and smiled at him. "See? Now I'm not sorry I came."

He laughed. "At least something good came out of your excursion." Something occurred to him. "Say, what were you doing up this way?"

She stretched her neck. "What do you mean, what was I doing up this way?"

"I can't think of any places you'd want to visit up here. It's all industrial. There's not much in the way of popular attractions."

"Archibald!" She tickled his side, causing him to squirm. "Do you really not know?"

He captured her wrists, planting her hands against his chest. "No."

She blew a lock of hair off her forehead. "I was coming here! To Nettlethorpe Iron." At his blank look, she made a sound of frustration. "I wanted to see your workshop, you silly man!"

He froze. "My... my workshop? You were coming to see..."

"Of course! I've only been begging to see it all week."

He struggled to process the fact that, on her first opportunity in weeks to leave the house and go somewhere, the place she had wanted to go was *his workshop*.

She kissed his cheek before climbing out of his lap. "Well, I suppose I'd better see it today. Goodness only knows when I'll be able to leave the house again." She scooped her stays up off the floor. "Help me get back into these, will you?"

Archibald obediently began fumbling with the laces. All the while, his mind was scrambling for an excuse to keep Izzie out of his workshop. It was bad enough that she had seen him covered in grime on the factory floor.

If she found out that his life's purpose was something as pedestrian as making *screws*, it would be the death knell for the budding regard she seemed to have for him. And, although he knew that eventually she would find out and come to despise him, he couldn't bear for it to happen quite so soon. He wanted as many weeks and days and minutes to bask in the glow of her affection as he could possibly scrounge before he entered the dark, cold night of her disdain.

Once they were both dressed, she took his arm and towed him toward the door. "Which way is it?"

He pulled her to a halt. "Izzie, I'm so sorry, but I think we need to get you back to the house with all possible speed."

Her face fell. "Surely we can spare a half hour!"

He shook his head. "Whoever is trying to kill you knows exactly where you are right now and exactly where you're heading. It's an ideal opportunity for them to prepare an ambush. The longer you linger here, the more opportunity they'll have to set their trap."

Her shoulders sagged. "I hadn't thought of that."

"I'm sorry," he said, and he was, in the sense that he was sorry she was disappointed.

Her blue eyes were pleading, which all but destroyed him. "I couldn't have the tiniest peek? Just five minutes?"

In truth, five minutes probably wouldn't make much of a difference. Not that he was about to admit as much. He pressed her hand against his heart. "There is nothing I prize more highly than your safety."

She heaved a theatrical sigh. "I suppose you're right. Well, then. Let's return the princess to her tower."

He led her back through the offices and down to the factory floor. Archibald noticed that four of the forge's wagons, which were normally used to bring in loads of the coke charcoal needed to fuel the blast furnaces, had been pulled up alongside the carriage. A group of around fifty men were milling about.

"What's all this?" Archibald asked.

"Her ladyship's escort," a caster named Josiah Digby said. He swung a sledgehammer up on his shoulder. "I'd like to see them try to take her."

There was a chorus of agreement. Archibald noticed that most of the men were carrying sledgehammers, pickaxes, or shovels.

"Thank you," Izzie said tremulously. "Truly, thank you for

risking your lives to protect me. Speaking of which, how is Jack?"

"He's fine," Digby said. "Surgeon gave him a few stitches. But it was a glancing blow."

"I volunteer to step in front of the next knife!" someone in the back called, and everyone laughed. Archibald took it that word had spread about Jack's reward.

Archibald opened the carriage door and offered his hand to help Izzie up. "Shall we?"

Izzie nodded crisply, and he was pleased to see resolve in her eyes as she accepted his hand. "We shall."

CHAPTER 34

They made it back to the Nettlethorpe-Ogilvy mansion without incident, which didn't surprise Izzie in the least. What sort of fool would attack a convoy of ironworkers armed with pickaxes and sledgehammers?

Of course, a man with a gun would change the balance of power considerably. But Izzie thought it noteworthy that, up until this point, none of the attackers had brandished a firearm, which seemed curious for a group smuggling those very weapons.

Izzie said as much to Archibald as a series of footmen filed into their bedroom with cans of hot water for her husband's bath. "It's enough to make me wonder if Mr. Cooper and his friends were really the ones responsible."

"He's denied any involvement. In fact, he claims to have no idea who you are," Archibald noted. The final footman exited the room, closing the door behind him, and Archibald peeled off his shirt. "Not that I'm much inclined to take him at his word. He's also refused to reveal the buyer of those stolen guns."

Izzie removed the coat of her traveling costume. The tear

was right along a seam, meaning it could be mended. She wondered if she would be able to wear it again, or if the mere sight of it would make her shudder. "I can't imagine what they would want with me, now that Cooper and MacDonald have been arrested. It's not as if I know anything about the men they were working for."

Archibald was unbuttoning his trousers. "Ah, but do *they* know that? They weren't there in the dark walks. They might believe you heard more than you really did."

Izzie followed suit, removing the long skirt of her traveling costume and draping it over the back of a chair. "That's the question, I suppose. Did the three assailants who were captured this afternoon reveal anything useful?"

"I'm given to understand that they did not," Archibald said, removing the last of his clothes and stepping into the tub. "They were reportedly of a similar ilk to the men who attacked you in Lady Waldegrave's garden—local delinquents well known to the magistrates but with no appearance of being part of any higher criminal order. All three say they were hired by a man with dark hair. This man appears to be of a somewhat higher social standing. They reported that he was well-dressed, and his hair was styled with pomade."

"That could be the man who tried to drag me into the carriage. The one who gave me this." Izzie gestured to the welt that had formed over her cheekbone.

Archibald's expression darkened. "What I wouldn't give for five minutes alone with him."

Izzie smiled as she removed her stays. "Five minutes. You could probably accomplish what you have in mind in five seconds. He wasn't much of a physical specimen, although he was stronger than me."

"The only information the men who were captured had about him was that he called himself George Smith."

"Which isn't much of a lead even if it is his real name."

Archibald hummed in agreement. "You can't think of anyone else who could be behind... Izzie! Wh-what are you doing?"

He seemed to notice for the first time that she had been undressing alongside him. Tossing the shift she had just pulled over her head on the floor, she climbed into the tub behind him. "Washing your back," she murmured as she took the sponge from his hands.

"Washing my... You don't have to do that." He promptly undermined his own words by groaning with pleasure as she went to work.

"I'd like to," she said honestly. "Just look at you, Archibald! I enjoy your appearance from the front so much, I don't spend nearly enough time admiring your back." She made an appreciative sound as she soaped some bulging muscles in his shoulders that she was fairly certain she did not possess. Truly, her husband was a magnificent specimen.

He sounded dazed as he protested, "I'm sure I'm not... smelling... like a rose."

She cooed as she ran the sponge down one of his arms. "You keep saying that, but really, you don't smell so bad. Besides, you'll be completely fresh in five minutes."

"Still, I wouldn't want to get you all—" Whatever he had been going to say was cut off by a groan as Izzie lay aside the sponge and started soaping his hair. She massaged his scalp, scouring it with her nails. Archibald's head lolled to the side, and she was pleased to see an expression of bliss on his face.

She rinsed his hair, then went to work massaging all those glorious muscles in his back. By now, he was making helpless sounds of pleasure.

She took up the sponge again, reaching around to soap his chest. She scooted forward so her front side was pressed flush against his back. His breath was coming in short pants, and she could see the tip of his erect cock breaking the surface of the water.

Once she was finished washing his chest, she set aside the sponge and began soaping up her right hand in a deliberate fashion. "Is there anywhere else you could use a rub... I mean, a scrub?"

Archibald's only answer was a groan.

She stroked her soapy fingers across his stomach, which had gone stiff as an iron plate. She made her voice teasing as she whispered, "Any places that are feeling very, very dirty?"

She slipped her hand beneath the water, finding him easily enough. Smiling against the back of his neck, she began to stroke her hand up and down his length. "Oh, my. It seems like you could use some help with this."

His voice had grown breathless. "You don't ha... don't have to..."

She giggled against his neck. "You keep saying that, too. You're normally very observant, so I'm not sure how it has escaped your notice that I *like* making love with you."

A strangled moan was as much response as Archibald could manage.

The soap dissipated quickly in the bathwater, so Izzie slipped around Archibald in the tub, straddling him. He groaned as she lined him up with her entrance. "I also enjoy driving you out of your mind," she said conversationally as she slid down the length of his cock. "It's becoming my favorite hobby."

She enjoyed the way her exceptionally brainy husband's eyes went out of focus and the fact that she seemed to have rendered him speechless. Smiling, she looped her arms around his shoulders for purchase and began teasing him with slow, deliberate strokes. "Do you like fucking me in the tub, Archibald?"

His whole body jerked as she said the naughty word. Being an upstanding sort of man, he tried not to use that sort of language in front of her. Not that he always succeeded when she was doing to him... what she was doing to him right now.

But, based on the pulse his cock gave inside of her, it roused him exquisitely to hear it on her lips.

She decided a little torture was in order. "I love fucking you. I love the fact that you can't resist me. I love teasing you until you get a cock-stand, and then I love how embarrassed you are about it. I love opening up your trousers while you're trying to apologize and making you feel good. I loved fucking you on your desk, with all your workers on the other side of the door. Do you think they all knew what we'd just done by the look on our faces? Because you walked out of there with the loose-jointed stride of a man who's just reached his pleasure? Do you think they all elbowed each other and grinned as soon as we were gone, because they knew I'd just made you come?"

Her little speech was having the predicted effect. Archibald had seized her hips and was doing most of the work for her, sliding her up and down his cock with quick, rhythmic strokes. He was so lost to the pleasure he looked almost drunk.

Izzie continued, enjoying herself. "I want to fuck you in the carriage. I want to fuck you on that same garden bench where we had our second kiss. I want you to pin me down and toss up my skirts and take me in the moonlight. I want to fuck you in the dark walks at Vauxhall. We can pretend it was the first night we met, that we bumped into each other unexpectedly. And you aroused me so much with your kiss, I just *had* to have your cock."

He was pumping into her desperately now. His entire body had hardened to stone. Izzie knew he was getting close.

She leaned forward and brought her lips to his ear. "I want to suck your cock at a crowded party behind nothing but a potted palm. I know you would try to decline that one, but we both know I could tease you until you got hard, that I could drive you so far out of your mind that you would be begging me for sweet, sweet relief. I hope someone would come along and catch us, would see the look of pure bliss on your face, and notice me kneeling at your feet. It wouldn't be *that* scandalous. We are husband and wife, after all. But they would titter, and the gossip on everyone's lips that night would be what a lucky fellow you are."

His big body was trembling beneath her. "Izzie… Izzie! Oh, my God, I… I…"

His hips bucked up out of the tub as he came. She clung to his shoulders as he pounded into her, making sounds of pleasure that were more animal than human.

Slowly, his strokes slowed until he collapsed, boneless, against the back of the tub, cradling her against him. She laid her head on his chest and enjoyed listening to the pounding of his heart as it gradually slowed back to its normal tempo.

After a few minutes, he shook himself, then rose from the tub in one smooth motion, lifting her up with him.

"Archibald?" she asked as he gently set her down and dried them both with a towel. "What are you doing?"

As soon as they were dry, he scooped her up in his arms and strode toward the bed. "Taking my revenge."

"Your revenge?" she asked as he lay her down upon the counterpane. "That sounds… intriguing. What do you mean your…"

He pressed her thighs open.

"Your…" she added weakly as she felt his warm breath between her legs. "Your…"

As his tongue found that little pearl between her legs, her

head fell backward, her question forgotten. And, indeed, Archibald had his revenge.

Three times.

CHAPTER 35

And so Izzie settled into a routine inside the house. After Archibald left for Nettlethorpe Iron, she would slip into John Nettlethorpe's sick room. He spent most of the day asleep, so it was a quiet place where she could write. Izzie wouldn't have said as much to Archibald, but the respite from his parents was a welcome one. Her new in-laws were not unkind, but they were extremely gregarious, and the notion that she occasionally needed some solitude in which to work was one they seemed to have trouble grasping.

When John Nettlethorpe did awaken, they would talk. He mostly didn't feel well enough for long stretches of conversation, although she enjoyed the stories he told her about Archibald's childhood, including the one about him disassembling and reassembling the pendulum clock in the corner.

They found themselves at an impasse regarding what he would call her. She invited him to call her Izzie, and he had muttered that *Lady Isabella* was more befitting. After some bickering, they landed on *Lady Izzie*, which suited them both well enough.

By now, she had read him her entire novel, *The Castle of Brynberian*, which he pronounced, "Daft, but a good sort of daft."

"Why, thank you," she replied. "That was precisely my aim."

Now when he awoke, she would read him passages of her current work and ask what he thought should happen next. He often made suggestions that never would have occurred to her, several of which she adopted. There was nothing like a plot twist, after all.

In the afternoons, her family was good about making sure she had visitors. Usually, they included Lucy and Diana, accompanied by either Izzie's mother or Lady Griselda. Her other siblings put in appearances, too, as did the Duke and Duchess of Trevissick, much to Mr. and Mrs. Nettlethorpe-Ogilvy's delight.

Then, in the evenings, Archibald would be home, so she didn't lack for company, and she would not have described herself as lonely. But even if her days were enjoyable, there was a sameness to them, and Izzie couldn't help but wonder how long she could keep this up before she grew restless in her confinement.

Five days after her attempt to visit Nettlethorpe Iron, her sisters Anne and Caro came to call. Lucy and Diana were there, too, along with Lady Griselda, who settled into a plush chair to doze in the corner.

Anne waited until Lucy and Diana were across the room poring over one of Izzie's new Gothic novels, leaving the three married sisters alone around the tea table. She leaned forward, dropping her voice low. "Are the more intimate aspects of your marriage going well?"

"If you have any questions, you can ask us," Caro added.

Izzie swallowed. "Things are going well. Archibald is… considerate."

Her sisters exchanged a knowing look. "Good," Anne said.

"Your wedding night wasn't too painful?" Caro asked.

Izzie considered her words carefully. "Archibald is… not lightly made," she admitted.

Caro made a sympathetic sound. "Poor dear. I should imagine he's not."

"But it turned out well in the end," Izzie hastened to reassure her sisters.

Anne giggled. "I'm sorry. I shouldn't laugh. But give it a week, and I daresay you'll be glad your husband is *not lightly made*."

Izzie's shoulders sagged. She *had* given it a week; in fact, two weeks had passed since her wedding day. Any remnants of her maidenhead had long since been obliterated. The act wasn't painful, but nor was it exquisitely pleasurable, as it was supposed to be. Although she very much enjoyed the other acts Archibald performed upon her person, she couldn't help but feel like something was wrong with her.

"Anne," Lucy called from across the room, "come and see this!"

Anne patted Izzie's knee as she rose to her feet. Once she was gone, Caro took her place on the sofa and wrapped an arm around Izzie's shoulders.

"Lucky Anne," she mused. "She's one of those women who finds pleasure in just about anything Michael does to her."

"One of those…" Izzie dropped her voice to a whisper. "Do you mean to say that you don't find your pleasure from… you know."

Caro's eyes flared with understanding. "Not usually. But there's a little spot on the outside—"

"I know where it is," Izzie said quickly. "Archibald showed me."

"Good! Very good." Caro studied Izzie's face. "What, then, is troubling you?"

"It's just…" Izzie glanced around to make sure no one was listening. "I feel like it's extra work for him. That I should be able to find enjoyment through the act alone. That there's something wrong with me," she added in a small voice.

Caro squeezed her shoulders. "There's nothing wrong with you, although I can understand why you feel that way. Married women like to jest about men with a large cock, or men with a small cock, but honestly? From what I can tell, there are more women out there like you and me, who don't much mind one way or the other. Far better to have a husband who takes the time to do the things that will actually please his partner than an indifferent man with a thick cock."

"I very much have one of those." Izzie sighed. She was feeling somewhat better after Caro's reassurance. But still… "I can't help but wish I were one of those women who found pleasure both ways."

"La, don't we all? But you are enjoying your marriage bed, yes?"

"Very much so," Izzie admitted.

Caro gave her a speaking look. "And you will not convince me that Thorpe is displeased to have you in his bed."

Izzie had to admit he had never given her cause to believe that, not for a single second. "No, he said that the minutes we spent making love were the best minutes of his day, and he would never object to having a few more of them."

Her sister smiled brightly. "I knew I liked him."

Lucy plopped down next to Izzie on the sofa. "May I

borrow this?" she asked, holding up the latest novel from Rosalia St. Clair.

"Of course. I finished it yesterday, and it's excellent. But you must promise to bring it back."

"Izzie needs all the books she can lay her hands on," Diana said. "She has floor-to-ceiling bookshelves to fill."

"Oh!" Anne exclaimed. "I haven't seen your new library yet. Would you show me?"

"Of course," Izzie said, rising from the sofa.

"There isn't all that much to see," Izzie explained as she led the group up the red-carpeted stairs. "We were feeling confident enough for a moment there that we brought in the architect. But two days later, I was attacked again."

"Has the work had to stop, then?" Diana asked.

"Mostly," Izzie said. "We're being very careful not to let anyone we don't know in the house. The architect Archibald has worked with before. But we feel less comfortable admitting a dozen strange workmen."

"That's probably wise," Anne said.

"Some portions of the project can proceed," Izzie noted. "My desk is being built off-site, and when it gets delivered, Archibald's men can carry it upstairs. The same thing goes for the window seat. His men are handy enough to install it. But my floor-to-ceiling bookcases will have to wait until the threat is resolved."

"Have your contacts come up with any leads, Anne?" Caro asked.

Anne shook her head. "It's strange—my network is usually able to uncover *something*. But there's not even a whisper of a plot against you, Izzie. Either whoever is behind this is unusually skilled at keeping their mouths shut, or your attackers are not connected to any of the usual criminal groups. I'm not giving up, though," she hastened to add.

Izzie sighed. Bow Street wasn't having any more luck. At

this rate, she would be imprisoned in this house for the rest of her life...

She reminded herself that she was lucky to be alive. That many people spent their lives imprisoned in a hovel, not by danger but by poverty, and they would have traded their lot for a chance to live in this mansion without a second thought. And that she was exceptionally lucky to have a husband who would move mountains to secure her safety and happiness.

She forced herself to smile as she pushed open the door to her future library. "This is it. Tell me what you think..."

A chorus of oohs and aahs erupted behind her. Lucy and Diana had visited the room several times, but it was Anne and Caro's first time seeing it. Izzie gave them the full tour, showing them where the window seat would be built, where her desk would go, and telling them of Archibald's plans for her floor-to-ceiling bookcases.

"It's perfect," Caro declared. "The only thing missing is a pet raven to perch on a stand beside your desk."

"Don't tell Thorpe," Diana said. "If you put the idea in his head, by this time tomorrow, she'll have a whole flock."

They all laughed as they filed out of the room.

As Izzie shut the door, Anne said, "And it will be lovely having your husband so close at hand."

Izzie tilted her head. "What do you mean?"

"This is Thorpe's workshop, is it not?" Anne asked, gesturing to the locked door across the hall. "Or have I misremembered the way? I've only been in there the one time."

There was a sudden roaring in Izzie's ears. "You've been inside Archibald's workshop?"

"Yes," Anne said, oblivious to the jealousy raging in her sister's gut. "It was when he first became involved with the Ladies' Society. I had just started my campaign against the use of chimneysweep boys, and he created this marvelous long-handled broom that could bend through the crooked corners so many flues have." Anne laughed. "He built it in one night. I thought that was impressive enough. But it doesn't hold a candle to his other inventions."

"What other inventions?" Izzie burst out. At Anne's surprised look, she modulated her tone. "It's just… Archibald keeps all his most impressive creations at his main machine shop. The one at Nettlethorpe Iron."

Anne waved a hand. "I'm sure you're right. This was more than a year ago. He's probably moved things around since then. But when I visited, he had one of his screw-cutting lathes in there!"

"His screw-cutting… what?" Izzie asked.

Her words were effectively covered by Diana, who said in the same breath, "Oh! I read an article about his screw-cutting lathe! It sounded absolutely fascinating, and the implications for precision-engineered machine parts are tremendous. Did he demonstrate it for you?"

"He did not," Anne said. "But I'll bet he's done so for Izzie."

Everyone turned to her expectantly. For once, Izzie was at a loss for words. Not only had she not seen Archibald's device in operation, but up until a moment ago, she hadn't even been aware that he'd built something called a screw-cutting lathe.

Even worse, she wasn't entirely sure what a screw-cutting lathe *was*.

And she knew that this was partially her own fault. That she tended to become so absorbed in the imaginary worlds she built inside her head, she didn't pay as much attention to what was going on around her as she should. Diana knew all about his invention without having a particular acquaintance with Archibald.

But she had asked him to tell her about his work multiple times. Now that she thought about it, he had changed the subject each time.

It was almost as if he was trying to avoid her questions.

But why? She could only come up with one possibility.

Because he thinks you're too silly to understand it.

Everyone was staring at her, waiting for her to answer. She scrambled to come up with a face-saving excuse.

They always said the best lie was the one that was closest to the truth…

"I must confess, I am yet to see it. As I mentioned, he now keeps most of his machines over at Nettlethorpe Iron. That's where I was heading five days ago when I was attacked. I was hoping to see all his inventions for myself. But I've been stuck here at the house."

The hallway filled with sympathetic murmurs. Lucy came over and wrapped an arm around Izzie's waist. "Don't worry. Bow Street will get to the bottom of this soon."

"And then you'll be able to see your husband's screwing-cutting jigamaree," Caro said brightly.

Everyone laughed, and Izzie felt a bit better. At least *everyone* didn't know more about her husband's invention than her.

But she resolved that as soon as Archibald got home, he was going to answer her questions.

And he was going to show her what was behind that locked door.

CHAPTER 36

*H*aving remembered to get washed up before he left Nettlethorpe Iron, Archibald went straight to his grandfather's bedchamber upon arriving home that evening. He paused outside the door but didn't hear any voices.

He felt a pang of disappointment. He'd only managed to catch his grandfather awake one time this past week. He knew his grandfather wanted him to keep Nettlethorpe Iron running smoothly above all things. But he hated having so few opportunities to speak to him now that the end seemed to be near.

Just as he placed his hand on the doorknob, he heard Izzie's voice, muffled through the thick wooden door. "Mr. Nettlethorpe? Are you waking up?"

"I suppose I must be," his grandfather returned. "Guess this means I'm not dead yet. So, what're ye going to read me this afternoon?"

Archibald paused. On the one hand, he did want to capitalize on this rare opportunity to spend time with his grandfather. But he had come to enjoy his wife's easy rapport with her grandfather by marriage, and he couldn't resist eavesdropping for just a moment.

"I do have some new chapters," he heard Izzie reply. "But, before I get to those, I wonder if I might ask you a question?"

"Go on, then."

"Could you tell me about Archibald's screw-cutting lathe?"

Archibald all but yanked the door off its hinges in his haste to get through. Why was Izzie asking about his screw-cutting lathe? How did she even *know* about his screw-cutting lathe? He had been so careful to avoid mentioning it.

One of the guards he'd brought over from Nettlethorpe Iron must've said a careless word. Goodness knows his parents wouldn't have mentioned it.

Izzie's and his grandfather's gazes snapped to him as he barged into the room. His focus was fixed on Izzie's face. Usually, it lit up when he arrived home after a day at Nettlethorpe Iron.

But this time, it fell.

Oh, God. His idyll of wedded bliss was already over.

She knew. Somehow, she knew about the screws.

He watched her draw in a breath, composing herself. She forced her face into a lifeless smile. "Good afternoon, Archibald."

He didn't know what to say other than, "Good afternoon."

She stood and began gathering her papers, not looking at him. "I know you haven't had much time with your grandfather recently. I'll leave you two so you can talk."

She was already reaching for the doorknob. "Izzie..." he began, then stopped. He desperately wanted to talk to her, to see if there was any possibility of salvaging their marriage, but he wasn't eager to have that conversation in front of an audience.

She must've read his consternation on his face because her expression softened. "We'll talk later."

Then she was gone.

Archibald pulled her desk chair around to face his grandfather's bed. He did want to spend time with his grandfather. Hell, it wasn't beyond the realm of possibility that this could be the last time his grandfather would be lucid enough for them to talk.

Yet he was wracked with anxiety, wondering what horrible thoughts were going through Izzie's head.

As he took a seat, he admonished himself to focus. He would never forgive himself if this turned out to be the last conversation he ever had with his grandfather, and he wasted it.

"How have you been feeling?" he asked.

"Like shyte," his grandfather replied, and Archibald couldn't help but smile. You could take the blacksmith out of East London, but you would never take the East London out of this blacksmith.

"So, what you're telling me is, dying isn't all fun and games?" Archibald asked.

"Something like that. I must say, though, your gel has made it a lot less dull."

"She has a way of doing that," Archibald said, his heart aching at the possibility that he might not be enjoying much more of his wife's sparkling company.

"That was the one thing that worried me," his grandfather noted.

Archibald tilted his head. "What was?"

His grandfather coughed, forcing him to wait for an answer. "You being alone. You've always been trapped between two worlds. The one yer parents want for you, and the one I brought you into. Maybe it was selfish of me to take you to Nettlethorpe Iron that day, to start you on this path—"

"It wasn't," Archibald said, meaning it. "I… I don't belong in my parents' world. If I had to choose, I would choose being an engineer." He paused. His grandfather wasn't much for sentimentality, but this might be his last chance. "You saved me," he said, his voice gruff. "By taking me to Nettlethorpe Iron that day. I would never have fit in, never would've been happy in the life my parents had planned for me."

"Good," his grandfather said, voice equally raspy. "That's good." He cleared his throat. "But if I'm tellin' the truth, I've been worried about ye. I messed up with yer father, ye see."

Archibald didn't know what to say. He could see his grandfather's point, yet he had no wish to insult his father. "I… well, I don't think Father was ever going to be an engineer."

His grandfather barked out a laugh. "No, that he wasn't. They say sometimes these things skip a generation, and maybe yer proof of that. But I could've pushed him to do something useful with his life. He might never have made cannons, but I could've forced him to learn the business side of things. He might've done pretty well hobnobbing with the princes and kings who come calling. But I was busy at the forge, and instead of taking the time to push him in a good direction, I left him to his own devices. You see where he wound up. Now, he likes to spend my money, but he decided I was an embarrassment. Then he went and married Anna-Maria Ogilvy—not that I'm meaning to insult yer mother. But both yer parents need a strong hand to guide them. Instead, they have each other, one leading the other farther astray."

Honestly, that sounded… about right. Archibald grunted.

His grandfather continued, "I know that's what they

wanted for you—to marry some fancy *ton* gel, who'd appreciate yer coin but never appreciate you. But somehow"—he barked out an incredulous laugh—"you managed to find yerself Lady Izzie."

Archibald sighed. He'd found her, all right.

And then managed to lose her a mere two weeks after their wedding.

Not that he was going to tell his grandfather as much, especially as he appeared to be drawing comfort from the notion that Archibald was happily settled.

Therefore, he asked, "You approve of Izzie, then?"

"I do. She's just like you." At Archibald's startled look, his grandfather continued, "She don't fit in her world, neither. She was never going to be someone's meek little wife, darning their socks and planning some eight-course dinner. Of course, you don't care about all that rot. And she don't care that yer not a man of leisure." His grandfather said the last three words with the same tone most people reserved for the words *traitor to the Crown*. Which was perhaps unsurprising. A man who had spent most of his life sweating next to a blast furnace so his king and country would have the means to win a war wasn't bound to think much of men with soft hands who rose at noon, and whose chief occupation was going to their club.

"Now, I know you," his grandfather continued, "and I saw the way you were looking at her while you spoke yer vows—like you couldn't believe yer luck. And I don't disagree. Yer lucky to have found her." He jabbed a finger in the air. "But she's lucky to have found you, too—someone who likes her as she is and won't go trying to make her change."

Archibald sighed. Maybe that would have been enough.

If only he wasn't a dull fellow whose great passion in life was making screws…

Still, he wasn't going to argue with his grandfather. "You think so, huh?"

"I know so." His grandfather gave a jerky nod for good measure. "Now, tell me what's been going on at Nettlethorpe Iron."

They spoke for the next half hour about the goings-on at the firm his grandfather had founded. When Archibald noticed his grandfather yawning and struggling to keep his eyes open, he patted his grandfather's knee. "I'll let you rest."

The only answer he got was a soft snore from the bed. He straightened his grandfather's blankets, lowered the lamp, and slipped from the room.

He was desperate to find Izzie, and he didn't have to look very hard as she was pacing the corridor outside his grandfather's room. He took three quick strides and met her halfway down the hall.

"Is anything the matter?" he asked without preamble, although he knew the answer before she spoke. The hurt was that plain upon her face.

"Anne was here this afternoon," she began, voice betraying that she was upset. "She said—"

She cut herself short, eyeing the two men from Nettlethorpe Iron assigned to the first floor. The man at this end of the hall, Stafford, was staring resolutely at the wall, clearly finding it awkward to witness their lovers' quarrel.

"You can head downstairs, Stafford," Archibald said. "I'm here now. Take Collins with you."

"Yes, sir," Stafford said, sounding relieved. He hastened toward the far end of the corridor to collect Collins.

Archibald turned back to Izzie. "What did your sister say?"

Izzie's blue eyes were full of hurt. "She mentioned that you received her inside your workshop once. You had made some kind of long-handled broom to help the chimneysweep boys, and you showed it to her in there."

"I did," Archibald admitted. Was that it? Was she jealous that her sister had been inside his workshop, but she was yet to have a turn?

Izzie drew herself up with wounded dignity. "Anne said you have one of your screw-cutting lathes in there," she said, nodding toward the closed door. "Is that true?"

"I do," he said in a clipped voice. "What of it?"

Izzie peered at him, as if she wanted to find something in his face that wasn't there. "Diana said she read an article about it. She said it was your most important invention."

He tugged at his neckcloth, which suddenly felt suffocating. "I consider it to be my most significant invention to date, yes."

"Then why did you tell me you didn't have anything of note in there?" she asked, her voice rising. "I specifically asked to see some of your creations, and you said there was nothing worth seeing. That it was just a hodge-podge, a room full of junk. Then I discover that you have your most important machine behind that door. You lied to me, Archibald!" She ran a knuckle beneath one of her eyes.

He dug his handkerchief out of his pocket and thrust it at her while he scrambled for something he could say in his defense. She accepted it reluctantly.

"I didn't mean to lie to you. It would be more accurate to say that I didn't think there was anything that would interest *you* in that room."

"Because I'm too stupid to understand it?" she asked, voice breaking.

"No!" he said, genuinely shocked. "You're not stupid at all. You're one of the most intelligent people I know."

"Then I'm what. Frivolous?"

"No! Of course not!"

She continued, undeterred. "With my silly little Gothic novels?"

"Your novels are not silly," he said, voice rich with feeling. "They're brilliant."

"This is why I don't understand you at all!" she cried. "You say all the right things, and I feel like you mean them at the time. And you do all the right things, too. But as soon as I ask you the simplest question about yourself, it's like getting a door slammed in my face. You always find a way to change the subject, or you do something to distract me. It's like you don't want me to know you!"

Because I don't. He couldn't say that, obviously. But if Izzie got to know the real him, she would discover that he wasn't the dashing fellow she'd built up in her head who went around saving her from roving brigands.

He was nothing but a tedious drudge whose greatest accomplishment was making *screws*. She would discover just how unworthy of her he truly was.

Although it sounded like it was too late. She knew about his screw-cutting lathe. Everything she needed to know was right there in the device's name.

She dabbed at her eyes with his handkerchief. "I can't tell you how small I felt standing here with my sisters. They knew all about your screw-cutting lathe. And I hadn't even heard of it! I'm your wife, and they knew more about it than I did. I felt like such an idiot!"

"I'm sorry," he said, meaning it. Because he had obviously hurt her, and that was the last thing he would ever want to do.

Even if this was the beginning of the end.

She was looking everywhere but at him. "I just... I love you. I love you so much."

The words should have made him feel elated.

Instead, they tore at his heart. Because he knew she only

loved the illusion he'd created, that he was some kind of hero.

That he was a thousand times more interesting than he really was.

"But I don't feel like you respect me," she continued. "I feel so confused sometimes, and—"

"You're right," he said, wrapping his hands around her trembling fists. "Not that I don't respect you. Because I do. But you're right that I should have shown you my workshop the first time you asked. I'm sorry, because I would never want to make you feel embarrassed in front of your sisters. I just… I fear that once you see my inventions, you won't find them all that impressive."

Her eyes were bright with unshed tears. "I am certain that I will. And I'd like to judge that for myself."

He nodded. "You will. I'll show them to you right now. Just… let me go in and clean things up a bit. Make it somewhat presentable."

"All right," she said in a clipped voice. "Thank you."

He unlocked the door and stumbled inside, closing it behind him. He lit a few lamps. He hadn't been in here in weeks, and, as he'd been keeping the door locked, the household staff hadn't been able to come in and perform any basic cleaning. It was a bit dusty, in addition to being a bit grimy, and he felt the crunch of metal shavings beneath his boots.

There wasn't much he could do about that. It wasn't as if he had a broom. But he grabbed a rag and started wiping down the screw-cutting lathe.

He wasn't doing a very good job of it on account of the fact that his hands were shaking. He managed to bump the pile of metal rods stacked next to the lathe, and half of them went clattering to the floor.

He threw down the rag, frustrated, and gazed around his

workshop. Tins of six different kinds of grease were scattered about the table, many of them staining rings into the scarred wood. Hammers, files, and lathes were strewn about, and papers were scattered everywhere.

He bent and began gathering the fallen rods. Who did he think he was fooling? He wasn't going to make this place presentable, not if he spent a whole week cleaning, and Izzie was waiting impatiently at the door.

Well, at least he had a moment to gather himself. When she made the horrifying discovery of what a dull fellow her husband really was, he would accept her rejection stoically. He would not beg, cry, or try to make her feel guilty about her decision.

He had always known this day would come, after all.

Resigning himself, he crossed to the door and opened it.

He squeezed his eyes shut. "All right. You can come in now."

She said nothing. The corridor was… strangely quiet.

He opened his eyes. "Izzie?"

He looked to the left. He looked to the right. He poked his head inside her library and called her name.

She was gone.

CHAPTER 37

One minute, Izzie had been standing in the corridor, wringing Archibald's handkerchief, wondering if she was making a mountain out of a molehill when a great metallic clattering came from behind the door to his workshop.

She had paused with her hand on the knob, wondering if she should go in, wondering if her husband needed her help, when a hand clamped over her mouth. She didn't have time to gasp, much less scream.

Another arm wrapped around her midsection, dragging her backward down the corridor. She tried to struggle, but she was at a bad angle, with her back to her assailant, and he propelled her easily along.

She heard a door open, and she was pulled inside a sitting room that the family seldom used. As her assailant turned to shut the door, Izzie brought her leg up and smashed her foot down on his, for all the good it did. Her flimsy slipper slid off his thick riding boot without leaving so much as a scuff.

He made no sound of protest at her attempt to defend

herself, not even a grunt. Suddenly, she felt the cold muzzle of a gun against the soft skin of her neck.

"One sound and you're dead," a male voice hissed in her ear. She couldn't quite place his accent. It wasn't the exaggerated vowels and clipped consonants of the upper classes, but nor was it the East London drawl of John Nettlethorpe. An upper servant, perhaps?

Whoever he was, he thrust a length of cloth into her face. "Gag yourself." She hesitated to take the cloth a beat too long, and he prodded her with the gun. "*Now.*"

Her fingers fumbled as she complied. Once she had finished, she turned.

Her eyes widened as she saw a familiar face.

Then, everything went black.

Archibald checked every room in the house—a time-consuming endeavor. Izzie wasn't in any of them.

She was gone.

Worry gnawed at him as he paced the foyer. He had tried to come up with some explanation, *any* explanation, other than foul play. But nothing fit. She wouldn't be hiding from him. To be sure, they had been arguing, but she was neither childish nor petulant. And she had been about to get her way. No matter how annoyed she might have felt with him, she wouldn't have taken herself off moments before he was going to show her his workshop.

Nor had she left the house of her own accord. He had his men watching every entrance, and they all swore up and down that they hadn't seen her.

There was only one plausible explanation, and it made him want to crawl into a hole and die—that someone inside the house had betrayed her. That one of the servants, or one of his men from Nettlethorpe Iron, had accepted a bribe.

That they would eventually find Izzie inside the house, but what they would find would be her lifeless body.

The mere thought made him want to curl up in a ball and die. This was all his fault. He had *sent the guards away*! Which had only been necessary because he had upset her in the first place. And then, after sending the guards away, he went and left her alone! How could he have been so careless with the most precious person in his life?

What was even worse… she had told him that she loved him. She had actually said those three little words that he had never dreamed he would hear, and *he hadn't said it back.* Which he had only done because he was so sure she would want to retract her declaration as soon as she found out about the screws.

But if he somehow survived this, somehow didn't die of a broken heart, he knew with absolute certainty that he would feel the crushing agony of not having told Izzie that he loved her, too, every second of every day, for the rest of his miserable life.

He shook himself. He couldn't think like that. He had to cling to hope that somehow, she might be alive, and he would have a chance to make this right.

From his post by the front door, Giddings called, "The Astleys are here, sir. I'm opening the door."

Lady Cheltenham swept inside, along with Lord and Lady Fauconbridge, Harrington Astley, a sobbing Lady Lucy, and Lady Diana Latimer. "Have you found her?" the countess asked. "Tell me you've found her."

"We haven't," Archibald admitted, his voice cracking. "I have no idea how this could've happened. I—I'm so sorry."

The countess nodded, unable to speak. Fauconbridge

offered his mother his arm. "We will find her. I sent notes to Anne and Caro."

"And I sent for Aunt Griselda," Lady Diana added.

"Thank you," Archibald said, although he didn't know what any of them could do to help. Still, it was good of them to come, if only as a show of support. It was more than his own parents, who had collapsed on a sofa, prostrate more at the possibility that they would become social outcasts than out of concern for Izzie's welfare, had managed to do. "I've also sent word to Bow Street."

Just then, one of his men, Collins, came sprinting into the foyer. "Boss!" he cried, gesturing behind him. "We found something. Follow me!"

He led a stampede of Astleys up the stairs to the first floor. "Whoever did this," Collins said, "I think he carried her out."

Collins passed by Archibald's workshop and rounded the corner. The rooms along this side of the house did not receive much use because they faced a narrow alley and therefore did not receive much light.

Collins opened the door to a parlor that Archibald had only been in once or twice. "It's over here," he said, gesturing to the window. "See?"

Leaning outside, Archibald saw that someone had tied a rope around the carved gargoyle that protruded from the side of the house. It dangled down to the alleyway below.

Collins was still speaking. "The window must've blown shut. That's why we didn't notice it right away. But this must be how they took her out."

Archibald squeezed his shoulder. "Strong work, Collins."

Hope flared in Archibald's heart. The presence of an escape route, instead of a corpse, suggested a kidnapping rather than a murder.

Maybe, just maybe, Izzie was still alive...

"Is everyone present and accounted for?" Archibald hated to ask the question, hated to think that one of his men might have betrayed him. But someone had done this, and he needed to find out who.

Giddings, the butler, answered, "All the servants and all your men from Nettlethorpe Iron are at their expected posts. No one has gone missing, sir."

Archibald rubbed his brow. That was a relief, but it didn't help Izzie. "Then who?"

Giddings' eyes were full of regret. "In addition to Lady Isabella's guests—her sisters, Lady Diana, and Lady Griselda, one other person was admitted to the house today."

Cold dread pooled in Archibald's gut. "Who?"

"The same man who came about a week ago to inquire about making over the front room. Who suggested redoing everything in chartreuse green. He said he'd come to take some measurements." Giddings dropped his voice low. "I'm terribly sorry, sir. I tried to turn him away, but your mother happened to be passing through the foyer, and she insisted that we admit him."

"Did anyone see this man leave?" Archibald asked, even though he already knew the answer.

Everyone started talking at once. It quickly became clear that the designer had not exited via any of the doors, nor was he still in the house. "It has to be him, then," Archibald noted. "What did he look like?"

Giddings was wringing his hands. "He had dark hair. Medium height and build. Brown eyes, I think? Not much to distinguish him." The butler looked miserable. "I am so terribly sorry, sir. I never should have let him in."

Archibald waved this off. "You could hardly gainsay my mother." He sighed. "I'll go and ask her what she knows about this man."

He found his mother prostrate upon a chaise-longue in

the front parlor. His father was fluttering about the room, bringing her cups of tea, handkerchiefs, and biscuits that were piling up, uneaten.

"Have you found her?" his mother moaned from the couch.

"We have not." Archibald pulled a chair up to the chaise-longue and sat, taking his mother's hands. "Mother, I need to ask you something. The man who came today about redecorating this room—how long has he been known to you?"

His mother gasped, sitting halfway up. "Surely you don't think he could be involved!"

"I'm afraid he is our leading suspect," Archibald said, struggling to hold his voice neutral.

"It wouldn't be him," his father said.

"He seemed very nice," his mother agreed.

"And he knew an awful lot about wallpaper!" his father noted as if this was an ironclad defense.

"When did you first meet him?" Archibald asked, attempting to steer the conversation back on track.

"Why, we've known him for a while," his mother said. "He first came to the house... what was it, my dove? A week ago?"

"Something like that," his father agreed.

"Did you seek him out?" Archibald asked. "Or did he come to you?"

"He turned up at the door," his mother confirmed.

"It was just a bit of luck!" his father added.

Oh, God. Archibald loved his parents. But could they possibly be more thick? A random stranger shows up at the door, peddling wallpaper, and they let him right in. It was probably no coincidence that the man showed up just as they were starting to let their guard down.

"Did he leave you a card?" Archibald asked. "Or any sort of direction?"

"He did not," his mother said.

"He said he would be back in a few days," his father noted. "But we do know his name—Mr. Smith."

Mr. Smith. That hardly narrowed it down, even if it was his real name, which Archibald very much doubted.

"Thorpe," his mother said from the chaise-longue, "you don't really think that nice Mr. Smith could have anything to do with Lady Isabella's disappearance, do you?"

"I suppose we'll know for certain soon enough," he said, trying to be diplomatic.

Stepping into the corridor, Archibald saw that Lord and Lady Thetford and Lord and Lady Morsley had arrived, as well as Thomas Daubney, the Bow Street Runner. "It was the wallpaper man," Archibald said. "I'm almost sure of it. He showed up at the door a week ago, and my parents let him in. Gave his name as Mr. Smith, didn't present a card or anything. It was probably a ruse from the start."

Lucy Astley seized Mr. Daubney's sleeve. "What do we do now?"

The Runner's face was creased in consternation. "We need to discover where they've taken her. I'll start by interviewing the neighbors. Perhaps someone saw something. We should also inspect the alleyway by which he made his escape. Perhaps he left some trace behind."

"But what if they didn't?" Lady Lucy cried as they streamed out the front door. "What if we can't find her?"

"Don't worry," Lady Diana said, patting her arm. "Aunt Griselda is coming."

"But what is Lady Griselda going to do?" Lucy sobbed.

Just then, the Trevissick carriage entered the far end of the square. Traffic was not light, but the horses were moving at a steady canter.

It pulled up to the curb, and the Duke and Duchess of Trevissick sprang out. "We came as soon as we heard," the duke said, offering a hand to his great-aunt, who descended with grave dignity.

"Oh, Lady Griselda," Lucy sobbed. "They've taken Izzie! We found a rope over there," she said, gesturing to the alley. "That must be how they got her out."

Lady Griselda peered into the alley. "You have discovered where she exited the house? Good. This is good!"

Hope flared in Lucy's eyes. "Can you really find her?"

"I cannot." Lady Griselda gave a command in German, and one of her brown and white speckled dogs leaped from the carriage and came to stand obediently by her side.

Lady Griselda's eyes held nothing but confidence as she turned to face Archibald. "But Inge can."

*I*zzie's maid ran and fetched the chemise her mistress had worn yesterday.

While Archibald, the Astleys, and a dozen of his men from Nettlethorpe Iron looked on, Lady Griselda led Inge to the very base of the rope, then gave her the garment to sniff.

Archibald scarcely dared to let himself hope. He knew hunting dogs were good trackers. But if the kidnappers had stuffed Izzie into a carriage, it seemed unlikely that she would've left much of a trail for the pointer to follow.

Holding his breath, he watched as Lady Griselda instructed the dog to "*Such.*" Inge immediately put her nose to the ground, sniffing the pavement. Archibald was terrified that she would track Izzie to the edge of the curb, and the trail would immediately go cold.

But instead, Inge started confidently down the pavement, heading away from the Nettlethorpe-Ogilvy mansion.

As one, the group gave a gasp of relief and began trailing the dog down the street.

At the corner, Inge made a sharp left turn, crossing the street and taking them south toward Mayfair. She kept her head down the whole time, her mind on her business, paying no mind to the carriages flying past her in the street.

"By jove," Harrington Astley said, coming up next to Lady Griselda, "that's remarkable."

Lady Griselda waved this off. "Inge is the best tracker I've ever trained. This is child's play for her."

Inge made another turn, leading them to the opposite side of the square. She marched up to number twenty-seven and would've gone right in were it not for the shiny black door barring her way. Inge seemed momentarily affronted but shook herself, then raised a front paw and pointed her muzzle directly at the door.

They retreated around the corner to formulate a plan.

"*Sehr gut*, Inge," Lady Griselda said, feeding the dog a treat from her pocket. "*Braver Hund*. You will be having steak tonight, yes, you will."

Lord Fauconbridge's face was creased in confusion. "But... is that not Andrew Milner's house?"

"Andrew Milner?" Lady Morsley asked. "You don't mean the politician? What could he, of all people, have to do with Izzie's disappearance?"

Lady Diana and Lady Lucy were jumping up and down.

"She saw him!" Lady Lucy hissed. "In the dark walks!"

"He solicited the services of a"—Lady Diana dropped her voice low—"a woman of easy virtue."

Lady Lucy turned to her friend. "I had all but forgotten that she mentioned it!"

"Me too!" Lady Diana exclaimed. "It never occurred to me that *Andrew Milner* might try to have her *killed* over such a thing!"

"To be sure," Fauconbridge mused, "he wouldn't stand a chance of becoming Prime Minister if word of it got out. Not after all the careers he's ruined on similar accusations."

"And I suppose that's all he cared about," Lady Cheltenham snapped.

Archibald only cared about one thing. "How do we get her out?"

The Bow Street Runner was the first to speak. "Normally, I would knock on the front door and demand to search the house. But Andrew Milner is an influential man, a member of Parliament. In this case, I feel the best course is to go before a judge and obtain a warrant."

Archibald only managed a snarl, but his words were not necessary, as the entire Astley cohort protested in angry whispers.

Daubney shook his head mulishly. "We must proceed with caution, must follow all the proper channels. Milner could make things extremely unpleasant for me if this turns out to be a false lead."

"Unpleasant?" Archibald took a step forward. His face must have been terrible to behold, because Daubney, who was two inches taller than him, shrank back. "Do you have any idea how *unpleasant* I will make things for you if my wife is hurt as a result of your timidity?"

The Runner swallowed. "Well, what would you suggest?"

"I shall knock on the door," Lady Cheltenham said. "We'll pretend it's an ordinary social call."

"Quite the coincidence for the mother of the woman he's just kidnapped to turn up," Harrington noted.

"I say we break down the door," Morsley offered.

"We can't just break down the door," Daubney protested. "It's bad enough that we're going in without a warrant!"

Morsley ignored the Runner. "Break down the door and take them by surprise. That's the way."

"They won't be surprised for long," Ceci noted. "We need something more subtle."

"We'll sneak in the back," Lord Thetford suggested. "We'll bring Inge. She'll be able to locate Izzie within the house."

"No," Daubney began.

"*Yes*," Diana said fiercely, giving him such a quelling look that the Runner, who was probably fifteen years her senior, took a step back. "My friend is in there, and if she dies because you were too concerned about following policies and procedures, then with God as my witness, I will make sure the whole world knows of your incompetence!"

Daubney's brow was creased, but he muttered, "All right."

Lady Diana turned to face the group. "What we need is a diversion. Mr. Milner is likely watching her like a hawk. We need something enticing enough to draw him away from the room." She turned and fixed her gaze upon her brother, the duke. "And I know precisely whom we should send."

Five minutes later, Archibald watched from around the corner as the Duke of Trevissick strode up to the door and knocked. It swung open. He couldn't hear what the butler said, but the duke's outraged response echoed down the street.

"Not a good time? What do you mean, it's not a good time? I sent a note over yesterday, informing Mr. Milner that I would call upon him this afternoon."

Archibald heard a mumbled reply from the butler.

"You mean to tell me that you didn't receive my note? I would have thought that a man with aspirations toward being prime minister could manage to organize something as simple as his household. I see that this is sadly not the case." He raised his nose in the air and sneered. It was an expression that would have looked patently ridiculous on anyone else Archibald knew but somehow looked natural on the duke's angular face. "Well, go and tell your master that if he wants me to sponsor the Forgery of Foreign Bills Act in the House of Lords, he had better find five minutes to speak to me right now."

Again, Archibald couldn't hear the servant's reply, but the duke was admitted to the house.

"He's so good at acting pompous!" Lucy whispered.

"He isn't acting," Ceci and Diana hissed in unison.

A moment later, the duke's voice was audible through a window on the house's corner. "Yes, I would like a drink." He was speaking loudly, as they had planned, so they could stay abreast of what was going on inside. The group hurried to stand beneath the window. Archibald heard it clearly as the duke asked, "Do you happen to have a 1795 Rausan-Segla? No? Well, try to find something that isn't swill."

After a few minutes, the duke said, voice dripping with sarcasm, "Mr. Milner, how kind of you to grace me with your company."

"I apologize, Your Grace. But this is not the absolute best time."

The duke *hmphed*. Archibald didn't want to risk peeking through the window, but he could picture Trevissick surging to his feet with a condescending glower. "Then I suppose it also isn't the absolute best time for me to co-sponsor the Forgery of Foreign Bills Act in the House of Lords. Thank you for helping me see that. Good day."

"You're considering co-sponsoring the bill?" Milner asked.

"Well, I *was*."

"Wait—please, Your Grace. I suppose I can spare just a few minutes..."

"Let's go," Harrington hissed.

Archibald nodded to Ceci and Elissa, who were to listen

beneath the window. Everyone else scurried around to the back of the house.

The back door came into view, and the group paused. "Should we just go barging in?" Lucy asked.

"Yes, precisely," Lady Griselda said, shouldering her way to the front of the group. "*Komm*, Inge."

She yanked open the door and strode through. The rest of the group streamed in after her.

A footman appeared at the top of the servants' stairs, bearing a bottle of wine on a silver tray. He paused, clearly flummoxed by the sight of two dozen well-dressed strangers and one dog striding in through the servants' entrance.

"You can't just barge in here!" the footman cried.

Archibald stepped forward, fists raised with the intention of knocking the man insensible before he could raise the alarm, but Morsley laid his hand upon his shoulder. "Wait, Thorpe." The earl's face was earnest as he said, "I should be the one to punch him."

The footman's eyes darted from Archibald to Morsley, full of alarm.

"I'm a peer, you see," Morsley continued. "If it comes down to an assault charge, they would try me in the House of Lords. I'll have an easy go of it there."

"You realize discussing this does not make things better!" Mr. Daubney snapped. "It only makes the assault premeditated."

"Fine," Archibald grumbled, ignoring the Runner. "I suppose you can be the one to do it."

Morsley squeezed Archibald's shoulder, then rounded on the footman, fists raised. Like most footmen, this fellow was around six feet tall and broad of shoulder. Still, he did not seem to relish the idea of being punched by the hulking giant that was Lord Morsley.

"Wait!" he cried. "There's no need to hit me!"

Morsley loomed over him. "Isn't there?"

"No, m'lord!" The footman set the tray down on a sideboard so he could hold up both hands. "I'll just sit over there in the corner. You won't hear a peep out of me, I promise!"

"All right, then." Morsley pointed a stern finger at him. "But you'd better not make a sound."

They left Morsley with six of Archibald's men to guard the back entrance. Lady Griselda gave Inge another whiff of Izzie's chemise. "*Such*," she whispered.

Inge paused, then headed toward the front of the house. The group tiptoed after her.

As they made their way toward the front stairs, a door opened, and a maid emerged. She gasped, hand flying to her heart.

Archibald froze. He couldn't let her sound the alarm, but his every instinct revolted at the notion of striking a woman.

He had just resolved that he would clap his hand over her mouth when Lady Thetford rushed over and gave her a conspiratorial wink.

"Shh!" the viscountess whispered. "It's a surprise!"

"A… a surprise?" the maid whispered back.

"Yes! For Mr. Milner." The viscountess, who admittedly didn't much look like a criminal miscreant in her frilly pink dress, hooked her arm through the maid's elbow. "Come with me. I'll explain everything."

Archibald shot her a grateful look, and they hurried on.

They reached the front entrance. Abruptly, Inge put her head down. Whereas she had been meandering about sniffing the air before, now she trotted up the stairs with resolution in her steps.

As he rounded the banister, Archibald could hear the Duke of Trevissick droning on about the Forgery of Foreign

Bills Act from the corner parlor. He hurried up the stairs on tiptoes.

Inge led them up two flights and down a corridor. Two men stood flanking the room at the end of the hall.

"What the hell!" one shouted, seeing Lady Griselda and the dog.

Archibald jolted as he recognized them as two of the men who had attacked Izzie in Lady Waldegrave's gardens. One was the man whose wrist he had broken, and surely enough, his arm was in a splint and sling. The other was one of the pair who had fled the scene rather than face him.

Archibald hurried around Lady Griselda. He marked the moment the two men realized who he was.

"*Oh, shit*," the man with the broken wrist said.

"Run!" his companion cried, fleeing toward the back of the house.

"We've got 'em, boss!" Collins called, giving chase with a trio of Archibald's men.

Inge led them straight to the door the men had been guarding. This time, when presented with a locked door, she did not calmly signal but began pawing excitedly at the varnished wood.

"*Braver Hund*," Lady Griselda said, feeding the dog another treat. "Lady Isabella must be inside. She would not be so frantic unless we were close."

A desperate sort of hope bubbled up inside of Archibald's throat. He rapped on the door. "Izzie! Izzie, darling, are you in there?"

There was no answer. Still, he had to believe Izzie was behind that door.

Of course, just because she was behind that door didn't mean that they would find her alive.

He pushed the thought out of his mind. It was too horrible to even contemplate.

He tried the knob. "Locked," he muttered. "I'm coming, Izzie," he cried. "Hang on!"

He took three steps back and was preparing to ram the door with his shoulder when Harrington laid a hand upon his shoulder. "Wait! That will make too much noise. Thetford can pick the lock."

"I can," Thetford agreed. "Somebody give me a hairpin."

"Breaking and entering," Mr. Daubney groaned. "Just what this afternoon needs."

"Come now, Mr. Daubney," Harrington said. "Don't be that way. In fact, why don't you join me for a moment in looking out this window. The view, I think you will agree, is very fine."

"The view is of a brick wall," the Runner muttered.

"Well, yes," Harrington agreed. "But looking at it will give you… what's the term I'm looking for?"

"Plausible deniability," Diana offered brightly.

Harrington snapped his fingers. "Plausible deniability, that's the one!" Slinging an arm around Mr. Daubney's shoulders, he turned him to face the window.

Lady Morsley gave her brother-in-law a hairpin, and Lord Thetford knelt upon the floor. Archibald probably could have done it himself. He had personally made all the locks in use at his family home. He probably understood their inner workings better than Thetford.

But, given how hard his hands were shaking as he wondered what he might find on the other side of that door, it was probably better to leave it to the viscount.

It took Thetford less than a minute. "Got it!" he cried, hopping up.

Archibald seized the knob and shoved his way into the room, terrified of what he might find.

It was a bedchamber. Izzie was splayed out on the bed,

gagged, with a wrist tied to each of the bedposts. Her hair was a mess, and it was clear she'd been crying.

But she was alive. She was alive, and the relief that flared in her eyes was unmistakable.

He rushed to the bed and began fumbling with the knot on the gag, but his hands were shaking, which rendered his usually deft fingers clumsy.

"Here," her brother, Harrington, said, pulling a knife from his boot. "Let me."

In a trice, Harrington had her free. Izzie drew in a gasping breath as she threw herself into Archibald's arms. "Archibald! You found me!"

He pulled her into his lap and buried his face in her hair. "Of course, I found you."

She was sobbing into his neck. "I was so afraid."

"*I* was so afraid," he said, voice trembling. "Are you hurt?"

"No," she said, giving a great sniff. "Just terrified. How on earth did you find me?"

"That was thanks to Inge." Archibald gestured behind him.

"Inge? Who is…" Izzie glanced over his shoulder, and her eyes flared with comprehension. "Oh, one of the pointers! Of course." Her eyes sharpened, and she clung to his arms. "You'll never believe who was behind all of this! It didn't have a thing to do with the guns being stolen from the Navy. It was—"

"Andrew Milner," Archibald said along with her.

"Yes! How did you know?"

"Fauconbridge recognized this as his address, and Diana and Lucy recalled that you had seen him in the dark walks."

"It was the same man who tried to kidnap me while I was on my way to Nettlethorpe Iron. The one who tried to drag me into the carriage. He somehow sneaked into the house.

He grabbed me from behind and put a gun to my throat. And then…"

Izzie proceeded to explain how he had forced her to gag herself, pulled a giant floppy bonnet over her head, and taken her straight out the window. "Then he marched me across the square with his gun digging into my ribs. He tied me up in here, and that was when Andrew Milner came in and explained that by this time tomorrow, I would be on a ship of convicts bound for New South Wales." Izzie shook her head. "I can't believe he was willing to resort to all of this to save his political reputation."

Andrew Milner's reputation was the least of his worries. He had just crossed one of the wealthiest men in England. Archibald was prepared to hire an army of barristers to make sure he spent the rest of his life rotting away in a dank cell.

He'd better hope he never got out of gaol. He needed those thick stone walls for his own protection. Because if he ever met Archibald in a dark alley, he was going to discover the true meaning of pain.

Archibald decided not to mention any of this. Izzie had already been through enough of an ordeal today. "Are you well enough to stand?"

"I am. And I'm eager to leave this place."

He helped Izzie up. She was immediately enveloped in a bear hug by her very relieved twin, followed closely by the rest of her family. After taking a moment to lavish praise and ear scratches upon Inge, Izzie was ready to depart.

They tromped down the stairs, this time taking no pains to be silent. Locating Andrew Milner proved to be a simple task, as the Duke of Trevissick was still lecturing him in a loud voice.

Mr. Milner, a sallow man with wheat-colored hair, blanched as Archibald strode through the door. He lunged toward a connecting door on the far side of the room, but the duke had the sword he wore at his waist out in a flash and held it against Mr. Milner's neck. "You, sir, are not going anywhere."

The rest of the party streamed into the room behind Archibald. Izzie seized his arm. "That's him!" she cried, pointing toward the butler, who was cowering in the corner with a silver tray bearing a bottle of wine. "That's the man who kidnapped me today and the one who slapped me across the face."

The butler wheeled around, sending the contents of his tray flying. He hurried toward a door in the corner, but Lady Griselda, who was the closest to him, managed to grab the back of his coat. He spun back around, raising the silver tray to strike her over the head.

Archibald was across the room in two strides. His fist connected with the blackguard's eye, and the man went down in a heap.

Archibald hovered over his inert body, fists at the ready. After a moment, Harrington peered over his shoulder. "I, uh… I think you finished him."

"Is he dead?" Lady Diana asked hopefully.

Harrington bent down and checked for a pulse. "No such luck."

"More's the pity," the duke sneered from across the room, where he was still holding Andrew Milner at sword point.

Harrington clapped a hand on Archibald's shoulder. "You can stand down now."

"I'm waiting for him to wake up," Archibald said tightly.

Harrington tilted his head. "May I ask why?"

Archibald cut him a look that said, *Isn't it obvious?* "So I can hit him again!"

Harrington shook his head sadly, patting Archibald's shoulder. "I'm afraid you finished him in one."

Archibald turned, glaring at Andrew Milner. "I don't

suppose you'd like to make any sudden moves? Perhaps lunge at me with a knife?" His voice was low and menacing as he added, "I would be *extremely* glad to have an excuse to hit *you*."

Milner's eyes were showing more white than blue. "I think I'll pass," he said in a reedy voice.

Izzie came over and tugged at one of his raised fists. "It's all right, Archibald. It's over now." The smile she gave him was tiny, but he was relieved to see that it reached her eyes. "Let's go home."

CHAPTER 39

hey left some of Archibald's men to secure the house while Mr. Daubney performed his investigation and made his arrests. The Runner waved off the rest of them. "I'm sure this has been trying for Lady Isabella. Go ahead and take her home. My interview can wait until tomorrow."

Archibald offered to carry her, but Izzie insisted she was well enough to walk across the square.

And so it was that a quarter of an hour later, after having bid Izzie's family goodbye, they strode through the front door.

Archibald paused in the foyer. "Do you want to rest?"

"Honestly?" Izzie gave a bleak laugh. "Before that elaborate disaster ensued, I was *finally* about to see your workshop. I would rather do that than lie down."

Archibald bowed his head. "Very well."

His heart was racing as he led her up the stairs. He still dreaded her reaction to his machines, but if there was one thing he had learned from their argument that afternoon, it was that Izzie wanted honesty from him even more than she wanted a personal library.

He summoned his courage. "I'm sorry I didn't show this to you earlier. The truth is, I've been nervous of your reaction to my workshop."

"Nervous?" Izzie looked surprised. "Why would you be nervous?"

"I've been worried that you won't find my machines all that impressive when you finally see them," he confessed. "Specifically, that you'll find them pedestrian. You spend all day dreaming up these fantastical worlds and marvelously creative storylines. I fear you'll find what I do decidedly humdrum by comparison."

Izzie gave a little huff. "I'm sure I won't."

Archibald didn't share in her confidence, but they had reached the door. This was it. "I guess we'll see," he said, holding it open for her.

The room was bright as he'd turned on all the lamps before his hasty departure. Izzie gasped as she entered the room. If she was bothered by the crunch of metal shavings beneath her slippers, she gave no sign of it.

She unerringly wandered over to his screw-cutting lathe, which made some sense. Archibald supposed it was the most sophisticated-looking machine in the room.

He tried to see it through her eyes. It was one of his smaller models, about two and a half feet long, its cutting mechanism raised from the bench by a stand on each end. Between a pair of slide rests ran a long screw that Archibald had taken pains to cut very, very precisely. There was a large wheel at one end and a variety of cutting tools resting on the bench around it that could be attached to the slide rests.

"You *built* this?" Izzie's hand flew toward the wheel, then froze. She glanced at him, her expression almost guilty. "Can I touch it?"

"Of course." Archibald spun the wheel himself, showing

her how it caused the central screw to turn. "This is one of my screw-cutting lathes."

"Your screw-cutting lathe," she breathed, staring at the machine.

She lapsed into silence while Archibald shifted back and forth on his feet. "Would you like to see it work?" he asked after a moment.

"Oh!" She shook herself. "Yes, please."

He loaded a short metal rod into the machine and adjusted the cutting tools to make a basic screw with eight threads per inch. Once everything was ready, he gave the wheel a spin.

Beside him, Izzie gasped. Archibald cringed. Now she knew the awful truth.

His greatest accomplishment was making *screws*.

He pulled the finished screw out of the machine and held it out to her. "So, you see, it's just what it sounds like. It literally cuts scre—"

"*This is the most perfect screw I have ever seen in my whole entire life!*" Izzie shrieked, snatching it out of his hands. "And you made it in four seconds!" She rounded on him. "However did you think to design such a thing?"

"It's not really an original design," Archibald confessed. "Lathes have been around for hundreds of years, and this isn't even the first one designed to cut screws specifically. What I've tried to do is improve upon previous designs, to perfect them. I have this idea..."

He trailed off, certain he must be boring her, but she was looking at him eagerly. "Yes?"

There was no helping it; he was going to have to tell her. "See, right now, virtually all screws are made by metalsmiths, by hand. No matter how skilled they are, it's impossible to make two screws that are precisely the same. So, you wind up with one box of handmade screws, and another box of handmade nuts, and you waste a tremendous amount of time trying to find a screw and a nut that pair together even remotely well. But if you can build them with a machine that is *precise…*"

He glanced at her, half-expecting to see her eyes glazing over. But instead, he found her watching him intently. "Go on."

"If you can achieve precision," he continued, "then every screw in that box will be precisely the same, and it will fit perfectly with each of the nuts as well. I realized the importance of precision a few years ago when I was obsessed with building locks. You see"—he picked up a file—"my grandfather started me working with hand tools at a very early age. I can build an unpickable lock by hand, but it takes me a full week to build just one. It's terribly inefficient. But if each piece could be precisely engineered, so they're interchangeable—"

"Then you could build a hundred locks instead of one," Izzie said.

"Exactly! It's not so much about making screws, although… that's literally what I'm doing right now. Making screws. It's about figuring out how to build things with *precision.*" He gestured to his lathe on the table. "Take the central lead screw here. I had to figure out how to cut it so the threads were *perfectly* even. This one is accurate to one ten-thousandth of an inch —"

"*One ten-thousandth of an inch?*" Izzie's mouth fell open. "How do you even measure one ten-thousandth of an inch?"

"That was another problem," Archibald said, grabbing a gadget that looked like a tiny brass table with a wheel on one end. "Because, of course, you don't know if you're building with precision if you can't measure it. So, I had to figure out how to build an extremely precise bench micrometer. See?"

He showed Izzie how to measure the screw with the

bench micrometer. "My men call it the 'Lord Chancellor.' Because if they're arguing about whether something they've made is sufficiently precise, you can't overrule the verdict of the Lord Chancellor."

"That's terribly clever!" Izzie said, seizing his forearm. She frowned. "But how did you cut the... the central screw, this long one—"

"The lead screw," Archibald supplied.

"The lead screw, thank you. How did you make it precise to one ten-thousandth of an inch? Surely you didn't do that by hand?"

"No. I'm good with a file, but nobody's *that* good. I had to invent another device specifically to cut the lead screw. It's over here if you'd like to see—"

"I would!" she cried.

Thus passed one of the most enjoyable hours of Archibald's life. Izzie didn't seem bored or unimpressed with his machines. Much to the contrary, she seemed delighted by everything he showed her. Standing behind his wife, with her framed between his arms, he demonstrated how you could change out the parts on his screw-cutting lathe, and even swap in a different lead screw, to make screws of all different sizes. She exclaimed in amazement over each variation and told him he was a genius six times. Archibald knew it was six because he counted. He even let her try her hand at making a screw, and she squealed with delight as it came off the lathe.

"I can't believe I made this!" She gazed at him, eyes earnest. "Could I keep it?"

He laughed. "Of course."

"Oh, thank you! I can't wait to show Mama! She'll never believe I made this." Her eyes sparkled. "I fear I'm your opposite in this regard. I'm possibly the least dexterous person you've ever met. I can barely darn a pair of stockings, and the less said about my embroidery, the better."

"That's all right. I didn't marry you because I wanted someone to sew my shirts and darn my socks."

She laughed. "That's fortunate. I know how severe the Duke of Trevissick is on your tailoring. I can tell you right now that any shirt I made would not pass muster." She peered up at him, her expression growing serious. "Say, if you didn't want someone to perform the usual wifely duties, then why, exactly, did you marry me?"

The timing of this question was fortunate because, for the first time, he had the courage to answer it.

He swooped Izzie up in his arms, ignoring her startled squeal, and carried her through the door. He made sure he was looking her in the eyes as he told her.

"I love you."

She gasped, looking genuinely surprised. "You... you do?"

"*So* much." He shook his head. "You have no idea."

She looped her arms around his neck. "Oh, Archibald, I love you, too."

He nodded. He was still having trouble fully believing those words. They seemed entirely too good to be true.

But he was slowly learning that he needed to trust Izzie and listen to what she said rather than assume the worst. His wife knew her own mind, and if she said she loved him, who was he to tell her she was wrong?

They had reached the stairs. He started up, as this was clearly going to end in their bedroom. "I fell horribly in love with you the very second I saw you."

She looked both startled and pleased. "Did you really?"

"I did," he said solemnly, turning down the hall. "It was the day of your sister's wedding to Thetford. I remember thinking you were so beautiful you didn't look human. That you looked like the daughter of the fairy king."

She giggled. "That's very fanciful for you, Archibald."

"It is," he agreed, striding into their bedroom. He kicked the door shut behind him. "I immediately concluded that you were the most beautiful woman ever to live. But then, it got even worse."

"How so?" she asked as he laid her down on the bed.

He followed her down, coming to rest on top of her. He raised a hand to her face and gently swept a lock of hair back from her forehead. "You probably don't remember, but I was seated just behind you at the wedding breakfast. I could hear every word of your conversation." He shook his head, rueful. "You were *so clever.*"

Delight swept across her face. "You thought I was clever?"

"Clever. Witty. Interesting." He chuckled. "I wished so badly that you were talking to *me.*"

"How I would have liked that!" Izzie exclaimed. "I was seated next to Lady Hering, who is—"

"A dead bore," Archibald finished for her. "I had to feign a bout of coughing when you told her as much."

"I'm surprised I didn't frighten you off. Most men think me far too outspoken."

"Most men are idiots. You're perfect."

"Perfect?" She laughed, incredulous. "I'm not perfect. I'm an odd bluestocking who pens stories about dukes pretending to be ghosts while living at the bottom of a well. Moreover, out of the basic skills expected of a wife, I do not possess a single one."

"Perfect," Archibald repeated. "Clever. Witty. Beautiful. Adept at managing my parents. Kind to my grandfather."

She tapped a finger against her lip. "Hmm… When you put it that way, I do sound rather wonderful."

They both laughed, and Izzie smoothed her hands over his chest. "But I think that *you* are the one who is perfect."

"Absolutely no one would agree with you," Archibald

noted. "I'm a glorified blacksmith. I get filthy every day doing manual labor at a forge. And my greatest accomplishment is making *screws*."

"Point the first—blacksmiths are dashing," Izzie countered. "The lords of the world pad their jackets so they can feign having the physique of a blacksmith. Point the second—I don't care whether you get your hands dirty."

"All of polite society would disagree," he noted.

She stuck out her chin, offended. "Since when have I given a fig for what polite society thinks? Returning to my list—point the third, I think your screws are marvelous. It's like the parable of the stonecutters. Have you heard that one?"

Archibald frowned. "I don't believe I have."

"A traveler came upon a group of three stonecutters. He approached and asked what they were doing. The first answered that he was cutting stones. The second explained that he was earning his daily bread. And the third said that he was building a cathedral." Izzie smiled up at him, her eyes sincere. "None of them were wrong, just as you aren't wrong when you say that you're making screws. But you're also building a cathedral. And I think you're going to change the world."

Archibald nodded jerkily, suddenly unable to speak. He should've known Izzie would see it that way. He should've trusted her. She'd never given him any cause not to.

She ran her hands over his shoulders. "And I truly think you're perfect. I never thought I would marry, you see, because the qualities I required in a husband were nigh impossible to find. Would you like to know what they are?"

Archibald nuzzled her neck. He did want to hear Izzie's list, but he also wanted to make love to her. "What?"

"Mostly, I wanted a man who wouldn't dismiss my writing as silly. I can't tell you how many men told me I should give up Gothic novels and write something 'important' instead or who assumed I would stop writing entirely after I married. I needed a man who didn't care that I wouldn't be a conventional wife, spending my days sewing his shirts and planning his parties. Because I fear I'll never be much good at those things."

She traced a hand across his shoulder, down to the bulge of his biceps. "Of course, if I had my wish, he would be built like a Viking. He would be just like one of the heroes in my stories—strong and brave, and willing to do anything to protect me. And, of course, he would kiss like a Viking, too. Like he was desperate to have me. Yet I would always feel safe in his arms."

She looped her arms around his neck. "I require a man who is intelligent and kind. I find I don't care much about what he does for work or if he gets his hands dirty. And I certainly don't care what high society thinks of him. It's not as if high society has ever approved of me, after all. In short, I want a man who loves me just as I am and who doesn't want to change me." She gave him a little smile. "That's all."

"But… but Izzie," he sputtered as something occurred to him. "That sounds like… like…"

"Like you? Of course, it does." She laughed. "You're my ideal hero. You couldn't be any more perfect for me if I'd written you myself."

Archibald thought his heart might burst. He'd always thought of Izzie as so high above him, as untouchable as a star in the sky.

Never in his wildest dreams had he imagined that she might love him, too.

"You really don't mind that I'm a blacksmith?" he asked, his voice gruff.

"Well, I don't think you're precisely a *blacksmith.* Engineer. Inventor. Captain of industry. Take your pick.

Although"—she twined her fingers in the hair at the nape of his neck and dropped her voice to a husky murmur—"I can think of several advantages to your facility for smithing."

"Oh?" Archibald's pulse was quickening, and his cock had hardened to iron. He began kissing his way across Izzie's neck. As much as he was enjoying this conversation, he needed his wife rather desperately. "Do you have something specific you'd like me to build for you?"

"It happens that I do." She leaned up to whisper in his ear. "Wrist shackles."

He had been aiming a kiss for her ear, but he missed entirely, winding up face-first in the pillow. "Wrist... did you say *wrist shackles?*"

"Yes! You see, there's a page in that book of Harrington's that shows—"

Now Archibald was really breathing hard. "I've a fair idea what it shows."

Izzie stroked his chest with teasing fingers. "And would you be interested?"

"*Yes.*"

She laughed at his hungry expression. "Good!"

She started to tug his lips down to hers, but Archibald paused, holding her delicate wrist up next to his thick one. "Wait... do you want me to build the shackles to fit your wrists? Or mine?" He couldn't decide which scenario sounded better. He obviously loved the idea of being able to do anything he wanted to Izzie, especially because he suspected such a scenario would arouse her unbearably.

But he found that the idea of being at her mercy was also *extremely* appealing.

She smiled up at him. "Why not both?"

Why not both, indeed? With this woman, he could be both a working-man and a white knight, both an industrialist and an intellectual.

He could be both a hammersmith and a hero.

He could be himself, and that was enough.

"Both it is." His lips found hers, and there was no need for conversation for quite some time.

~

Keep reading for a special preview of *Romancing the Rifleman*, coming in 2025!

~

Wondering what Izzie and Archibald will be getting up to with those wrist cuffs? Subscribers to my newsletter will receive a second epilogue short story so you can check in on their happily-ever-after. This one is extra steamy! Sign up at courtneymccaskill.com/newsletter/ .

PREVIEW: ROMANCING THE RIFLEMAN

She's the one woman Harrington Astley can never have.

Lady Diana Latimer might be everything Harrington Astley has ever wanted. But her older brother, the Duke of Trevissick, despises him, and would never give his approval for them to wed. The beautiful girl who makes him feel like he's more than just cannon fodder is as unattainable as a star in the sky.

Diana Latimer has had it with fops and fortune hunters.

Making her London debut seemed like a lark three years ago. But after her brother saddled her with an absurdly large dowry, Diana has found herself besieged by fortune hunters. There's only been one man she's truly liked—Harrington Astley, a handsome army lieutenant with an irreverent sense of humor. Now Harrington is back in London, but thanks to her brother's meddling, he's convinced that nothing can ever come of the attraction flaring between them.

When the Foreign Office asks Harrington to attend a

house party to try to ferret information out of a Swedish prince he befriended during his last deployment, Diana sees her chance. Harrington doesn't speak a word of Swedish. But Diana does. Of course, a young, unmarried lady cannot attend a house party without a chaperone… which is why she informs Harrington they need to marry. For King and country.

Sometimes you have to fake it 'til you make it!

Harrington promises Diana's brother that they will annul their fake marriage just as soon as their mission for the Crown is complete. But Diana never agreed to that plan, and she's not giving Harrington up without a fight. She's going to do everything within her power to seduce her husband and turn their fake marriage into a love that lasts a lifetime.

Romancing the Rifleman will be coming to your favorite bookstore in 2025. Pre-order your copy today!

HISTORICAL NOTE

-Lest anyone thinks Izzie's Gothic novel is too ridiculous to be believed, I based it on the actual plot of *The Castle of St. Donats* by Charles Lucas, which was published by the Minerva Press in 1798. It really does contain guard bears, naked pirate sword fights, and a duke living at the bottom of a well pretending to be a ghost! Just as modern romance novels have different subgenres, Gothic novels came in different varieties, including Gothic parodies which were intentionally over the top, poking fun at the excesses of the genre. In fact, Jane Austen's *Northanger Abbey* is considered to be a parody of Gothic parodies!

-Likewise, if Archibald's engineering accomplishments sound too good to be true, I based them on the achievements of a real engineer named Henry Maudslay. Born in 1771, Maudslay was the son of a wheelwright for the Royal Engineers who later worked at the Royal Arsenal at Woolwich. His father died when he was nine and so at age twelve, he went to work at the Royal Arsenal himself, starting as a powder monkey filling cartridges by hand and working his way up to the blacksmith shop. It was immediately obvious that he was a prodigy with an amazing facility for using hand tools.

At the age of eighteen, he was hired by Joseph Bramah. You may have heard of Joseph Bramah's unpickable lock; Maudslay was the one who actually built it. Bramah's workmen at first shunned Maudslay because he hadn't completed a formal seven-year apprenticeship. Maudslay proposed a challenge—he would have one day to repair a hopelessly broken bench vise, and if the workmen were not impressed, he would leave of his own volition. When the other men saw how skilled he was, they agreed that he should stay. By the time he was nineteen, the same men who had demanded he leave made him head foreman by unanimous consent.

Maudslay and Bramah worked together for eight years until Bramah refused Maudslay's request for a rather modest pay raise, and he left to open his own shop. Like Archibald, Maudslay had a passion for building things with precision, and he did indeed build the best screw-cutting lathe of its age. He built several prototypes over the years, some of which can be found at the Science Museum in London and the Henry Ford Museum in Michigan. He also pioneered the bench micrometer and did indeed create one that could measure to one ten-thousandth of an inch.

My favorite story about Henry Maudslay involves the creation of his block making machine. The Royal Navy needed a huge quantity of rigging blocks (which, to my layperson's eyes, look like pulleys)—130,000 per year. They could not hire enough craftsmen to keep up. Sir Marc Isambard Brunel (father of the famous engineer Isambard Kingdom Brunel) had designed a series of forty-two machines that would churn out the blocks. But he couldn't find anyone capable of building such a complex design.

Then, one of his friends, M. de Bacquancourt, happened to pass by Maudslay's shop and saw a five-foot-long brass screw, made on his screw-cutting lathe, naturally, and precise to one ten-thousandth of an inch, displayed in the window. He ran straight to Brunel and told him he'd found the man who could build his machines. It took Maudslay six years, but they were finished by 1807. There were forty-three machines in the final design, which performed sixteen separate tasks. You put a piece of wood in one end, and a finished block would come out the other side. There was nothing else in the world like it at the time, and they worked so well that the Royal Navy continued using them until 1965.

Today, Maudslay is honored as one of the founding fathers of mechanical engineering. He leaps from the historical record, a hundred years ahead of his time.

-Historical Accuracy Confession: At one point, Michael comments that he should be the one to punch a footman, because he is a peer and would therefore be tried in the House of Lords. To be sure, Michael is known as the Earl of Morsley. But because his father is still alive, Michael's title is what is known as a courtesy title, and he is not yet considered to be a peer, with all of its accompanying privileges. He would therefore face trial in the same court as Archibald. But I thought the joke was funny, so I put it in there anyway.

-The country of Salaria is my invention.

ACKNOWLEDGMENTS

I would like to thank everyone who has helped me bring this book into the world: my wonderful editor, Diana Bold; my indispensable beta readers Linda and Melinda; and my brilliant cover designer Bailey McGinn. I'd like to thank my author buddies, both over in The Brazen Belles and at Regency Fiction Writers for always being there to commiserate with me about this crazy writing life! I would also like to thank all of the readers who go above and beyond to support me, especially my ARC readers and the members of my street team. Melinda, Gloria, Anne, Jessica, Mariah, Lindsay, Julie, Nicole, Jocelyne, and Kesha: you are THE BEST, and I appreciate you more than I can say! As always, I want to give a shout-out to the University of Texas Library, which is pretty much the only thing standing between me and bankruptcy via research books. I also want to thank my wonderful family, especially V and J. How did I get so lucky as to have you guys in my life?

It is a well-known fact that engineers make outstanding heroes. They are both logical and cool under pressure, say, if the model rocket their youngest child launched in the middle of Zilker Park went off course and almost crashed into someone's car. NOT that I have any experience in this area! They can fix literally anything, and they enjoy performing tasks such as capturing rats and killing poisonous snakes (or so I am reliably informed.) And when the zombie apocalypse comes, they will be completely prepared, living large in their solar fortress. What I'm saying is, this one's for you, Dad! I love you bunches. Thanks for everything.

ABOUT THE AUTHOR

After reading *Black Beauty* for the 1,497th time, Courtney McCaskill was inspired to write her own stories. Reviews of her early work were mixed, with her fourth-grade teacher, Mrs. Compton, saying, "Please stop writing all of your essays from the point of view of a horse." Perhaps she is improving, however, as her book, *The Duke's Dark Secret*, was recently selected as a finalist for the 2024 Maggie Award in the category Published Historical Romance.

Today, Courtney lives in Austin, Texas with the hero of her own story, who holds the distinction of being the world's most sarcastic pediatrician. She is reliably informed by her son that she gives THE BEST hugs, "because you're so squishy, Mommy." In 2022, Regency Fiction Writers honored her with its Lady of the Realm award in appreciation of her volunteer work, both on its Board of Directors and as the Coordinator of the Regency Academe. When she's not busy almost burning her house down while attempting to make a traditional Christmas pudding, she enjoys playing the piano, learning everything there is to know about Kodiak bears, and of course, curling up with a great book. Visit her online at www.courtneymccaskill.com.

ALSO BY COURTNEY MCCASKILL

The Astley Chronicles

Book 1: How to Train Your Viscount

Book 2: What's an Earl Gotta Do?

Book 3: The Sea Siren of Broadwater Bottom

Book 4: The Duke's Dark Secret

Book 5: Let Me Be Your Hero

Book 6: Romancing the Rifleman (Coming in 2025)

My Favorite Mistake: An Astley Chronicles Novella

The Weatherby Wallflowers

Book 1: A Wallflower Never Surrenders

Book 2: Snowbound with the Scoundrel (Coming November 12, 2024)

Book 3: One Bed for the Bluestocking (Coming in 2025)

Book 4: How He Won His Wallflower (Coming in 2025)

The Wicked Widows' League

Book 1: Scoundrel for Sale

Book 2: A Very Roguish Boxing Day (Coming December 3, 2024)

Other Books:

One Fine May (The Rake Review)

For more information, visit www.courtneymccaskill.com.